Chasing the Bear

Jeffrey Recker

Saguaro Publishing Co.
Denver, CO

Author's note
This story is purely a work of fiction and that all characters, including the main two, are solely derived from the author's unbridled imagination. The only exceptions to this are the occasional encounters and quotes from notable personalities.

Additionally, the names of some real race winners were occasionally substituted in favor of characters mentioned in this novel. In no way does the author wish to depose the hard-sought achievements of these real-life athletes. For example, the real winner of the '93 Bolder Boulder women's citizen race was Carol McLatchie of Houston, Texas, not the fictitious Jennifer Ledge.

Published by Saguaro Publishing Co.
690 Pennsylvania St. #4
Denver, CO 80203
(303) 832-6524

Jeffrey Recker
Chasing the Bear

Library of Congress Catalog Card Number: 96-92998
ISBN 0-9655984-0-3

a source of kindling...

As with any beginning, there lies a purpose...

Years ago I boldly announced to a close friend that I was going to run a marathon. He patted me on the back and said, "go for it." I saw a blank look in his eyes that told me he really had no idea what "it" was. When I mentioned this intention to my parents my mother said slack-jawed, "that's about six miles, isn't it?" *Oh, and then some...* The more I ran the more aware I became of a line that separates a runner from a nonrunner--and that line is in no way thin. In it lies a valley of misunderstanding and ignorance--innocent and not.

So one day I stared at a blank sheet of white paper, incessantly inspired, and began to write with the purpose of gaining the understanding of my nonrunner friends and family. But even in doing so, I can only expect to achieve a meeting of the minds--a compromise perhaps--somewhere in that valley. *After all, some things have to be experienced to be fully understood.*

Soon I realized that runners too would enjoy this story because it is, after all, about them.

So I give this to my parents: my father, who often tells me just how proud he is of his "marathoner" son; my mother, who once told me not to be disappointed if I didn't win the Boston Marathon! "I hear there's a lot of good runners in that race," she said. Well, Mom, a few more than four thousand runners beat me to the tape that year. And no, I wasn't heartbroken.

It is also given to my brother, Ken, whom we share an on-going thought: long live the Clydesdale Division.

And to my friends; some of whom run, some who do not. Without our shared experiences (which they will recognize a few) this story would not have been possible.

And finally, it is given to my wife, Kathaleen, a twenty-five year old, 2:51 marathoner at the time of this writing, and the true inspiration behind my writing. She is--and will always be--my running partner in sport *and* in life.

WARMING UP

"A thinker's weight is in his thought, not in his tread.
When he thinks freely
his body weighs nothing."

- Henry David Thoreau

A sufficient light is delivered by a swollen, imperious moon and the spackled, white swath of the Milky Way. The occasional stone, bump, or crack in the road is easily negotiated.

The lone athlete runs through the canyon with the speed and agility of an animal at play.

A pitter-patter of footsteps is laid to ground with perfect cadence, providing a beat which nature's symphony accompanies. Locust and other desert creatures sing from the depths of the encompassing darkness. A wide-eyed owl lets its presence be known and coyotes howl in the distance celebrating a kill. A moderate run-off from yesterday's rain is heard splashing its way down the rocky, canyon wash, and a slight breeze rustles the branches of a Palo Verde tree. It seems that all the elements are here to sound a splendid melody.

Out here, the runner thinks, it is difficult to imagine that Tucson is just five miles to the south.

A feeling of isolation engulfs the runner since the city lights are held at bay by the box canyon and the road leading in is closed to private vehicles. The Parks and Recreation Service runs a tram for tourists each day but it shut down at five o'clock. So earlier, when the sun gave way beneath an explosion of pink and orange, and an empty blackness fell over the sky, the runner set out expecting to see no one else. It is now, in the cool late evening, that the four mile stretch of granite walls breathes a life of its own.

Saguaro cacti spiral upwards casting their silhouetted, human-like forms against the backdrop of the night sky. Some are over forty feet high and embody ten or more arms. The runner thinks they resemble sleeping giants, keepers of their domain.

The runner comes to the belly of the canyon where an imposing wall-face signifies one's retreat. The descent offers an increase in leg turnover and the ability to stride out with little effort. It brings a smile to the runner's shadowed face. It feels like flying--flying in the dark--

1

with the only engine that of the heart. The runner's feet never really seem to touch the ground.

Folklore has it that more than one hundred years ago the Spanish named this place Sabino, after talk of a magical, roan horse which was seen running through the canyon when the moon was full. The runner now glides through an exceptionally fast mile in full appreciation of that lore. Perhaps, one day, there will be stories told of a runner who ran with that horse. It is a sweet thought.

The mile which follows seems even faster. The next one even faster, perhaps. It is difficult to judge since the surrounding darkness exaggerates the sense of speed. *...But that had to be...*

And soon the runner's thoughts surrender to the depth of both fantasy and expectation. One day the runner will compete and match strides with the great ones of the sport; hearing their labor, seeing their sweat, and feeling their pain. Of course the runner too will feel the pain. And in the final meters of the race the competitors will hurl themselves forward and the finish line will draw closer. And the runner will reach deep within and search for a refuge of fuel in a depleted supply. And the runner will kick, and perhaps feel the surge being met by someone. But the runner will kick again and somehow break free. And the runner will win. But tonight the runner races alone, accompanied only by their ghosts. *"One day..."*

ONE

On a desolate, far reaching stretch of dirt road in southern Arizona is a sign that reads: ORACLE: 22 MILES. *God must have placed it here to taunt me.* What other purpose could it serve in the middle of this dusty, rarely traveled land where my aged and dented Jeep suddenly coughed and died?

So, I weigh my options. Thumb it? I haven't seen another vehicle all day. Forget it.

From the West cumulus clouds rise like dough in an oven and take shape in the form of giant pastries. The tops of them--cast against the brilliant blueness of the sky--look as white as bone, but their nearly flat bottoms look more like tooth rot; black and sore. Below them, virgas of purple and gray hang like unfinished curtains that manage only to tease the arid desert floor. It's been too dry to produce any real rain. But the turbulent afternoon sky is plenty strong enough to kick up a gusty wind. It blows in carrying a pungent scent of deer weed and sage; inviting smells that have only recently touched my senses in many years. Thorny skeletons of dead bushes tumble across the road, one actually coming to rest on the Jeep's grill. It's a bad omen, I'm thinking. Then I look up holding my breath in search of smiling vultures.

When I lived in this part of the country I had often heard about people who became stranded in the desert and consequently died from dehydration or a basic lack of conditioning as they tried to walk to town. As I drink the last bit of juice I've been nursing for the past hour I remember that many of these unfortunate souls were found within a short distance of help. I wonder if that too might be my fate? I doubt it. The passion that has transformed my life over the past seven years has prepared me well.

So really, the choice is simple. I might even laugh at the irony of it all if I wasn't pressed for time. I have less than four hours to catch a flight leaving from Tucson. I figure I can run to Oracle and from there I'll be able to catch a taxi or just pay someone--anyone--to drive me to the airport, some forty minutes further. If I'm lucky I'll make my flight. So within minutes I abandon the Jeep, carrying with me a worn, leather day pack which I've stuffed with a change of clothing and my wallet. "The buzzards can have the rest," I say.

Twenty-two miles... I've run that distance--and greater--more times in my life than I can remember. Still, it's a hell of a long way, quite beyond my view. How apropos, I suppose. So much of life is exactly that: quite beyond one's view.

3

The transformation I underwent in my mid twenties will carry a weight that will last me a life time. It's as if I crawled inside a cocoon that years later spat me out in my present form.

I begin my run; the most important run of my life, I'm thinking. Along the way I know I'll have plenty of time to think about what brought me to this point and place in time. And what a ride it's been!

*

They're out there. They tear through your streets hungry and wide-eyed in the early morning when you're still asleep dreaming about a cushy life filled with new china patterns and maid service and lottery winnings. They pass by your home in the evening when you've just taken the chicken out of the oven and lounge by the television with the remote control comfortably in hand. You don't notice them but the sound of your dog barking in the back yard makes you question what's out there. Occasionally they annoy you at intersections since you're forced to cover your brake pedal as one unexpectedly dashes out in front of your car. You're upset because in this day of age vehicles should have the right of way. Roads are meant to be driven--not to be run, by God! But mostly you don't notice them. They tend to go about their own business, willing to flush your dreams for theirs in a heartbeat. It might be ten degrees and blowing snow outside--you might be comfortably sipping wine in front of a fire inside--but make no mistake about it; they're out there--running again. They're a breed of animal--a fraternity no doubt--of athlete who diligently trains day-in and day-out and dutifully races on any given weekend, at any given location, often traveling at their own expense, using vacation and sick days in order to do so. And most doing so for lack of money or fame, but for reasons altogether different.

And me? Well, I'm one of them.

But it wasn't always that way. By my mid-twenties, a sedentary life style left me wondering what I was going to do about the little tire that had gradually enveloped my waist. Finally, one day in the fall of '88, I woke up next to several Taco Bell wrappers and six empty bottles of Tecate beer. I grabbed my soft belly, belched long and hard. Yeah, I grossed myself out. Of course, having been a procrastinator my entire life, it took that much to get me into a pair of running shoes. Nonetheless, that's exactly what I did.

So then, there I was, starting anew. Committed to exercise and the right to thinness. Ready to tear across the surrounding desert and run down wild game. It all sounded great until I actually sped out my front door and came to a staggering halt with the numbers on my mailbox still in view. Exhausted, I bent over, resting my hands on my knees, and spat. *Oh baby, this wasn't going to be easy. Yak.*

In retrospect, that ill attempted first day was the best thing that could have happened since it fueled my self-disgust. So I set out the next day, and the day after that, again and again. But not because the weight was coming off--which it was. Something else had taken hold of me. A feeling so deeply rooted that I dared to call it--love? Yeah, that's what it was--love! Years later I would read a quote from George Sheehan stating that "running was the cause, fitness was the effect."

Understanding that, the fact that I was shedding pounds really didn't matter at all, because that was merely a by-product of this thing I enjoyed. And the bottom line was that I had quickly found myself in love with the simple action of placing one foot in front of the other and watching them turn faster and farther.

Unfortunately, another by-product of that love was obsessiveness. Within two years the sport had become all-consuming. I fed on miles the way a pregnant woman might feed on chocolate.

Indeed, a summer morning in '91, I quenched this overpowering hunger with a twenty-eight miler. It was nothing, really. Perhaps like Donald Trump adding another million to his billions; it was nice but was it really necessary? I had run more than three thousand miles that year which included one particular span of six weeks when I *averaged* thirteen miles a day.

It was during this time when I really felt myself begin to gel, my body taking on the daily toil of miles with exceptional ease. It seemed that running became easier than brushing my teeth, more natural than urinating. I ran day-in and day-out, sometimes twice or even three times in a single day. I ran in the mornings when the desert heat wouldn't dampen my energy and melt the soles of my shoes on the concrete sidewalks. Though, I must admit that on more than several occasions I found myself in the middle of a ten miler with the afternoon sun directly overhead. I ran in the evenings, down dark streets, through parks, and the entire length of Speedway Boulevard. I ran through trashy alley-ways, past the County Animal Shelter and Ernies Auto Body and Bobo's Restaurant and the Little League baseball field filling my nostrils with the scent of freshly cut grass. I ran along Miracle Mile as prostitutes smiled at me while cowboys snickered at my skin-tight Lycra shorts and coyotes howled in the nearby foothills. Basically, I ran all the time, any time, any where and any distance.

I was doing intervals on the local track when most Americans sat in front of their televisions and watched President Bush announce his decision to liberate Kuwait. I was driving out to the desert to run my favorite trail when Magic Johnson announced he was retiring from basketball because he carries the HIV virus. When a close friend of mine died I ran twenty--*Escapism*. When the Berlin Wall came tumbling down I ran twenty--*Celebration*.

The day I forgot to show up at work for my six month review I was out running. I had other things on my mind; my mileage was down for the week. When I got home there was a message on my machine from my boss. I showered quickly and rushed in to the office. I hadn't stopped sweating when I arrived. My boss never realized how nicely he set me up when he asked me why I generally looked like "shit." "I've had chills and a fever all morning long," I told him. Certainly, I looked the part. He sent me home, wishing me to get well. That afternoon I logged another eight. I never felt better.

When I wasn't running I could think of nothing other than the run; an upcoming race, a past performance, my diet--too much fat? too few carbs? split times and final times; things like that.

I did a lot of wishing back then too, dreaming of a time in the near future when I would be better, faster. Even during the stretch when I averaged thirteen miles a day I was entirely convinced that I could improve a great deal. I could always run a little harder, a few more miles, perhaps. I knew of more than a handful of professionals that ran in the neighborhood of one-hundred and fifty miles per week. *If that's what it takes, well...*

And naturally I was convinced that there was nothing perverse about this thing, this need, this life of running. After all, I was going to kick some ass eventually and battle the bear some day, wasn't I?

And at some point in the fall I had to admit it: I was in the best shape of my life. I was physically peaking and exceptionally confident that I could run my best race ever in an upcoming marathon.

And I did it too!

On a smogless day in California I ran effortlessly through mile after mile of the San Diego Marathon and crossed the finish line in just over two-hours and forty-eight minutes. I had run a PR (personal record) by nearly twenty minutes and in doing so had--get this-- qualified to run in the women's Olympic marathon trials! *All the miles logged, all the time spent in preparation, all the personal sacrifices....* They had finally come to fruition in the form of success.

It would have been the perfect argument in favor of my obsession, had I been the other sex.

But while a two forty-eight over twenty-six miles is a fine time for a man, it wasn't exactly going to strike fear in the hearts of anyone with natural talent. Hell, I was going nowhere except home.

It was a strange day; that one. The joy I felt pouring out of me from having run a PR--and by so much--was equalled by a veritable sense of devastation that hung on me like the sweat-laden singlet bearing my unseeded race number. I had run the race of my life and there-in lay the point. On that day, when I was at my best, no fewer than one hundred other runners beat me to the tape.

In the eyes of the few spectators who lined the streets I was nothing more than an also-ran, someone to wish well, to encourage in the final miles of the race. They'd say such trivial things: "hang in there; you're almost there; you can make it Buddy!" I mean, honestly, I've never heard anyone say to the leader of a race, "you can make it Buddy."   .

In retrospect, I should have seen this impotence, this collision between my desires and abilities, and the self imposed sentence which followed, long in advance.

And perhaps I did.

I was never blind to the fact that if I finished well I might squeak in just under two-fifty, some thirty minutes after the race winner. I knew that much going in and it didn't bother me in the least. But afterwards this knowledge churned in my stomach like rotten fruit. It's like the married couple who diligently saves for years and years and finally has enough money to buy the dream house; the one with the two spare bedrooms, only to move in and discover the wife is expecting triplets. It's just not enough and it's not going to get any better! So I'm an also-ran. Move on. Deal with it.

And as time came to pass I did deal with it. Quite easily. I rationalized that it was much easier for me, a well-to-do club runner with obvious limitations, to accept my position in this pecking order in the food chain, this hierarchy of running where the slow-of-foot is left to accept the role of Dog Meat on weekends than it is for someone who runs much faster and closer in the chase to be occasionally labeled "Thoroughbred" or "Big Dog."

In fact, I've come to enjoy my positioning among the pack. But not for reasons that a nonrunner might think; perhaps the notion that if I was indeed a talented runner I might one day wake up and find myself washed up, labeled a "has-been." All that kind of thinking is pure nonsense. It is inevitable that we all age and the great runners of today will not win the big races of tomorrow. Yet, unlike many sports, like football and baseball, running is something that one, barring injury or other misfortune, can continue to perform well into age at the level of his contemporaries. My solace came to me with the knowledge that I will always run and compete for the pure pleasure of the sport-- nothing more. My talent, or lack of, will always see to that.

7

Unlike others who I came to know--one which I came to love--I will never have to run because others expect me to. I will never have to run to appease a sponsor or a coach. I'll never have anyone scrutinize, judge and evaluate my every race and every workout.

I'll certainly never have to worry about disappointing the American public with a sub-medal performance in the Olympics, like Patti Sue Plumer did in '92. I remember watching TV with several nonrunner friends of mine, watching this woman turn sixty-five second quarters. It was an amazing sight in my eyes. Yet when she finished fifth one of my friends yelled out, "she sucks!" Sure, he was ignorant and so I shouldn't have been bothered by his outburst. Yet, I was. I thought about how many people across our sports-crazy nation must have echoed those exact same sentiments at that exact moment. It was disheartening to hear her life summed up so emphatically with not so much as a minute understanding as to what she had accomplished to earn her the right to have been in that race in the first place. How many lung-searing quarters had she run over the years in practice? How many victories had she notched before that race? How many competitor's spirits had she squashed along the way? In this country of nearly one hundred and fifty million women she was simply the best of them all! Yet somehow she'd earned the right for my friend, and God knows how many others, to frown at her, to say "she sucks!" The fifth fastest woman in the entire world that year--*sucks?*

Furthermore, I'll never have to worry if the results of a race I ran poorly in will appear in the Sunday paper. Nor will anyone ever ask me to run faster than the day, or month, or year before. I'll never be faced with suffering the consequences of plateauing at an unacceptable level. Nor will I ever have to do battle in the pit, where the Big Dogs cruise at sub fives and attack at will. The pit can be exceptionally cruel--but I'll get to that later.

Of course, the devil's advocate will point out that if I am never to experience these pressures then I will never know the beauty that also accompanies them. I whole-heartedly agree. And I suppose I might sacrifice all that I have to trade places--even for a short time--with a great runner so that I might experience those things first hand. I wonder what it would be like to, just once, feel the victory tape break across my chest; one time when my hands would be held high over my head and not hitting the stop on my watch. But that is neither an option which I can choose or a path which I can follow. So you will see that while I haven't competed on that level I have experienced it from the outside looking in. A different perspective certainly, but a perspective abundant of worth nonetheless.

8

*

All of this isn't to say that I stopped living the run after that memorable day in San Diego. I clearly did not. Though I've become humbled and obedient to my own limitations I still continue to run almost every day, averaging about forty miles a week. I continue to have difficulty finding anyone in my personal telephone directory that isn't a runner. I continue to search for articles on the thoroughbreds of distance. And finally, I keep sending in my renewal to any fluff publication on running--a mystery that I may never figure out.

I left Tucson in '92 and moved to Denver. My love for the run, though quelled somewhat, was certainly alive and well. I looked long and hard for an area to live that would provide me with many options in which to run. The task had proved difficult.

I had been in Denver for nearly two months staying in a Holiday Inn and living out of a suitcase. I was starting a job as a sales representative for a small furniture manufacturer. Most of my time was tied up on the learning curve, particularly meeting with dealers that were scattered throughout my three state territory. There was little time for apartment shopping.

Yet within weeks I knew I wanted to live close to the university. It was ground zero for an excellent selection of runs of varying lengths and terrain.

Unfortunately, rents in the area were excessively high. I became frustrated rather quickly.

The local economy was booming and there seemed to be an uncanny attitude by corporate owners and landlords that there was an endless supply of prospective tenants floating about. This bred a very uncaring attitude. "Either you want it or not," I heard more than once. In one instance I found the management staff so rude and scant that I walked away mumbling inflictions at them. It was very unlike me, but I was growing rather impatient and tired of living in a hotel.

On that particular day I became so frustrated that I cut short my search and chose to go for a run to clear my thoughts. I'd noticed a cinder track nearby during my search.

After two miles of a slow warm-up I began a series of four-hundred meter repeats. Seventy-five seconds around. "I'll take it," I said. It hurt badly. I hadn't acclimated to running at altitude yet and before long the workout had trashed me. I took refuge on the grassy infield of the track and began some gentle stretching exercises.

That's when I saw it. Adjacent to the track, a sign hung in a window of an old brownstone building: LOFT FOR RENT.

I memorized the number and called it later that night.

A man with a heavy east coast accent answered. I recognized the foulness of South-Philly english. The man, who introduced himself as only the landlord, described the apartment as "olda, but widout da bugs. Wid characta, yoos understand?"

About the only thing I did understand was that this guy sounded like he moonlighted as a second-rate plumber. But things being as they were I decided to meet with him the next day.

Just as I suspected he carried a supply of plumbing equipment in a greasy, brown leather bag.

"Sorry bout da gear," he offered. "I just fixed a lady's pipes befa ya shown up." He smiled revealing dirty, yellowed teeth.

I do believe his remark implied that he'd just gotten laid which nauseated me. The man was unkept, wearing an unlaundered white T-shirt and tan, polyester trousers that threatened to fall down. He had a large, soft belly and several poorly shaved chins. Don't get me wrong; everyone's got a right to get laid but when I was actually forced to imagine this man screwing I had to squirm a little under my skin.

He finally introduced himself as "Harvey." He held out a small, round hand and offered it to me.

I felt like he was sizing me up.

"What's ya name, kid?" He had a low, raspy smoker's voice.

"Paul Jeffries," I offered.

"Yoos ain't no student." It was an observation, not a question.

I told him that I had graduated college back in '85, and said nothing else. It was a bad decision to come here, I thought.

Harvey led me into the building and up the stairs to the top floor; the third floor. He griped about the tenants the entire way.

"I'm glad you ain't no college kid," he said. "Ya don't know what it's like to manage a place like dis!"

Yeah, whatever. I said nothing.

"And dey never give me a damn notice win dey leave!" he said louder. He added that he planned on keeping the boy's deposit who had vacated the unit in question. "Every damn penny of it!"

If he was doing his best to sell me on the apartment he sure had an odd way of going about it. I doubted that he had ever returned a deposit.

He opened the door. "Dis is it."

Like I needed an explanation. He was really getting on my nerves!

I stepped inside. Everything leading up to this point suggested disappointment, but to my disbelief I was thrilled. It had ten-foot high ceilings and hardwood floors that made my voice reverberate when I spoke. And I was totally surprised to find that there really was a sense of charm about it; just as Harvey had said. Oak moldings framed the doors and two large southerly exposed windows. White French doors opened up to a moderate size, wooden balcony.

"How much did you say it was?" I asked, calmly.

"Six-fifty," Harvey said, flatly.

I inquired about the noise level though I didn't care. "Theres a lot of students living here," I said.

"Dere's a lot of professionals too," he said. He was a bad liar.

I walked out to the balcony. I couldn't believe my eyes.

The view was great. Anyone looking out would notice the red brick, university clock tower rising high above the campus buildings. Mature oaks and elms, most of which were in the firm grasp of autumn's colorful foliage, mixed with rows of Victorian Tudors. Seventy-five miles to the south, snow capped Pikes Peak loomed.

I, on the other hand, didn't notice any of this. My eyes were glued to the four-hundred meter track barely a stones throw away.

Harvey stepped out onto the balcony with me as I was still taking in the sight of the track. He produced a plastic smile.

"Looky here," he said. "Yoos look like a good kid and I think ya'd like it here..." He pointed a hairy knuckle in the direction of the track. "...dat is if ya don't mind havin that fuckin track in ya back yard widda distraction of all dem God-damn joggers screamin' at eachudda."

Quite a salesman I thought again.

Personally, I've never known runners to be that loud, I mused. "Well, I do work out of my home quite often. Again, the noise--"

"Whadya say I give it to ya for six bills on a two year lease?"

Two years? He was really going for broke. I wanted to ask him for five. I rubbed my chin and thought of how Linus has his blanket and how I'd have my track!

A long silence followed.

I turned and faced Harvey. He looked uncomfortable. Perhaps he was feeling his bowels move.

Finally I accepted. I would have paid eight. It was perfect.

I'll always think it amusing that Harvey never noticed my Nikes and my shirt which read: San Diego Marathon.

Now, having a track in my backyard was exactly the magnet that I did not need in my life. I had just gotten over a serious relationship with the run and even though I came to grips with the fact that I would never be anything other than an average club runner my love for the run would always haunt me, always test my will. So this track acted as the bottle in the refrigerator of a recovering alcoholic, always there, calling to me, teasing my senses.

And I knew of the complications this toy could pose. But I swore I could separate excitement from obsession. So I used the track, but only sparingly.

More than that I found myself looking out at it every so often like a proud new owner or caretaker, perhaps. I was like a teenager who had just layed down his life savings of six hundred dollars for his first car; even though it was rough in spots, an occasional pothole or raised surface in the dirt, it was still a beautiful sight: four hundred meters of screaming rock and roll!

Then in November the storms came and buried it with snow. It would remain dormant for the remainder of the winter, just lying there like some coiled, sleeping snake waiting for the speed demons to heat it up again in the spring.

When it finally did thaw out in the spring it received an overhaul.

As a "gift" from the alumni of Rocky Mountain University, the track was reconstructed with a rubberized top that promised to be very durable to the changing weather conditions.

As I understood it, the university didn't own the track and therefore never used it for meets, but its close proximity to the school presented the alumni an opportunity to show goodwill in restoring it.

The unofficial truth behind the reconstruction was that the Mayor was an avid, and frightfully slow runner, who logged nearly twenty miles a week, and the gift was not at all intended as a present for the community as much as it was for the Mayor to take care of some "concerns" he had with certain segments of the student body. It seemed some fraternities were participating in on-going violations which included, but not limited to: drinking under the legal age, playing excessively loud music at all hours of the night and practicing random acts of vandalization. Of course, there were always the multiple charges of date rape to be buried and forgotten. "All for the sake of upholding the fine stature of the university, you understand?" said a deep-pocketed alumni, and member of one of the fraternities the Mayor had inquired about.

It was most likely one more gift in a long line of them but as usual it served its purpose and the Mayor was a happy man for the time-being. After its completion the Mayor even went so far as to have a red-ribbon cutting unveiling the new track. He was shown on the news that night, dressed in dated jogging sweats, taking a "victory" lap for his efforts in getting the job done. I watched this live from the comforts of my own balcony. Later that night when I watched the news I strained to see if I might be seen in the background mouthing my sentiments; "what a moron," I'd said. I couldn't believe that in a city this big he was making such a hoot about a simple track

12

reconstruction, but given that most politicians would never even consider the running community to be a populi worth targeting for campaigning I was happy that he'd thought of it.

To my surprise I often saw the Mayor out at the track for several weeks that followed.

Looking back, I'll enjoy the vision I carry with me of him; turtle slow, making his way around the track, trying to fight back the tide of fat which loosely blanketed his waist. Hadn't anyone had the nerve to tell him how tight his sweats were? When he moved his ass looked like two Sharpai puppies fighting each other. I felt sorry for him. Then my pity turned to humor. What was he doing on the track anyway? The track is for speed work (intervals) and not for jogging in place. It equates to driving a golf-cart at Indy; it just doesn't fly. Now, don't get me wrong; I'm always pleased to see people of all abilities out and running. But I wanted to shout down at the Mayor from atop my balcony to get off the track and enjoy the myriad of trails and parks the city has to offer. And perhaps, one day, the Mayor shared this thought with me because after April 1'st I never saw him on it again.

What and who I did see on the track interested me a great deal. I'd sit on my balcony and watch people of all shapes and abilities circle it.

With the recent improvements it became a magnet for the local runners to gather, including myself. It was there that I met Barbara, the president of a local running club that I would join later that spring.

Barbara, a petite, blonde with a long face and crowfeet pulling at her eyes told me that a group of very talented women--including herself and aside from the club--were going to start using the track once a week for interval training.

I soon found myself out on my balcony every thursday night watching their workouts. I was fascinated with them. More than that, I was attracted to them.

But my attraction was for reasons that undermine the obvious; the toned bodies and hearty souls they often exemplify.

Women in sport have always had to battle a pessimistic attitude in society that is slow to change and unwilling to accept their position as athletes. Why? Who knows. I could probably fill my thoughts for days with theories on this. One reason might be because women, from the time they are infants, are taught passiveness and complacency. Sport, in a general sense, is an aggressive action. The two contradict each other. So, I'll just say this: the female athlete represents an enigma in a society that is too wanting of rule and order and status quo.

This makes the female athlete a natural rebel. When I look into the eyes of one I see a purpose behind them. Sure, I'm attracted.

13

Other than Barbara I didn't know any of their names but I soon came to recognize them by their talent level. Gender aside, they were some of the finest athletes I'd ever seen.

On one particular evening, about a month after they had started using the track, I was relaxing on my deck in anticipation of their arrival. I glanced at my watch: five o'clock. Too early yet. They wouldn't be coming for another twenty minutes or so.

But just then I noticed a young woman walking in the grassy infield of the track. I'd not seen her before but I knew in an instant I would always remember this moment.

TWO

"Hey! you with the group today?" asked a loud, wild voice from behind.

The sheer abruptness of the question startled Jennifer. Before she could turn around it came again.

"Hey! you with the group today?" Even louder this time.

Jennifer saw a towering woman with a crooked smile fast approaching her. Each step ate up yards of turf. "I think so," she managed to say between the woman's breaths.

"Hi, I'm Melissa Jones, but everyone just calls me Mel." She giggled twice, then quickly extended her arm--which was as long an arm as Jenny had ever seen on a woman. Mel had straight, black hair wound tightly around her head, pulling on the skin around her eyes and causing them to bug out considerably. She was an odd one by anyone's standards.

Jennifer's eyes got wide as well, mimicking the look that Mel had on her face. A subconscious need for acceptance, perhaps?

Mel shook hands vigorously and in one enormously large breath said, "Toni I talked with her earlier said she had invited someone new to run with us tonight God tell me you're her before I make a complete fool of myself like I always do have you ever done that like I always do?"

Jennifer's mouth was open from being baited with certain responses that never came. *Oh my, she thought. Who is this nut?* Nonetheless, she tried to match her exuberance.

Jennifer stuttered twice in anticipation of being interrupted. She saw that Mel's eyes were fastened on her lips as though she was going to either read them or eat them. Jennifer felt uncomfortable and stuttered a third time. "Yes, I guess that would be me," she finally said with the biggest smile she could muster. "I was beginning to worry--"

"Oooh no!" Mel screamed. "We're here every Thursday evening at five-thirty..."

"ta, ta, ta, to--" A complete sentence would be out of the question, Jennifer realized, watching Mel deeply inhale, another verbal explosion on its way.

"You're early I bet Toni told you five-o'clock just in case you had a hard time finding the place like I did the first time I showed up and drove around campus for thirty minutes until I thought I was going out of my mind from circling and circling and circling and circling..."

And as Mel's words became tangled Jennifer's attention began to wane. She fought to decipher the nonsense spilling from this woman's mouth.

"...but you must have just driven right up to it I guess..." Mel moved closer to Jenny, choking her space.

Jennifer stepped backwards.

Mel followed, gapping the space, nearly on top of her now. "...I think that's really great Toni told me you were new in town and that you were really nice and fast too and like a lot of us including myself has a great interest in..."

It was no use, thought Jennifer. The woman's words were a web of nonsense. *Scream and run away!* she thought, understanding that years and years of running had not been spent in vain. She would use her talent now to run away, far away.

But as if someone turned off a faucet the words no longer spilled from Mel's mouth. Instead, Mel's eyes were quickly fastened on Jennifer's lips again, anticipating some sort of an answer.

Oh no, thought Jennifer. Did she ask me a question or has she just run out of air?

If it was possible Mel's eyes were wider now.

"Sort of, yeah." A safe answer, she hoped. Jenny diverted her eyes and kicked the ground.

"Huh?"

"What?"

"I asked you your name," said Mel.

"I'm sorry, I was just..." Jennifer kicked the ground once more. "It's--"

"Look it's the other girls," Mel interupted, pulling back now to greet them.

Apparently she had the same effect on others, Jennifer noticed, as she saw eyes being tossed in every direction but Mel's.

Still, she felt ridiculous. She'd just been made fool of by the most socially inept person she'd ever met; someone she would probably end up knowing and running with for years to come. She still wanted to run and hide.

A Hispanic woman with shiny, black hair that fell loosely down to the small of her back approached Jenny. Although she looked to be exceptionally fit she had a fuller figure than most runners Jenny knew.

"I'm Luz Diaz," she said, revealing a quarter-inch gap between her front teeth. "You must be Jenny Ledge?"

"Yes," she said, surprised. "How did you know that?"

"I saw your results in the paper this week." Luz spoke in a soft, Spanish dialect.

"And from that you were able to--"

"And I also placed third behind you and Toni at the Washington Park race," she cut in. "I guess I was interested in finding out," she said innocently enough.

"I had a good race," Jennifer said, playing down her results. "Luz, that's a pretty name."

"Thanks, it's not my real name. It means 'light' in Spanish. My mother started calling me that when--" Luz stopped short of finishing the sentence. "Well, you don't want to hear about that. Let me introduce you to the others."

There was Dee Smith, a top triathlete in the state. Jennifer recognized her name from several race results she'd seen in a past issue of a local fitness magazine. Dee was a sponsored athlete and an intimidating figure to most pure runners. At five-eight she possessed a very muscular figure and broad shoulders spent from time in the water. Her chlorinated hair was wiry and white and fell four inches straight to a square jaw line that seemed sharp enough to cut bread. She said nothing to Jennifer other than "hey", which added to her intimidating character.

Barbara Duff greeted Jennifer next. Barbara was the president of Spiridon Running Club, named for the first Olympic gold medalist in the marathon, Spiridon Loues.

"Welcome to track," Barbara said. There was a tone of excitement in her voice like she was getting ready to sell her something. "I saw you talking to Mel and some of the others. Don't be shy. Everyone here is really nice, so if there's someone you haven't met just go say hello."

"Thanks, I will." Jennifer looked in the direction of the other women. They were all fit and exceptional athletes.

As if reading her thoughts Barbara said, "I'm sure your first day here can be a little intimidating. But don't worry, you look like you can hold your own unless--"

"Unless what?"

"Unless you get into a conversation with Mel." Barb laughed. "I saw you lose that one."

Jennifer laughed. "I'm so glad you said that. I thought it was just me."

"No. She drives us all crazy."

Barb was an older woman, late-thirties perhaps. She was charismatic and looked at Jenny straight in the eyes when she talked.

Jenny took an immediate liking to her.

"And after track I want to talk to you about joining Spiridon Running Club. We need more talented women in the club."

So then, she is trying to sell me something, more or less, thought Jennifer. "You mean this has nothing to do with Spiridon?"

"No, not at all, except that most of the women here belong to the club," Barbara said. "This is just Toni's group she's gathered to remind us who's number one around here."

Jenny's eyes got big.

"Just kidding," Barb said. "Speak of the Devil."

Toni showed up. Toni had fiery red hair. Some would say it was her hair that earned her the nickname "Torch." Others would say it was her awesome speed that earned her that name. Immediately the other women approached her and said hello. It was obvious the other women in the group held her in high regard.

"Well, there she is," Barb pointed out. "Of course you probably don't need an introduction. Nobody does." And just as quickly as Barbara had said something about not being intimidated by the level of talent at the track, Jennifer saw her swallow hard.

Within minutes the group of ten began a slow warm up around the track. Jenny ran next to Toni and thanked her for the invitation to run with the group.

"I'm sure you'll enjoy yourself," replied Toni, with a touch of sarcasm in her voice.

It was the double-meaning tone in her voice that Jenny would hear a hundred times over in the course of the next few years. But this was the first time she heard it and it startled her. Jenny dropped back to run with another woman and questioned the intent of Toni's words. Through years of competitive running Jenny was not naive to mental intimidation by other runners; it's not prevalent but it exists as a game that few play. Still, Toni's comment made little sense. Toni had just beaten her soundly in a race five days ago and had nothing to prove.

So Jenny quickly deduced that there was nothing to be made of Toni's comment. After all, Toni had befriended her at the race and had extended the invitation to run with the group. She concluded that the whole scene, with ten different personalities that included a certain share of large egos, was just a difficult one to digest all at once. Just do the workout and stop thinking, she said to herself.

Ten of Denver's finest women runners circled the track that night. And when it was over Jenny felt as spent as she'd ever felt in all her years of running. She was filled with a great sense of satisfaction having been pushed by the most accomplished group of athletes she'd ever had the opportunity to run with. She knew the high would last all night.

A month had passed since she'd moved to Denver and she finally felt like she'd made some friends and was settling in.

From the balcony, a mere stone's throw away, I had watched the entire workout. *Junky that I am.*

*

Jennifer Ledge was a year out of college and new to the city of Denver by way of Las Vegas, Washington D.C., and upstate New York. She was recruited out of college by the Department Of Energy as part of a program created to interject talented, enthusiastic college graduates into areas of management in hopes that they would lend new ideas to a government which recognized its own staleness. Unfortunately, for the exact same reason why the program was created it bombed. With each level the program passed through its focus filtered, eventually drowning in its own bureaucracy. One low-level supervisor was so surprised to hear that Jennifer had been assigned to his office he greeted her by saying, "why fix what ain't broken?" Jennifer thought about pointing out that while the "machine" still moved its wheels were falling off. But instead she just left it alone. It was obvious that the demand was not recognized or simply not wanted at this level. And of course when that is the case supply is inevitably pushed aside. So her assignment failed that time, as it did each time, and she was sent elsewhere.

This time they had moved her, "permanently" to Denver to work at the Rocky Flats Nuclear Plant to be the understudy of Janet Kurth, Director of Public Relations.

A new body was needed at the plant. Janet Kurth was constantly under great emotional and physical strain to answer to the press and special interest groups regarding the safety of the Plant. She was also looking to retire in a few years.

"Send me a talented young individual, who's bright, energetic, follows instruction well, career minded, and willing to relocate," said Janet Kurth. At least that's what they had told Jenny when she agreed to accept the position. Janet had actually asked for someone who could "put up with a lot of shit and who isn't afraid of getting buried in it!" But basically, "any warm body will do! Just ANYONE!" she'd said.

So when Jennifer was told of the opportunity in Denver she was excited. "You're just the person we're looking for," Janet had told her over the phone, "being that you..." Janet rolled her eyes and shuffled through some crap on her desk locating a note pad with Jennifer's work experience listed on it. "...worked at the Yucca Mountain site and have a basic understanding of nuclear waste and storage."

Yucca Mountain is a project about a hundred miles north of Las Vegas where the Government hopes to store nuclear waste someday. Currently it is undergoing testing.

"Yes, I worked there for six months," Jenny said encouragingly.

"I'm sure that experience will come in handy," said Janet, picking wax out of her ear.

"Thanks for the opportunity," Jenny had said. "I won't let you down."

I don't really give a shit, thought Janet. I'm out of this toxic dump in a few years anyway. "I'm sure you'll do a great job."

Next, Jennifer had called her parents in upstate New York and told them the good news.

"I'm being slated as the next Public Relations Director at Rocky Flats," she'd said excitedly. "Janet told me she'd looked at dozens of possible choices but in the end she just kept on coming back to me."

"Imagine that," said her father.

"Yeah, someone must be looking out for me up there," Jenny said, "because I didn't even have to fly in for an interview."

"That's wonderful," her mother said. "Now, where exactly is Denver?"

"It's closer than Las Vegas."

"But it's not New York."

"Mom, DOE doesn't have any locations in New York," Jennifer reminded her. "Besides, Denver seems like a great place."

Jenny had been told that Denverites live a very active lifestyle. Certainly the ski industry is a major influence in the state. And there didn't seem to be a lack of talented runners along the front range either. One could be in Boulder, shopping for groceries, and be standing next to a current or future world record holder. She knew that once she began to enter races she would toe the line with the likes of talented runners whom she'd only read about. The notion was both frightening and exciting.

The evening run with the likes of Toni Jamison proved that point. She could hardly wait for next Thursday's track session.

When she returned home from the track workout she showered and changed into a favorite pair of jeans and a green sweatshirt that read: Golden Griffins X-Country. Jenny is a small girl, not even a hundred pounds, and her small frame was forever lost in it. She sat on her only piece of new furniture--a floral chintz sofa--and took inventory on her life. Her apartment was small and her belongings were few but she felt a sense of pride in her well-being. She thought of how her parents scraped their pockets to send her to the state college where she would eventually help ease the burden by competing in cross-country and earning a full scholarship in that sport her final two years. She thought of how her parents instilled in her a strong work ethic and how that had enabled her make the Deans List every semester and eventually graduate with honors, and how she continued to use that same drive and motivation to improve on her running. But most of all she thought about what a crazy, yet exciting year it had been; the people she had met, the young men she had dated--all of whom lasted only a short time after finding out how difficult it would be to date a girl with greater ambitions, higher goals, and a strong addiction to running. "You're getting up at five a.m. to run?" one once asked, fearing he might be asked to come along.

She laughed at the memory of that.

And then she laughed harder at a memory that came back to her full and strong. It was of a time many years ago, when all of this craziness first started...

...."I'm spitting up blood!"

"Me too!" the twelve year old with curls said, launching a wad of spit that landed several feet from her. "See!"

There wasn't really any blood mixed in with the saliva but when the wad landed in the powdery dirt it turned thick and saucy, enough to convince the two imaginative children.

"Yuk," the other girl commented, black hair, Italian descent.

"I can't help it," curly hair replied. "If she makes me run another hundred yards I'm going to spit up an entire lung!"

They were hidden under the protective confines of the bleachers. A safe haven for two children in gym class looking to escape the burden of physical endurement. As they watched their classmates run by, their eyes were illuminated by a ray of sunlight which breached their dark castle. At the far end of the track stood their teacher, an imposing woman by the name of Mrs. McCoy, staring down at a hand-held stopwatch calling out times for the children as they crossed the finish line. "Good job girls," she yelled. "Jenny and Teresa, you're up!"

Teresa ducked low, unwilling to surrender to the teacher's invitation. "She can't make us run again, can she?" A pouty look, lips turned down, sinking brows. "Why, that would be...." Her eyes darted back and forth until she was able to remember the word her mother had used the previous night. "...incredulous!"

"Yeah, it would be...in--credallis," mimicked Jenny.

An infectious laugh spread between the two, having stumbled upon such a gigantic word, and more, a meeting of two young hearts.

But the shrill of the giggle was just enough to reveal them. The next sight they saw was a pointed finger in their direction. "They're in there!" shouted the finger's owner.

Their cover blown, they crawled out from under the bleachers and stood in ridicule of their classmates. "Slow Pokes! Wimps!"

One of the better "athletes" in the group, a girl with braces on her teeth, approached Jenny and yelled in her face, "you're afraid to run a hundred yards!"

"Am not!" said Jenny, defensively, "but I'm spitting up blood!"

To prove her point, she once again launched a wad of spit that not only flew an impressive ten feet from her but managed to find the top of Mrs. McCoy's white athletic shoe.

Suddenly the classmates were dead silent, aware that the teacher was not at all pleased about being spat on.

For several seconds that followed the only sound that was heard was Jennifer swallowing hard. *Gulp!*

"I think you owe me a hundred yards," said Mrs. McCoy, not bothering to wipe the spit off her shoe.

"She can't run a hundred yards!" the girl with the braces blurted out. "She couldn't outrun a goat!"

Now all the girls were laughing hard again, at Jennifer's expense.

"Can too!" shouted Jenny.

"Can not!" the other said.

They were standing toe to toe--all eighty pounds each.

"Can too!"

"Can not!"

It's hard to say who pushed who, but a moment later the two were on the ground, pulling hair, wrestling.

Mrs. McCoy abruptly pulled them apart, despite the appetite for fight of the young classmates.

"I'm not going to tolerate fighting in this class!" said the teacher, sternly. "If you want to challenge each other then do it on the track. Both of you line up for the hundred yard dash!"

Jennifer and other girl exchanged an evil glance, possibly a sneer.

Even at the age of twelve one understands the feeling of dignity and the need to prove your worth to yourself and others.

When the two girls lined up next to each other and the teacher blew the whistle to start running Jennifer spurted from the line so fast that the other girl just simply stopped in her tracks to watch. A moment later Jennifer would lay claim to the fastest hundred yards clocked all year in the gym class of Mrs. McCoy.

The previous night Jenny had seen the ending of Casa Blanca while channel surfing and now couldn't resist a near quote from Bogart. While walking away from the track with her new best freind she turned to her and said, "Teresa, this could be the start of something beautiful," referring to the run. Indeed, it was the day her life changed forever and she began the chase of a lifetime.

It was a great memory, that day. But she was suddenly aware that she had no one else to share it with at the moment, and specifically the loneliness of being so far from home.

She was troubled by the miles that separated her from her parents. But the economy in the Northeast had taken a turn for the worst in recent years and good jobs were hard to come by. Under better circumstances she was confident that her education could afford her a high salary in the private sector. But many of her friends who stayed at home were working for wages far beneath their potential. So she took comfort in her decision to come to work for DOE. They had promised her a bright future which she now seemed on the verge of realizing.

At least she hoped so. Three moves in one year was wearing on her.

But even still she looked on the bright side. She'd at least had the opportunity to see several areas of the country.

She reflected on the downside as well. Budding friendships had went by the wayside with each move.

But even that had a silver lining. A while back she decided to use the transient period in her life to improve on her running. After all, running skills were something she could take with her where ever she might be sent. Friends and relationships had a way of slipping under. Her resolve turned out positive.

While in Las Vegas she'd shunned the intoxicating night life for which the city is known, went on few dates, and chose to spend her time training hard in the surrounding desert canyons and mountains. Weekends were often spent in search of old mining roads which seemed to go on forever and lead nowhere.

Then, just as she thought would happen, the Department moved her again, to Denver. She brought with her a confidence which she had never shown. Although the drastic change of running at altitude threatened to choke her supply of oxygen, she had, just days ago, tied her PR at the 5K distance, placing second to Toni "Torch" Jamison. She was running times that only a year ago she dreamed about.

Her thoughts were interrupted by the ringing of the phone.

"Hi Jenny. This is Barbara Duff."

"It's nice of you to call. What's up?"

"Are you planning on running the Sneak on Saturday?"

Jenny had heard some of the women at track talking about the race. She was already tempted but undecided. Racing on two consecutive weekends so early in the season probably wasn't smart. She put her hand on her right thigh which was stiff and under arrest from lactic acid; recovery time at altitude seemed endless. Yet she didn't want to come right out and say no. Her social life had been almost nonexistent. "I don't know. It's a good race though, isn't it?"

"It's the first large race of the season around here. Most of the girls from track will be running. I heard you placed second to Toni last week in that 5K." Barbara continued with curious speculation in her voice that resembled something between a question and a statement. "This could be your chance to, uh, beat her."

With that, Jenny had to laugh. "Toni killed me in that race and there was no one there to push her. I wouldn't come close to her in a competitive race. But thanks for the boost in confidence. Will you be racing?"

"I thought I'd give it a try. It's early in the season and I've always found it to be a good barometer as to what kind of shape I'm in." Barbara laughed, and added, "or how bad of shape I'm in."

"You look like you're in fine shape," said Jennifer.

"Got to stop eating so much, you know?

"I suppose."

"Also, it's interesting to see who the new competition will be each year, like yourself," said Barbara. "And afterwards I'm throwing a party for Spiridon Running Club. It should be fun."

"I'm not sure if I want to find out how I stack up to a good field this early in the year. I mean, it could get really ugly," said Jenny. "Especially with the way I've been feeling."

The comment took Barbara by surprise. "You mean you've been sick and still ran as strong as you did earlier tonight?"

"No, nothing like that. It's an altitude thing," Jenny paused "You, being born and raised here, wouldn't understand."

But in a way Barbara did understand. She knew from other conversations with runners that acclimating to altitude wasn't easy. Runners often talked about battling the effects of less oxygen: slower race times, quicker into oxygen depth, longer recovery time. It seems like everything is slightly slower at altitude. Even water takes longer to boil!

The funny thing about running at altitude is that after you have acclimated it hurts less, but you still run slower than you might at sea level. I've personally noticed a difference of ten to twenty seconds slower per mile. Runners who live at altitude typically carry two sets of PR's: an altitude PR and a sea level PR.

They both laughed and continued to talk for nearly an hour.

By the end of the conversation Jenny agreed to run the race. Her dating life had been nonexistent for months now and the party afterwards sounded promising.

THREE

The ringing carried a weight to it that pounced on me from every angle of the room, shaking me from my slumbered state. Without raising my head from the pillow, my eyes still shut, I located the source.

I whispered a groggy "hello." It barely came out.

"Is this Paul Jeffries?"

I didn't recognize the voice. I managed to open one eye. The bedside clock read: 7:10. God, what's happened? I wondered. Someone in my family must have had an accident! "This is," I said. "Has there been some--"

"Hi," a cheerful voice erupted through the line. "This is Linda Lockey with Southern One Bank. I was wondering if you've had a chance to send this month's payment in on your installment loan?"

I grabbed my head with my free hand. I suppose that's the universal symbolic reaction to most puzzling situations. Something inside me screamed to ask what the purpose of this call was at such an offensive hour--and on a Saturday! Yet I was still groggy and unable to take an indignant stand. The next words out of my mouth were apologetic in tone. "I forgot." Which was the truth. "I've been busy and it slipped my mind. I'll mail it today."

"So then I can expect to receive it by when?"

This struck me as odd. It was bad enough that she called at such an early hour but now it seemed as if she was doing her best to piss me off. Still, I was unable to fully gain my faculties. "Well, I suspect you'll get it in a few days," I said. I was beginning to gain my wits. "If I stick it in the mail today wouldn't it make sense that you'd get it shortly thereafter? I don't deliver the damned mail."

But the woman seemed impervious to my sarcasm. She was just an employee doing her job--a pawn in a game. She said indifferently, "I'll make a note of that. Thank you and have a pleasant day."

And with that the line went dead.

Well, I *was* planning on having a pleasant day. I just didn't expect it to start out so rudely. It was the twenty-eighth day of April and the day of the Cherry Creek Sneak five miler. I had planned to run it until earlier in the week when I pulled a hamstring. Given that, I changed my plans and decided to sleep late--and sleeping late certainly passed for pleasant, didn't it?

I was quite beside myself. The call had really angered me. If only I had my senses about me when she called I would have told her a thing or two! But then I suppose that's why creditors often call so early in the morning; to catch us deadbeats off guard. I fumed over this for several minutes and tried to remember her name. Linda. Linda what? Then it came to me. Linda Lockey.

I sat up in bed and contemplated laundering the soiled mound of clothing in the corner of my bedroom. Suicide would be less painful. I had watched it grow for the past week like it was some kind of bacteria experiment in a school project. I'd gotten lazy. Laziness evolved from depression, I suppose. I always get that way when I come down with an injury, no matter how slight it may be. This one was going to keep me from competing in the first big race of the season.

Then I thought about the girl I had seen at track the other night.

She was young and pretty. Twenty--twenty two years old, tops, I was thinking. It was difficult to tell from a distance. Runners often appear to look younger, especially from afar when one can only witness their slender, athletic builds. Still, I could make out a few details: chestnut colored hair, braided and pulled through the opening in a white cap, fell a quarter of the way down her back; her face was lit with excitement and she seemed to hold a smile longer than not. Months later she would tell me that endless smile stemmed from nerves--she'd been so intimidated that day that her stomach had turned into one giant knot.

I was taken back by her physical prowess. She, so simply put, looked fast. There is no other way to tell you. But I'll tell you why later on.

And was she racing today? I suddenly wondered. There was only one way to find out.

I took one last look at the pile of dirty clothing before making my way from the bedroom and out the front door. The laundry would have to wait for yet another day, now aware that I had only thirty minutes to get to the race.

*

Jenny's mouth was agape as she watched nearly ten thousand runners flock to the starting area of the Sneak. Many runners stretched their calves and hamstrings, leaning against buildings, street signs, and even each other. Some ran fifty yard striders out in front of the start line, others simply jumped up and down. Still, others seemed to be in deep thought and many talked and exchanged nervous laughter with each other. In all, the scene looked rather chaotic.

"How do you feel?" asked Barbara, who had given Jenny a ride to the race.

"Nervous. You?"

"Hell yes."

Jenny was no stranger to pre-race jitters, but she never knew how she would feel prior to a race. After all, each race had a different flavor, a disposition of its own. And because of this, new emotions were always mounting in her. In the past she'd experienced both vigor and sadness. Sometimes strength, other times weakness. But now, in this chaotic mass of bodies, she felt feel sick to her stomach, and oddly enough, out of her element. She didn't even know where to line up.

In smaller races she'd always search for somewhere close behind the elite male runners, usually about two or three rows back. But she'd never been in a race of this magnitude. Lining up too close to the front she'd risk getting trampled by hoards of inexperienced male runners who often jump from the starting line like Sears is having a lawn and garden sale. But if she lined up too far back she wouldn't stand a chance of catching the other top women who would surely have a hundred meters on her before she even reached the official starting line.

"Come with me," Barbara said.

The two pushed their way up to the front as far as possible. Ten rows back they realized it was useless to try any more.

"This is hell!"

"Tell me about it," echoed Barb. "If I hadn't had that extra piece of pizza last night I'd be able to squeeze up a few more rows."

Jenny assumed the comment was thrown out to ease the rising anxiety of the moment, but there wasn't a hint of humor anywhere on Barb's face: horizontal lines from cheek to cheek. Jenny looked away immediately. It was an odd time to notice but Barbara seemed obsessed with her weight. She spoke of food each time Jenny had talked with her.

Just then a very large man, dressed in black Lycra tights, fat hanging over each side of his waist, stepped in front of her. Jenny and Barb squeezed to his side. "Look, there's Toni, Mel, and Luz."

The three were tucked in nicely behind the elite male runners in the second row.

"Lets see if we can get up there." Jenny's voice trailed off at the end of the sentence, realizing how ridiculous it would be to try.

Unexpectedly the gun sounded. She didn't even hear the countdown. Was there one?

Within seconds Barb was no longer at her side.

Away in a flood of bodies Jenny was swept.

Runners bore in from every angle. Elbows flew finger-close to her face. A child, perhaps ten years old suddenly appeared directly in front, causing her to sharply veer to her left. How did a child get up here? She nearly fell but a strong hand, which she never got to place with a face, grabbed her elbow and steadied her. It was useless to try and thank who ever it might have been. She could only keep her eyes fixed straight ahead.

Just as she suspected, exuberant men, whom she guessed must think they're out to run a hundred meter dash flew by her on either side. The rage she felt quite suddenly turned to helplessness as the undulating sea of bodies pushed forward.

She felt her stomach churn. A warranted fear consumed her. She wanted to vomit.

She glanced left, desperately wanting to seek refuge somewhere on the side, but she was too deep within the current of runners. Any attempt to fight the forward motion of the field, to veer at any angle, would surely result in disaster and injury. She felt most vulnerable when both feet were in the air, when even a small bump from behind might send her sprawling.

Then it seemed as if the flow of runners began to thin.

A half mile into the race the pretenders and the inexperienced, unpracticed runners began to drop back. As they did, her anxiety began to fade as well.

Minutes later Jenny found a comfortable stride and was able to gain control of her breathing.

She'd never been in anything like that before--ever!

She gathered her composure and soon the competitor within emerged. A tallying look to the front resulted in a count of three other women. She wasn't in bad position after all! Although she realized that there were probably a few women hidden behind the fifty or so men who still ran in front of her.

Jenny recognized Toni right away. Her bright red hair stuck out like a flashing beacon in the fog, appearing and disappearing in the pack of men who surrounded her. Toni had a graceful, half-moon stride which Jenny, even in this moment of competition, fell victim to notice and envy.

Between Toni and herself was a shorter, plumper girl with a long, blonde pony-tail whom Barbara had pointed out as one to keep an eye on. Jenny was shocked by the girl's ass; it was rather large for a talented runner. Yet the girl continued to plow through the field like a run-away locomotive.

Up ahead, Jenny could hear a race official calling out split times for the first mile. "Five-fourteen....fifteen...sixteen..."

Jenny went through the opening mile in a five twenty-seven. "Oh shit!" Considering the slow start she was shocked by the time. The adrenaline must have really kicked in. She wondered if she would die and ugly death in the minutes to come. Yet, it wasn't the first time she'd gone out too fast in a race.

She cognitively slowed her pace to what she believed was something she'd be able to hold for the next four miles.

At some point before the second mile Mel pulled up next to her.

Between breaths she blurted out, "Hey! Jenny! I, thought that was you. Let's run together."

Given that Jenny was going about as fast as she could manage she really had no choice.

They cruised along at a capable pace, although Mel was lanky and awkward, brushing Jenny's side twice in two miles. Still, they worked well together and managed to pick off dozens of competitors including the pudgy girl with the blonde pony-tail.

From the side Jenny heard: "fourth and fifth women!"

She was satisfied with her position. The women in front of her were too far ahead to catch. Indeed, she hadn't seen the "Torch" since the third mile.

But then she began to tire rapidly. *Hang on.*

With well over a mile to go she found herself hurting badly. Within seconds Mel put ten meters on her. Then twenty. Then fifty!

She'd gone out too fast after all and now she was about to pay the piper.

She ran the fourth mile in a lethargic six-forty. She felt sick and dizzy. Her world spun around her as a surreal quality filled her head. Her legs felt callous, like two inanimate objects along for the ride. She fought to just keep them moving.

The pudgy girl passed her. Then Luz Diaz pulled up next to her and said, "only four more minutes, hang on!" *I must really be falling apart for a competitor to say such a thing, thought Jennifer.* She couldn't say anything in return and Luz ran on by. Dozens of men swarmed on both sides of her. *Am I even moving at all?* Another girl passed, and still another one! It seemed as though all ten thousand runners would eventually pass her.

Jenny's lungs were hot and dry and rebelled against her every attempt to expand them. At long last, the finish line was in sight. Four hundred meters, then three. She wanted to stop! Then one hundred. Close to the finish chute Dee Smith ran by her smiling and said, "wonderful race, wasn't it?" Jennifer couldn't even acknowledge her, otherwise she would have told her to fuck off. Her mind swam in a sea of delirium. Her eyes were glazed and washed over, like an old woman with cataracts.

She had no idea how many women passed her in the final mile. She was sure she hadn't see them all. She was glad she hadn't seen them all.

*

I was standing alone under the expanse of an enormous Elm passively observing the dozens of athletic figures gathered at the party. I brushed away pretzel crumbs that had gathered in the folds of my shirt. I was suddenly conscious that my shirt read: BREAKFAST RUN. Below the caption was a drawing of two pieces of toast and several eggs, all of which had human legs attached; they were racing. How ridiculous, I thought. I can't believe I wore this shirt! I took a large swallow of beer from a plastic cup and another bite of the pretzel, now hoping to hide the shirt by replacing the crumbs I had just brushed off with new ones. Some race T's are really lame, I thought.

I recognized a few of the talented runners from the Sneak but since I had never met any I found it awkward to approach anyone in particular. Mostly, I was content to eavesdrop.

I was suddenly aware of what an odd sort of bunch us runners must appear to nonrunners. We must irritate the hell out of them! We, like no other group other than proctologists perhaps, can laugh and hold a lengthy conversation about pooping. "If I could race every day I'd be as regular as clock-work," one man was saying, "I get so nervous." When we see someone in motion we immediately critique them. Movie stars are easy targets because, with the exception of Bruce Dern and few others, they're not real runners. Once I watched the movie Ten with a good runner-friend of mine. Perhaps you remember the scene: gorgeous Bo Derek, running along the beach in slow motion, breasts bouncing and everything. "She'll never be any good," my friend said. "Her knees knock." I agreed. Somehow I think we were missing the point. We talk of things like PR's and splits and negative splits and get upset if we're two seconds a mile slower than we were last year. Some monitor their heart rates closer than doctors monitor terminally ill patients in a hospital. We all wear those funny shorts that are, lets face it, way too short to go anywhere but out for a run. It's not like we decide to go to church and throw a pair of them on. Our pets are named Chase, Bullet, Rocket, Comet, or after some legendary runner like Pre. We even talk in meters! Didn't anyone tell us the "new" math miserably failed in this country?

Although many of the conversations were about the earlier race. "I went out too fast.....I could have knocked off thirty seconds if..." I enjoyed hearing the ones that ended in "if." I wanted to finish the sentence for them. *If I didn't eat that double cheeseburger....if my parents hadn't passed on legs made of coal.* But I bit my lip and held silent. The beer was good company for now.

I reminded myself of what a bad attitude I'd developed in the past week since pulling the hamstring. Although, to my own defense, it did seem like every person there had a reason, an excuse, why they should have run better.

"Paul!" Barbara Duff had come out of nowhere to greet me. "I'm glad you decided to show."

Barb was the only other runner I knew at the party. She was the President of the running club, host of the party, and a welcomed site.

"I thought you'd never show," I said.

"I've been at the awards ceremony. Ninth place!" she screamed, beaming and holding up an age group trophy.

"Congratulations," I said.

"Must have been those two extra pounds I lost last week," she said, laughing. "I take it my boyfriend, Mike who lives here also, has shown you around."

I quickly scanned the crowd for him although I have no idea why. I wasn't even aware that she had a boyfriend much less what he looked like. I looked back at Barbara. If it wasn't for her weathered appearance she'd be damned cute, I thought. She smiled constantly and if one didn't know her well enough might assume that the lines on her face were some lasting effect of all those smiles. But in reality the lines represented--more than anything else--a difficult life. *She's an interesting one, alright.*

At the time of this party Barbara Duff had held the position of president of the club for several years. She was a good club runner who lacked the physical genes to ever be an exceptional one. But that hadn't stopped her from trying.

I felt a certain comradery with her (or perhaps it was pity) since I had also obsessed about the run but lacked the physical qualities to ever live up to my expectations. Still, to each his own, I suppose. My obsession with the run hadn't led to the returns I expected. Perhaps hers had. I didn't know her well enough yet to decide.

But I did know one thing that would keep me from ever raining on her parade: her enthusiasm for running was unmatched by anyone I had ever known. Because of this I felt like she would always be the perfect choice for president of the club.

She battled both alcohol and drugs in her twenties. And while she was still known to throw back a few from time to time she claimed that her drinking was under control. "All those calories are bad for my running," she'd told me on our first meeting.

At one time she weighed a hundred and sixty pounds, was proud of drinking her male buddies under the table, and found herself bankrupt from having spent all her money on a serious cocaine addiction. Her problems came to a head one late October morning when she woke up in the intensive care ward of a hospital, diagnosed with a viral infection, inflammation of the lungs and pneumonia. She had spent the previous night lying face down on her lawn in below-freezing temperatures. She had lost another bout to the almighty bottle.

A change in her life-style was needed to--well--stay alive. That was ten years ago. Barbara now weighed a hundred and ten pounds. "I'm still pudgy," she'd say, searching for the least bit of looseness about her. But asked or not, Barb loved to tell the story of how that time spent in the hospital was the turning point in her life, and anyone who listened would undoubtedly believe her because she simply gave them no other choice. One could see the truth in her eyes.

"Thanks for the invitation," I said. After meeting her that first time at the track she had talked me into joining the club. "It looks like a great bunch."

Barb introduced me to several members. Most of the people were exceptionally pleasant and I felt a twinge of guilt for silently mocking them earlier.

After an hour the party was in full swing. A hundred people swapped stories and laughter on the same front lawn where Barbara had once passed out and nearly died.

At one point I found myself standing in a group of runners next to the tall red head from the Thursday night group. I didn't even know her name as of yet. I wanted to introduce myself and tell her that I had seen the Thursday night workouts but I suddenly felt at odds in doing so. How could I tactfully reveal that I had been watching her from my balcony every week now since the weather turned nice. If worded wrong it might come out sounding rather strange: "I've been watching you..." So I chose to say nothing.

Later, as I was about to tell the punch line of a joke to a few captive listeners, the new girl from track appeared in front of me. I found myself unable to remember the line. Since my timing was thrown off I sensed that the joke would bomb anyway. I thought about starting over for her sake as well as mine. But an impatient listener who probably needed to relieve his bladder briskly asked me to continue.

"And so--" But it was no use. The punch line had completely escaped my thoughts!

"And so--Oh God, it seems as if I've forgotten," I finally said.

The impatient man made a dash for the bathroom. The others politely laughed with or at me--I'm not quite sure.

I was rather embarrassed. I wanted to say something to the new girl but I sensed that I had just made an irrevocable fool of myself. *Great first impression.*

Still, my eyes found her eyes and I fought for something to say. But what's to say? From my balcony I'd witnessed her awesome talent and from the street I'd seen the focus in her eyes as she pitted herself against the clock, but I realized now that I was truly seeing her for the first time.

I'm bias, but...

She's beautiful, I was thinking. Her eyes were coral brown, flecked with tid-bits of green. There was a certain sensuality about them that left me breathless. Her face was thin, but the structure was not extreme, not gaunt like some other runners I'd seen; ones whom strangers might take pity on and offer food in a humanitarian way. The spring season was evident on her skin--a faint shading from having spent time under the sun. It looked soft to the touch--I wanted to reach out to do so, but naturally refrained.

Her lips were full and lush and easily curled to render a smile when she held out her hand and introduced herself.

"Jenny Ledge, sorry to blow your joke."

"Paul Jeffries and it would have bombed just the same."

"Doubtful," she said. "My timing always seems to be off."

"Mine too," I replied. "Look, I've scared them away."

It was just the two of us now, face to face. So intimidated that I found it difficult to look her in the eyes.

"Bathrooms, beer, a bad joke," she smiled. "Don't take it personally."

"Yeah, but I don't know anybody," I said. "Other than Barbara," I added.

"Well, we're even then."

"Not really," I said too quickly. "You know--" I spotted a few of the women she ran with on Thursday nights, "--them!"

A confused expression washed over her face. "How'd you know that?"

Oh God, I searched for a way to diffuse this bomb. I couldn't very well tell her I'd seen her workouts. That I'd jumped out of bed this morning to specifically see her race. She'd think I was a lunatic.

"I saw you in the race today. You're a fast one," I said, nervous smile. "I figured you must know them." Innocent enough, I figured.

"You really think I'm fast?" She actually giggled when she asked this.

"Fourth woman," I said, like a school kid proudly knowing the answer.

"Fourth woman at mile three," she said. "Fourteenth woman at the end! Yeah, I really kicked some ass today," she said with heavy sarcasm.

"Fourteenth out of four thousand women," I replied, putting it in perspective. Nonetheless, it was obvious she wasn't happy about being passed by ten women in the final two miles. She suddenly looked glum and didn't respond to my optimism. Suddenly aware that we were headed south on a conversation that promised to move forward with the grace of a three legged dog, I searched for something new to say, a better topic. *Your hair, your eyes, your lips, your legs. Damn!*

"You'll get 'em next time," was my only offering.

"Yeah, I might," she replied. "If I don't blow up again."

"We've all blown up at races," I said.

She shook her head in agreement and smiled an appreciative smile.

Common ground.

*

Later that evening I was back in my apartment. I reflected on what a great day it had been. I wanted to prolong it.

As the hours passed I thought more and more of Jenny, occasionally saying her name just to listen to it roll off my tongue. I had felt so uncomfortable with her in the beginning, but soon after we had talked freely. I was happy and I wanted to ride that high as long as possible.

I picked up the phone and dialed information.

"Operator?....Denver....Do you have a listing for....."

Seconds later, at exactly one twenty-eight a.m., a very groggy, but recognizable voice could be heard on the other end of the line.

"Who's this?" the voice asked, unamused.

"This is Paul Jeffries," I said. "I wanted to let you know that I forgot to send that payment off to you today which means you probably won't get it 'till Wednesday."

"Excuse me?" the voice was slightly more awake now, angry.

"This *is* Linda Lockey, isn't it?" I laughed.

FOUR

The Bolder Boulder consistently ranks as one of the finest 10K road races in America. Because of the more than thirty thousand participants and a similar amount of spectators, many view it as more of an event than a race. There's no argument from me on this point, knowing that it takes the average entrant over an hour to complete the course. They must be doing something other than racing out there!

The course winds through both residential and commercial sections of Boulder, Colorado. Along the route, bands, belly dancers, and a group of high-kicking, chorus senior citizens are just some of the well-wishers who entertain the runners. In good spirit, the locals blast music from their front yards, spray water on the runners, and taunt them with cold beer--I was once offered a joint. The course ends in Folsum Stadium on the campus of Colorado University, where the runners and spectators celebrate for hours afterwards.

The event actually consists of four separate races. It starts with a citizen's race--which is run in waves that can total over thirty, beginning with the "A" wave saved for the better men and women. Then the wheel-chair race takes place, followed by the women's elite race, and finally the men's elite race which is run around noon.

A healthy and deep purse always ensures a large field of world class runners for the elite races. Yet, in years past, the late start has seen many of them complain that the often hot and muggy conditions combined with the altitude takes a toll on their times. One year, after Jill Hunter won the race in just over thirty-four minutes she apologized for her slow time. She might have been concerned about what the flat-landers back in her homeland of England would think. Nevertheless, the elite *do* appreciate the event. It's not often when even the great runners receive the recognition they do at the Bolder Boulder, having the opportunity to finish in a stadium filled with nearly forty thousand screaming, appreciative fans.

In the elite race, invitations are also extended to the areas top runners, giving them an opportunity to showcase their talents in front of the hometown fans.

That year several members of Spiridon were invited.

Jennifer was not one of them.

I lined up next to her at the start of the citizen's "A" wave. She told me she was glad she didn't receive an invitation.

"I haven't earned it," she said, the disaster of the Sneak still fresh in her mind.

She seemed rather indifferent about the whole notion. If she was upset for not being invited it didn't show. If she was relieved I couldn't tell. I didn't dare dig too deep--I hadn't earned that right either.

"Besides," she said, "I'd probably come in dead last in the elite field."

There *was* that possibility, I suppose.

"Even in the Olympic games, someone--some phenomenal athlete--has to come in last," I said. "It wouldn't be anything to hang your head about." But even as I said it I questioned my comment. Finishing last, or near last, even in an elite race is nothing to take lightly. I'd talked with a woman who had been one of Denver's finest distance runners but finished near last at the '84 Olympic marathon trials. She tried to compete for some time afterwards, but eventually, her will broken, she stopped running altogether. In any case, Jennifer's comment took me by surprise and I left it alone.

We were lined up towards the middle of our wave when the gun sounded. Though, unlike the Sneak, it didn't seem to matter; this wave consisted of quality runners who knew how to pace themselves, were considerate of other runners, and able to keep a straight line. So our poor starting position didn't do much to hamper our path out of the chute.

It took Jenny less than a minute for her to humble me, leaving me in her wake and take up with the lead pack of women.

Then, after the first turn I lost sight of her.

*

Barbara Duff had warned Jennifer about the Bolder Boulder course. "It's deceptively hard and not one to expect a PR on," she'd said. It has many turns, a few hills, very crowded, and often hot. "...above all, don't go out too fast or you'll find yourself hanging on like you did at the Sneak."

Despite the warning Jennifer bolted from the starting line like she was being chased by a butcher. It had been nearly a month since the Sneak. She felt a certain need to prove to herself that she could hang with the best of them, that the Sneak had been a terrible goof.

Now in the race, she thought back to her training during the past month: fifty miles a week including a speed session each Thursday. She was race ready.

Her legs felt battle hard and she turned them with the fluidity of well-oiled pistons.

The first mile approached. She was one of six in the women's lead pack. They went through in 5:25. She thought of Barbara's warning.

Don't go out too fast...don't go out to fast... She rejected it. On she went--*get out of my way!*

The third mile marker was clearly in her sights. The lead pack had dwindled to four. Of them Jenny only recognized one: Luz Diaz.

But Luz had faded in the Washington Park 5K. She was big and had thick, muscular thighs; more of a sprinter's build. Her breathing was ragged and heavy. Jenny knew it wouldn't be long before the pack would consist of only three. Within the next quarter mile it had.

Many of the men who'd gone out too fast began to fade as well. This added a new, tangible element to the race. The road to victory now looked like an obstacle course latent with slower men whom they would have to negotiate their way around. Up until this point the pack had run closely knit, able to sense each other's strengths and weaknesses. But now the tightness of the pack was challenged. Jennifer wondered if the other two women were as frustrated as she was.

She didn't have to wonder for long.

The other two women were wearing matching singlets from a track club Jennifer didn't recognize. They exchanged looks and said something Jennifer wasn't able to hear. From years spent on the cross-country team in college (where victory is determined by placement and not time and therefore teammates "help" each other by racing together) Jennifer thought she was being set up to be torn down; the two would work together from here on to try and break her.

Running as a team has its advantages. Even in a sport that is nearly always seen as an individual effort there lies that hidden element. In the years that Jennifer had run cross-country she had been spat on, intentionally elbowed in the face and ribs, and often thrown off stride by opposing teammates who had purposely cut in front of her. Once an opposing team went so far as to soak their singlets in foul smelling perfume to nauseate the other runners if they dared to pass.

"Teaming" outside of cross-country racing is rare but Jennifer was getting a good taste of it now. These two frustrated her by crowding her in the turns; throwing her stride off.

The three came to a left turn, Jennifer was on the inside. There was a man directly in front of her who seemed to be barely moving. She tried to swing around him on his right but the other women held their position, giving her no space, and ran her into the back of him. At that point they surged and took a ten meter lead.

Jennifer came back on them within a minute. Yet another incident occurred.

At the four mile mark an aid station was set up. It came at the top of the longest hill on the course. Many runners slowed to take on water. But a man who was running directly in front of Jennifer stopped--cold turkey! Jenny plowed into his back and nearly went down. The incident cost her precious seconds and added to her frustration. Once again the other two women took advantage of her misfortune and surged on her.

Within the next quarter mile Jenny was up on them again. She thought about sarcastically thanking them for their concern. It was one thing to employ teaming tactics on her but to take advantage of an unfortunate incident that might have possibly caused injury was nothing short of unsporting and vile.

Instead, Jenny went by them, putting ten meters on the two. Yet the attack wasn't successful and they reeled her in within seconds. It would be impossible to break them now, she thought.

They turned onto Folsum Street with just over a mile to go. The noise level began to sear as the crowd grew larger. The applause propelled the three forward in a battle of will. They matched each other stride for stride.

Turmoil filled Jennifer's body. Perhaps the two are finally going to break me, she thought. I guess there is something to be said for cheap racing tactics, after all.

Just when Jenny was about to slip off the pace one of the other women let out a loud, exasperating sigh and quickly fell back. Now it was only two. I can't give up now, she thought.

The two entered the stadium elbow to elbow. The crowd went crazy. Over the loudspeaker an announcement was made. "The first woman...no...the first two women have just entered the stadium. They're in a heated contest with only a hundred meters to go! Here they come..."

Jennifer didn't hear any of this. The screams that came from within were louder. Her body was withered in pain. She no longer cared about winning the race. She just wanted to stop. Still, she pressed onward, propelled by the need to defeat the bitch next to her.

The finish line drew close.

Closer now. Kick it! Hang on! She's closing on me--hang on! Can't! Blacking out! Do it! Push! Puush! Puuush!

*

Spiridon Running Club reserved a room at the host hotel of the race. The club members were able to shower, party, and even catch the elite race on TV if they choose not to watch it live. Some members

38

planned to do both, catching the finish in the stadium a short five minute walk away.

Spirits soared throughout the room as word passed that one of their own members had won the women's citizen race, even though most had not yet met Jenny.

After an interview with several local journalists Jennifer came over to the party. She was greeted with cheer and high-fives from people she had never met. The whole scene was a bit overwhelming for her.

I was thrilled for Jennifer.

The race had been quite exciting. I had lost sight of Jennifer early on, but after the first mile, when the A wave began to thin, I was able to spot her again. She was running in the women's lead pack about fifty meters ahead of me.

Since I typically run about the same speed as the better women club runners, I have developed a great pleasure in watching them, seeing their race unfold before my very eyes. Like I said, I'm very comfortable with my positioning in the hierarchy of running and this, perhaps more than any other reason, is why. I compare it to riding in the press truck, with one huge difference; I'm on the playing field! I can experience first hand what the observer on the press truck can't. I can tell in an instant when someone's will has just been broken. I can feel the slightest incline on a course that might make the difference in a race. I can spot the slightest compromise in a runner's stride. I can hear their labor and sense the level of confidence in a given athlete. I can run in their shadows and experience the attacks, the denials, and the relentless surges meant to break a competitor's spirit and understand in an instant why someone, perhaps only ten meters in front, might be uncatchable.

I felt I had seen and experienced many of these things during the race. For nearly a half an hour I had been able to keep the lead pack of women in my sights. I had run in their shadows and witnessed the attacks and counter-attacks over and over again. It was a perfectly brutal race.

And when Jennifer nearly went down at the water station I honestly felt the race was over for her. If she had decided to drop out at that moment I would have too and walked with her off the course. But of course that did not happen. I felt so helpless as I watched her stumble, wishing I was close enough to have steadied her. But I was too far back to do anything.

Shortly after that the course took a hard left and I lost contact with them for good. Then, nearly two miles later, I heard the low roar of the crowd coming from the stadium. I could only wonder if Jennifer was still in the hunt for the win. I felt I knew the answer. When I finally entered the stadium I scanned the crowd in an attempt to find her. And when I did I saw that a race official had his arm draped around her shoulders and was escorting her up to the press box. I knew then it was her; that she had won. God, I was so happy for her.

Now in the hotel room I gave her a cold beer and a warm hug.

"Thanks Paul," she said. She was beaming. Even her eyes were smiling.

"You earned it," I replied.

"I've waited a long time for this."

I didn't know if she was referring to the beer or the victory. Perhaps both.

Just then, a few cheers went up from the club members who were gathered around the TV. The elite women's race was nearly underway.

Spiridon had two entrants in the race: Toni Jamison and Melissa Jones. There was a great amount of excitement as the club members were seen lining up next to the invited world class runners.

Toni looked exceptionally fit. There was a certain invincibility to her that I'd not seen before. But I think TV has a way of doing that; of dehumanizing a person and making them appear to be larger than life, untouchable in a sense. In person, she was vulnerable, human, she had a voice and real emotions. You could pinch her skin and watch it redden. But on TV she appeared altogether different. She'd taken on a hard facade and I saw her in the only way I could; as an athlete, an exceptional one at that, capable of running me and anyone else in the room into the ground. Her figure was daunting, intimidating, a mere apparition of a perfect running machine right there on the tube for everyone to witness--like it or not.

Others in the room felt the same thing. Comments were thrown back and forth about how "ripped" she looked, how determined and confident she appeared. We all saw her in a different light now. We saw her playing the role she was expected to play, quite simply, as one of the finest distance runners in America toeing the line with her peers.

And at this level she was no longer one of us; a member of Spiridon. She was someone entirely different, someone with a sponsor's name printed boldly across her chest, someone who's name was recognized in every running circle across America. So perhaps she *was* larger than life, as I knew it.

When the race finally got under way Toni could be seen throughout much of it running just off the pace. It was frightening to think that even at her level she was eventually outclassed. *Just how good were these other women? I wondered.*

Toni ran well and finished seventh. Mel--well--just a mile into the race she clipped another competitor's heals and the two went down. *Melissa Jones: DNF--did not finish.*

The elite men's race was the most exciting one in the history of the Bolder Boulder, with local favorite and Mexican Nationalist, Arturo Barrios pulling out a gut-wrenching, come from behind victory over fellow countryman Martin Pitayo.

*

Later that day Jennifer, Barbara and I were at a coffee shop on the Pearl Street Mall in Boulder still dressed in running attire. I was in a great mood since I hadn't expected Jennifer to accept my invitation for coffee before the thirty mile drive back to Denver. All she asked was if Barbara could come along since they drove up together.

Now an interesting thing about Boulder is its back to basics flavor. If you think "flower-power" died in '70 you haven't visited Boulder lately. Outside the coffee shop was a parked VW van crudely painted with peace signs and flowers, a relic from a time I thought had since disappeared. Just about anything that is grass-roots based goes in this town. A live and let live attitude prevails among the locals. So I was a little surprised to be getting stared at from other patrons.

"Don't look now," I said to Barbara, "but that girl with the nose ring, pierced lip, and black lipstick apparently doesn't like how you're dressed--or any of us for that matter. She's staring at you."

"I'm amused," Barb responded, looking back at the girl. "I guess she wasn't awake when thirty thousand of us ran through this town."

"Perhaps the stampede woke her and she's carrying a grudge into the afternoon."

"Most likely she just thinks were odd," said Jennifer, referring to the other patrons who looked and dressed similarly to the staring-girl. Personal hygiene was not high on the list of importance here.

Barbara lifted her coffee mug in the direction of the girl and smiled at her, who in turn stuck out her tongue, showcasing a silver ball that was pierced through it.

"That's disgusting!" Barb voiced, turning her attention back to Jenny and I.

We all cringed and laughed.

Obviously, we felt quite out of our element. So I decided to bring up a comfortable topic: the race. Specifically, the men's elite race, where Arturo Barrios pulled out an improbable victory.

"I heard him at a seminar," I said. "One thing that struck me was how soft spoken and reserved he was. Not at all how I envisioned the former world record holder in the road 10K to act."

"He's just a person," Jennifer said. "What did you expect?"

"Someone a little more intense, aggressive," I said. "You saw the look in his eyes when he passed Pitayo. Did that look conjure up thoughts of a mild mannered reporter?"

I could tell that Jennifer and Barbara weren't following me. They had never heard him speak. They had only seen the fierceness in him on the roads.

I told them that Arturo, in street clothing, seemed cool and relaxed, but in racing flats had the ability to drive a hammer into the heart of a competitor. So I explained that it was difficult for me to see Arturo as both Dr. Jeckle and Mr. Hyde.

"He seemed uncomfortable talking about his achievements in front of the group," I said, gathering my thoughts. "Although we stared at him with blank expressions for the better part of an hour like he was some kind of a God or something."

Jennifer and Barbara laughed.

"Under those circumstances I think anyone might be a little benign," said Jennifer.

Barbara noted how ironic it is that Arturo can command such respect from other runners, yet not even be recognized in public. "At least in this country," she said.

I was suddenly aware that Jennifer's eyes had not left me while Barbara had spoken.

I reached for my coffee and in doing so knocked over a water glass. Fortunately it was empty and when our eyes were no longer wide from having been startled we all had a good laugh.

"Anyway, I don't know how someone can stand up in front of a crowd for the better part of an hour and talk about running," said Jennifer. "It seems a little boring."

"I've been to several seminars that *were* boring," I commented, "but Arturo opened the discussion up among the running club. We talked about whether great runners were born or made."

"What was the conclusion?" Barb chimed in.

"Most everyone agreed it took both entities, with the emphasis being on being born with the right genes. In other words, choose your parents well," I laughed, suddenly having a vision of me standing naked in front of the mirror, my thighs too fat, my bones too large.

"That's depressing," Barb said, looking down at her own lap, sharing the same thought.

Then, as if on cue, Barb's and my eyes gravitated towards Jennifer's body, critiquing it in our thoughts.

Jennifer noticed immediately and crossed her arms in a modest reaction.

"Stop it!" she said.

"Sorry."

"So what about the other half of the equation?" asked Jennifer, getting back on track.

"The part about runners being made?" I asked.

"Yeah."

"Well, there's no question about that," I said. "Having the right genes is a nice start, but even *that* person will drown in mediocrity without the will to win. And if you need proof of that think about the race today--specifically the *moment*.

Jennifer and Barbara knew of the *moment* which I was referring. The race had been extremely tight throughout with Martin Pitayo, Arturo Barrios, and the defending champion from Kenya, Thomas Osano, exchanging leads. With a little more than a half a mile to go Pitayo surged, taking a commanding lead. Neither Barrios or Osano were able to respond. In distance racing if a surge is not quickly answered there's a good chance that it may never be answered, especially late in a race. It seemed like a sure sign of victory for Pitayo. The surge had devastated Osano who fell quickly off the pace, leaving only Barrios to challenge.

But Barrio's face revealed only pain and contempt. He barely clung to a ten meter gap. The television commentators had already conceded the race to Pitayo. And then I witnessed the miraculous.

Barrios began a kick from over three hundred meters out. He went by Pitayo and on for the victory.

In the fleeting seconds it took Barrios to pass, one could see the expression of disbelief on Pitayo's face.

Later that afternoon Barrios had commented on the bold move. "This is it; I knew I was either going to win the race or die trying."

Anyone who witnessed the event and the *moment* would think nothing less. Many of the runners from Spiridon said it was the most gut-wrenching victory they'd ever seen.

"A picture is worth a thousand words," I said. "At the seminar Arturo spoke of sacrifice, will, guts, and courage. He talked about hunger--not the feeling one has for lunch at noon--but the strife one might feel to overcome odds, to climb from the depths of poverty, for example. He suggested Americans haven't produced a winning distance team in ages because 'American's aren't hungry.'

"He talked about an earlier time in his career when he flew from Mexico to Phoenix to run the 1986 Continental Homes 10K. It was a ambitious venture since all he could afford was a one way plane ticket. He'd have to finish in the top 8 and rely on the prize money to get him home."

"Nothing like a little pressure," said Barb.

"It gets worse," I said. "He had little or no money left when he arrived in Phoenix. Thinking he'd have to go to bed hungry he was relieved to find that the elite runners were given a complimentary pre-race dinner. Later, in the hotel room, Martin Pitayo would allow him to share his bed so he wouldn't have to sleep on the floor."

"Pitayo?"

"Yeah, the same guy he outkicked today! So much for returning favors," I said, laughing.

"So how'd he do?"

"Well all he wanted to do was place in the money," I reminded them. "But when he toed the line at the race, looking around, he realized it was a virtual who's who of running."

"Again, the pressure--"

"Yeah, he'd actually been given the last seeded number in the field," I said. "Anyway, as the race grew old and pack dwindled he found himself amongst the leaders. He began to calculate his earnings with each runner dropped. He knew the exact amount for each placement--five grand to the winner. 'Five grand could feed a family in Mexico for a year he told us, putting it in perspective."

"He won, didn't he?" asked an impatient Barbara.

"Of course he won," I said. "He set the state loop course record with a time of 27:41 in the process. Imagine, here was this relatively unknown runner with a high seed leaving a world class field in his wake, kicking everyone's ass. He was suddenly in the big time!"

"Now that's hunger," commented Jennifer.

"I agree. And today, when his heart was strewn across the road for everyone to see, I think I finally understood what it means to have the will to win. It would have been so easy for him to follow Pitayo into the finish and settle for second place. Everyone would have told him what a great race he had run and that he should be happy to have placed second."

I looked at Jennifer. "You ought to know what I'm talking about. You spent time in the pit today and pulled out the victory."

"Thanks for the praise," Jenny said, blushing. "But I didn't really care at the end. I think I just outlasted the other girl."

Neither Barbara or I believed her. With the finish line in sight, battling for the win, one doesn't just outlast the other. The win is always earned.

I'd seen the race close up, following in her footsteps. I'd seen her competitiveness. The two others relentlessly surged on her and each time Jenny had answered, finally breaking them. So I could see the fire that, while dowsed by her own modesty, smoldered beneath her skin.

Jennifer turned to Barbara. "Besides, we all had heart today."

"Yes we did," I said. "Here's to the chase."

The three of us held our coffee mugs high in the air and clanked them together. "To victory!" we said.

We attracted more strange looks from the patrons.

Us runners! For God sakes we must irritate nonrunners.

*

The following day I learned that Arturo's victory at Boulder was on the heals of battling the flu just days prior. What's left to say?

FIVE

"Do you think we runners bother nonrunners?" I asked Jennifer.

"More than they bother us?" she laughed.

"Seriously," I said. "We're always talking about lowering our PR's and how many miles we're putting in and so on."

I could see that Jennifer wasn't really giving the question much thought.

"I mean, one time when I was skiing up at Winter Park I heard two stock brokers talking about the market," I said. "It made me really uptight to hear business being discussed at a place created for relaxation and enjoyment."

"Perhaps that was enjoyable for them," she said. "What's your point?"

"There's nobody I can ever talk to about my running goals, other than other runners," I said. "When I told my mother I was going to run a marathon she thought I was out to run six miles."

"I know what you mean," she said. "When I told my mother that someday I want to qualify and run in the Olympic trials she said to me, 'that's a tough race with all those Kenyans in it.'" (The women's marathon trials are held every four years in this country. Obviously, only American women run in this race, from which the top three make up the team that will go on to represent the United States in the next Olympiad.)

Jennifer slurped up the last noodle of what was a large heaping mound of Seafood Tortolini. "It sounds like you've got something on your mind," she said.

"Something," I admitted, leaning forward and glancing at her ninety-five pound frame. "Where did you put all that food?"

She was amused. She held her stomach in and refused to exhale until I sat back in my chair.

She let out a long sigh and said, "I have no idea but I know where your's is going."

This time it was her who bridged the gap. She poked a finger in my stomach. While my six foot, hundred and eighty pound frame is considered rather large for competitive running most nonrunners wouldn't consider me a large person. Still, like a thick fog, I could feel my waist close around her finger. "No fair," I said, "I wasn't ready for that!"

"I'm going to start calling you Jello Boy," she said.

We laughed.

The first date was going well.

We were sitting in Josephinas, a trendy, Italian restaurant in Larimer Square, downtown Denver. Live R&B was playing in an adjacent room and the words of a soulful singer echoed in our ears. *"...Seems like the real thing baby, seems like the thing I love, couldn't be nothing else baby, cause it's you I'm dreamin of..."*

We finished our dinner and made our way to the other side of the restaurant to be closer to the band.

Jennifer had never been here before and she commented on the eclectic decor. All kinds of things hung from the ceiling and the walls. It looked like the owner had a field day at a garage sale. Two badly dented trombones hung above us. Prints of turn-of-the-century posters adorned the red brick walls; one of Uncle Sam, pointing a board-straight finger and asking for your investment in government bonds to support the war.

My favorite item in the bar was a life-size, black and white print of ten young women in a beauty contest. I estimated that the original photograph was shot in the thirties. The women were dressed in loosely fitting bathing suites that hung just below the knees; the garments were not in the least bit flattering by today's standards. My first reaction was to laugh but I then I looked a little deeper and saw that the women were really quite stylish. They wore their hair short, curled and closely pasted to their heads. All were brunette and thin; full figures wouldn't become fashionable for another fifteen years or so. Eyebrows were pencil-thin; some were drawn on, full lips, sleepy eyes. Dorothy Lamour and Heddy Lamarr imposters, I thought. Glamour in its infant stages; raw yet disciplined, innocent yet sensual.

And where are they now? I wondered. What were they thinking at the time of the photo? Did they dream of fame or fortune? The expressions were timeless. Each set of eyes told a story. They were maidens on the cutting edge of their time. An auspicious photo, I concluded. The women in it were full of promise, favor and prosperity, but in the end held captive by the claim and peril of time and mortality--like all of us. *Moments in the sun*. Appreciate them while you can.

We spent the evening talking about life, love, the future and past. She was so easy to talk to, I thought. It became clear that we had much more in common than running.

We talked about work and the demands that our jobs placed on us. We came to the same conclusion that our bosses drowned in ever-increasing responsibility and that misery loves company.

"If my boss is having a bad day," Jennifer said, "then I better not be smiling."

She revealed that she had invented a "scream meter" with which she measured each work day. "It's an intangible device that measures my level of frustration. See, I'm being groomed for Public Relations Director at the plant."

She told me how she's constantly putting out "fires," trouble shooting, issuing press releases, and sometimes defending the actions of Secretary O'Leary. "They all have their place on the meter."

Jenny sighed in response to her own admission of a sense of helplessness. "The bureaucracy in the government is endless. You can try and try to make a difference but decision and change are slow to come, if at all."

She changed the subject abruptly. "Did you run in college?"

"No," I said. "I've never had any talent."

"You're a good runner, Paul." She said encouragingly.

"I'm an ok runner," I replied. "Running is something I discovered years after I graduated. However, for the sake of staying in shape I occasionally ran while I attended the university--but nothing competitive."

I took a sip of wine. I watched it breathe in my glass. "Although, once I was out on a run and two guys wearing university issued track singlets passed me like I was standing still. Well, I guess I'm competitive by nature because it really pissed me off. I went after them. They saw me chasing them and laughed, turning up the speed a little more. I never came close to catching them but I chased them hard for over a mile. In the end they left me boiling in my own sweat and blood."

"Ahhh, the old sweat and blood story," Jenny laughed. "What happened next?"

"Nothing," I said. "The chase had taken me too far off campus. I wasn't in very good shape back then. I was exhausted and had to walk much of the way back home. I was petrified that they'd pass me on the way back, that I'd end up having to chase them again."

Jennifer smiled in appreciation of the story. She had run competitively in college and hadn't heard many running stories from the other side of the tracks.

"When did you start to run competitively?" she asked.

"Competively?" I laughed. "That's a relative term, isn't it?"

"Ok then. Seriously?"

"Seriously?"

"Yeah."

"Six years ago. I was out for a run, trying to take off a few extra pounds, and realized that I'd been out everyday for the past three weeks. I'd gotten hooked without even knowing it. I signed up for my first 10K the following week."

I told her about the race and how being inexperienced I'd gone out too fast, actually competing for the lead for the first half mile. I had no respect yet for distance or the "thoroughbreds." Hell, I didn't even know they existed. I was literally one of those high-hoping first timers who jumps off the starting line too fast, quickly slows, and gets in everyone's way. "I once was a roadblock," I told her.

"I paid the price in that race," I said. "I ran the last half a full ten minutes slower than the first half."

I took another sip of wine. More bubbles rose to the top. "Still, I enjoyed myself, the race, the competition, and the feeling of accomplishing something new."

Jenny smiled more. She'd run competitively nearly half her life. What could she remember about first time debacles?

"So, back to this thing you eluded to earlier," she said.

"What would that be?" I asked, having already forgotten.

"In search of goals and such," she prompted me.

"Well, as I said, I discovered my interest in running about six years ago," I said. "And with most interests there's a source of kindling."

I turned bright red with embarrassment. "Now don't laugh at me," I said, holding up a finger. "It's a terribly disturbing thing for me to reveal to you on our first date."

"It's not like you're--"

"That's right," I said. "I'm--"

"What?" she giggled.

"--a dreamer."

We were both feeling light headed from the intoxicating wine. We laughed a lot.

"So let me get back to the story," I said. "I can remember sitting in my dorm with my college roommate. We were watching the Boston Marathon and I was fantasizing about racing in it. Naturally I won."

"We all do in our dreams," she added.

"Well, I guess it must have been a strong fantasy because it's one that I've carried with me for years."

"What?" Jennifer's eyes were wide. "You want to win the Boston Marathon?"

I nearly lost a mouthful of wine with that thought. "God no!" I said, turning red in the face, choking. "Well, actually yes, I 'd like to win it. Who wouldn't?"

"You'd rival the odds of the Buffalo Bills winning next year's Superbowl," she joked.

"That's comforting," I responded. "Actually, I'd just like to qualify this year and run in it." I mentioned that I had qualified once already in San Diego but had chosen not to go that year. I was relieved when she didn't ask me why I had made that decision. How could I have told her on our first date that I had experienced a serious reality check after San Diego and chose not to run because of some self-imposed sentence that I bestowed upon myself in recognition of my stupidity?

"It's a wonderful goal," she said. "You shouldn't have any trouble qualifying."

"You never know," I replied. "I need to run a sub three-ten. Anything can happen over twenty-six miles."

That much is true. Every runner who has ever trained to race a marathon understands and accepts the cruel fact that all the time and effort that leads up to the event can be dashed by a cold, injury, or simply having a bad day. In a shorter race, say a 5K, a bad day might account for a slower time by only a minute or two. In a marathon, a bad day might result in a half an hour or so, or not being able to even finish. Additionally, if you've trained properly you've trained to peak at just the right time. So if you do indeed have a bad day you won't be able to bring yourself to another "peak" for several months afterwards. Marathoning is discouraging in this way.

By the evening's end we were happily drunk and floated in the lyrics of the singer on stage. He was passionately wailing about matters of the heart. *"...One fine day I'll reach that higher ground, cause I've got you by my side baby, and I aint ever lookin down, yeah, yeah, got you by my side baby, and I'm gonna reach way up high..."*

SIX

Jennifer and Barbara didn't notice the disgruntled looks they received from other runners as they ran through the park. While they held a pace slow enough to converse they still managed to pass handfuls of slower, recreational runners along the way. The fact that they did so while talking about the latest issues of their favorite magazines, an episode of Seinfeild, and some "dirty laundry" commanded a great amount of attention in the form of envy and jealousy.

Barbara couldn't wait any longer to hear about the date.

"Sooo--?"

Jennifer had been waiting for Barbara to ask.

"You know--" Barb said between breaths. "Don't hold out on me." It was Barb's second run of the day. "I don't know how much longer I can go and I don't want to miss any details!"

Jennifer enjoyed playing the game. It was nice to have a new friend. "Well, you might say there were a few sparks."

"Really now," being baited. This would be a game of twenty questions. "And just how big were these sparks?"

"How big would you like them?"

"As big as you can make 'em," Barb said. "Elaborate a little."

Jennifer wasn't accustomed to talking freely about the physical side of her dating life. Some things shouldn't be openly talked about, she thought. Nonetheless, she was enjoying the inquisition. "We kissed a little."

"And--?"

"And that was it."

"Oh." Barb sounded disappointed.

"If you're dying to know that much, it was the best kiss I've ever had."

"Getting better. Go on..."

"You won't stop 'till you hear what you want," Jenny laughed.

"Look, I haven't had a date since Mike moved in.

"I'm sure Mike appreciates that."

"You know what I mean."

"Sure," said Jennifer.

"Besides, I need the satisfaction."

Given that... "It rocked my world. It was total chewing satisfaction. I smoked a pack of cigarettes afterwards."

"Now we're getting somewhere," Barbara said.

"That's about as far as it's going to get."

"So, you didn't....you know..."

"Good God Barb, what on Earth do you want to hear?" Jennifer was amazed at Barb's fortitude. "We stayed up all night long and made passionate love in every room of my apartment."

Just as the words escaped her lips two elderly men on bikes rode by going the opposite direction. One veered dangerously close to the curb while he turned his head to see the face behind the words.

Jennifer turned apple-red. "Oh, my God! Do you think--?"

"Yes, they heard you alright," Barbara finished. "You should be a popular figure around here for now."

They both laughed easily, but Jennifer wondered whether or not there might be any truth to it. She also wanted to set the record straight. "Barb, of course nothing else happened. I don't want things to develop too quickly."

"That's good. Besides, I was just joking with you." Barb's breathing was now heavy and she was running a step behind Jennifer. "I take it you'll see him again."

"Better believe it."

"So when's the next date?"

"We're running a fifteen miler together on Wednesday."

"That sounds romantic," Barb said, sarcastically.

"Paul wants to make it to Boston. I told him I'd consider running it with him."

"That's more honorable than marriage."

"I know what you're thinking," said Jenny. "We'll see each other in some pretty bad moments. But I don't mind. Paul needs someone to train with. And if things develop between us, or even if we just remain friends and he makes it to Boston, we'll always have that bond between us."

"Forget what I said," an exhausted Barbara said. "You...give it...a romantic flare."

"Yeah, who knows?"

Jennifer sensed that Barb was really struggling now. "Why are you doing two runs today anyway?" she asked.

"Had an extra slice of pizza last night," she replied. "Got to watch my girlish figure."

SEVEN

I was out on a run in Washington Park. I wasn't going very fast and other less experienced, less talented runners swept by me from time to time. A few years ago that would have driven me mad but it really didn't bother me now. I knew the park was a breeding ground for weekend warriors who were intent to fulfill their athletic fantasies. I'll get 'em back at the races, I thought. Besides, I had more important things on my mind than who's backside I was staring at.

I was having one of those self-revelation type of moments. Nothing so deep as to ponder the meaning of life or anything, but more on the scale of my immediate future, a relationship with Jenny perhaps. She seemed to good to be true. Which was a scarry thought in itself. As the saying goes, if something seems to good to be true it probably is. But I quickly discarded that notion. I had never been in a relationship which I was truly happy. Perhaps this was it, I thought. After all, as another saying goes, good things happen to those who wait. I was thirty years old. I felt I had waited long enough. I also thought about achieving goals in my business life. And finally, I thought about achieving goals in my personal life.

And that of course meant running. It had become such an important part of my life and I knew I needed to decide in what way, if any, I wanted to steer it. Specifically, what goals I might set that would constitute a victory.

But I was aware that first I needed to define victory.

I was aware that victory meant many things to many people and to try to homogenize the term would be like trying to fit a thousand runners into one size of shoe.

Even at a personal level, my definition of victory had changed on more than one occasion. When I first began running my goal was to make it around the block. A year later my goal was to run a marathon. Then, to run one faster; to actually race it. And after I ran my PR in San Diego and internally combusted my goal was to not obsess so much about running--to put it in perspective and in its place. But now I was focused on a new goal. "I want to qualify and run Boston," I'd told Jennifer.

And achieving that goal would certainly constitute victory, I decided now. But only if I did so while keeping the run in perspective.

I was acutely aware of the position I was putting myself in; the spell I might fall under once I seriously began training hard--being that I am a self-admitted obsessive-compulsive. Basically, the logic goes like this: if it's worth doing, it's worth overdoing. I thought about the will it takes for a recovering alcoholic to hold a bottle of beer in his hands without popping the top. That in essence, would be the equation I would face as I trained for the marathon.

I couldn't go into a marathon undertrained and expect to do well, much less qualify for Boston, I knew. But, I couldn't afford to fall victim to the same set of circumstances I did while living in Tucson; risking my job and everything I had for the purpose of running. So I delved into this venture with a new attitude which I was cautiously optimistic about. I'd rely on past experience to get me through, to recognize obsession, while still allowing me to train hard.

Most of all, I'd rely on my recognition that the run is, above all, a beautiful thing. Its action is to be enjoyed.

George Sheehan once asked the question; "why in sport is the emphasis always on the product rather than the process?"

I took this to heart as I circled the park. The sun felt good on my face. Occasionally it would slide behind the long shadows of oaks and elms on either side of me. That felt good too. I ran past a field of deliciously colored flowers that stretched for nearly a quarter mile. I ran past a family hand-feeding squirrels, and fishermen casting lures into a reflective lake. I ran by couples holding hands, children playing frisbee, owners playing with their dogs, and dogs playing with their owners.

Then I came across a shaded area of the park where a small orchestra was set up and getting ready to play. I didn't exactly stop to smell the roses, as they say, but I did stop to listen to the music. A percussionist slowly struck a timpani drum with a heavily gauzed stick. The sound which emanated was soft, yet full and vibrant, offering a hint, or rather a promise of something yet to come. A chorus of trumpets then delivered a fanfare of notes so fine and pristine that I turned to a woman and asked her what I was listening to. "Copland's Fanfare to the Common Man," she said. The melody the trumpets carried wasn't really a melody at all, but rather a string of notes placed so evenly you would swear someone was sure-handedly setting them down like fine china on a dinner table. A moment later french horns accompanied the trumpets in the same series of notes, but an octave lower. Their sound was distinctively less sharp, nearly muted, and blended depth to the fanfare like a voyage through a spacious, airy tunnel. The timpani drums still stable and proud in the backdrop. Then, as if the third and bottom layer of this musical cake had just been applied, the rich, bass resonance of trombones blended together with the other horns, still carrying the same tune, but offering completeness to the mix. It was the most beautiful thing I'd ever heard.

I swear to God I thought birds were going to come pick me up and carry me out of the park.

Finally, there came the recognition of an appreciation I found for that day in the park and all the things I had come across while under the simple transport of just my own two feet.

So, I asked myself, is it possible to enjoy the run yet diligently train hard at the same time? Of course it is, I said.

But I knew it wouldn't be easy. Anything worth having never is. After all, victory is not an enigma. It doesn't just happen because of blind luck, through some inexplicable occurrence. It is neither puzzling or questionable and in its absolute form takes root in the cumulative effect of one's finest efforts leading up to that particular happening; the payoff being equal to the sum of input. So chasing victory would surely be a fathomable toil. It would call for a recipe more complicated than my mother's stew: mileage and perseverance, speed-work and spunk, hill-work and heart, and a dash of common sense--just for flavor.

Boston seemed like a great goal to shoot for. And victory would surely be found on its starting line.

I exited the park with a positive outlook on my objective.

EIGHT

Toni Jamison lived in a five bedroom, four-thousand square foot, Georgian styled mansion in North Cherry Creek, an exclusive and prominent historic district in the heart of Denver. Ivy climbed the red brick structure and life size marble lions guarded the entrance to the cobblestone driveway. A purebred Golden Retriever by the name of Lucy guarded, rather passively and certainly by chance, the front entrance of the estate.

Through years of observing Toni's morning ritual, which began at exactly a quarter of five, Lucy had reserved her spot directly in front of the large hand-crafted oak doors in hopes of being taken on the morning's outing.

This morning was certainly no different than any other. Toni descended the stairway and saw Lucy anxiously awaiting her in the foyer. Toni greeted her in the same manner she'd done so for the past several years; a pat on the head and a kiss to her cold and wet, fat and black nose. "Good morning, girl." Lucy's tail swung fast behind her smacking anything in its way.

"I swear, Lucy, I don't know who's more addicted to this crazy sport, you or me?" She stroked Lucy's head and gave her a good squeeze. After she let her out to do her "thing" she called Lucy back inside. "I'm sorry, I can't take you with me this morning. I'm going for a tough one." Lucy's head sunk and her tail stopped wagging. Toni would swear that the dog could understand English. But the truth was that Lucy was getting on in years--white patches of hair on her face now replaced the gold coat of yesteryear--and had heard the apologetic tone in Toni's voice hundreds of times.

"You be a good watchdog while I'm gone," she said with one last pat on her head. Those were always her last words when she left Lucy behind. Just saying them bought a grin to Toni's face as she envisioned her eight year old Golden, which would probably greet a pack of hungry wolves with a wagging tail, actually trying to guard anything at all.

Toni walked across the front lawn to the edge of her property. It was plenty dark out but she was still able to see her feet disappear beneath the dense thick grass. She turned left past the marble lions, Rocky and Bulwinkle she liked to call them, and started her run down the familiar pathway of her street which was lined with a variety of stylish, expansive estates, similar in size to her own. A street lamp allotted a final glance behind her, revealing the need to call the lawn service--again. Mature trees, bushes, and hedges covered the property;

they were in need of trimming. An unusually high amount of rain had fallen that summer adding to the growth of the grass and plants. The upkeep was draining her account. If she chose to let it go she'd surely hear from one of her neighbors in the form of a nasty, anonymous letter stuffed in her mailbox in the middle of the night. Her neighbors were tremendous communicators when it came to sharing their differences--which were in no way different than their dislikes.

The estate was a giant financial burden. The previous year a new roof had to be put on. Two years before that the plumbing needed to be updated. Contrary to most of her neighbors Toni was not money-rich and couldn't afford such costly repairs. The estate had been left to her when her parents died in a car accident, five years earlier, along with a small trust fund which paid her just enough money to get by on--but only if she worked too. Her position as an assistant manager of a running store paid even less than the fund. But she had no thoughts about leaving since the owner appreciated her stature as a runner and let her set her own schedule, allowing her to train as she liked and fly off to races on a whim. There had been more than one occasion when she toed the line at a race depending on winning prize money to pay her bills.

Over the years she had constantly struggled with the idea of selling the estate. Indeed, she'd be able to live comfortably for the rest of her life if she chose that route. But she knew that that was not an option which she would ever consider with any conviction. Four generations of her family had grown up in it. She felt an incorporeal sense of obligation to push through the difficulties of caring for the estate so that one day a fifth generation might appreciate the home.

Toni loosened up slowly, merely throwing one foot in front of the other for the time being. At this early hour she witnessed the other estates in a slumbered state, before they came alive with bright lights, swinging doors, and noisy cars.

Other than the same street address she had nothing in common with the occupants of these other estates. She was often made to feel like an outsider, perhaps even a tourist, on her own block. She was aware of the different lives they led. "You don't belong to the country club?" a neighbor once asked, horrified. "How on earth do you manage?" Consequently, this left her with very little to say to them. Conversation was reduced to congenial pleasantries: "have a nice day;" "your lawn looks really nice this spring." At times she thought about adding, "and please tell your husband that I will not, under any circumstances, sleep with him because he seems to think you no longer understand his needs."

There had been several instances when she fought not to say *those* words. Dr. Wiler, father of three and husband to one, once went so far as to offer to send her to Boston to run the marathon if he could just "cop a feel for how hard that ass is." Mrs. Wiler would enjoy hearing that one, she thought, wryly. But in the end she would always keep such things to herself, understanding that if she was to make a big stink of the unwarranted and unwanted approaches she would inevitably come out the loser. After all, she surmised, she was an easy target for her neighbors to slander; being young, pretty, fit, single, and according to the circles of power, spoiled rotten with the inheritance of the estate.

But even by keeping a low profile she was certain that rumors still spread about her. "You'd better watch out for that one, she'll steal your husband out from under your nose." "That little thing has men coming and going all night long." Well, she thought, such are the words that come from the mouths of aging housewives with too much time on their hands. Once, at a neighborhood block party, she heard two women refer to her as "an eccentric, flat chested runner who runs for the pleasure of seeing the men turn their heads. After all, why else would she jog in those little shorts that ride so high?" By then she had given up hope of trying to fit in. So the following day she waited until late morning when many of the neighbors were up and about and circled the block for nearly an hour in her racing outfit; "bun-huggers" and a shortly cropped singlet that exposed her washboard stomach. Within minutes she had gained an audience. Dr. Wiler had actually given her the thumbs-up sign before his wife slapped his face and told him to go inside. Toni was the talk of the block for weeks.

Fortunately, this division was something she could live with. Her life revolved around different circles--the running community.

But even in this environment she felt odd at times. For just the opposite reasons she'd find herself not wanting to reveal where she lived for fear of being labeled in the same way she saw many of her neighbors; rich and privileged. And when a new acquaintance did find out she'd make it clear that she sometimes had to look for change under the cushions of her sofa so that she could buy lunch. Fortunately she found that most runners didn't bother to ask. For better or worse, runners may know little else about members in their "fraternity" other than how fast they are. "That's Toni Jamison, I've known her for years, she ran a sixteen minute 5K at Footlocker and placed fourth at Peachtree." "Really, what does she do for a living?" "I've got no idea..." And so the conversations went. Indeed, a runner's constitution of success is usually based on personal endeavors rather than accolades of money.

Ten minutes into her run Toni turned on to the Cherry Creek bike path--which was grossly misnamed in favor of those who preferred pedaling, she thought. At this point she quickened her step to what felt like a five minute mile pace. She backed off after holding it for several minutes. The first one's always the toughest, she thought. Such a shock to the system. She ran the next "pick-up" at precisely the same speed and length of time as the first. Then two more minutes of easy running. She continued this pattern over and over again, never yielding the intensity. At the half-way point in the workout she turned around and began running west, towards home.

The sun had crept up behind her, casting her shadow directly in front of her in elongated form. She studied it and liked what she saw-- the fluidity of her gait, the straight-ahead pumping action of her arms, her head held steady and high. Then, for several minutes, she fantasized that her shadow was a competitor--one she would wantingly chase during her next pick-up. And as this fantasy grew old and the sun climbed the sky directly behind her the shadow began to shorten. *Sure enough this ghost-competitor was starting to come back to her-- like they always do.*

But more than anything, she fed on the fact that during the workout she had seen no other runner on the path. And this, particularly this, was a feeling she fed on. It gave her a competitive edge knowing that many of those she'd race against on the weekends were in a slumbered state getting soft and slow. The harder she worked the greater her edge. Another three minute pick-up made it six. She thought perhaps that *that one* had been the most difficult. She'd think the same of the seventh, eighth, nineth, and tenth.

At six a.m. when much of the city was just rolling out of bed, she found herself back at home. She saw two things; her door open wide and an exceptionally angry Mrs. Wiler standing in front of it, pointing back at her own estate. Somehow, Lucy had gotten out and was now across the street and in the process of pissing on Mrs. Wiler's rose garden.

NINE

The summer came and went before I knew it. Almost overnight President Clinton had become America's most celebrated runner. Soon, Oprah Winfrey would claim that fame. Never mind that Bob Kempainen would soon run a 2:08:47 in Boston and in doing so set a new American record in the marathon. That achievement would scarcely make it outside of the local Boston newspapers. Never mind that within the year Arturo Barrios would announce his decision to become an American citizen. Few outside the running community would even know the name. And finally, never mind that such legends in running like Fred Lebow, founder of the New York City Marathon, and George Sheehan, runner-writer extraordinaire, would both die soon, their warm hearts--which they gave so much to others and the sport--replaced by metal statues to be used by nesting pigeons and ignored by most people.

It was early Sunday morning and I was out on my balcony reading the newspaper. In fifteen minutes I'd meet Jennifer for a long run in the park. I hadn't been in town much lately and I was excited about seeing her.

Lately I'd been putting in a lot of hours at work and taking advantage of good weather and dry mountain roads by traveling from city to city visiting my accounts. These trips would often take me away for a week at a time, sometimes two. When possible I tried to make it back to Denver by Thursday night.

I hated to admit it but I liked to watch the women's Thursday night workouts from my balcony. A while back I'd confessed this to Jennifer and she told me to "knock it off and get a life." After that she said the other women at track began to notice and wonder why she was always staring up at my apartment building. "I'm too embarrassed to tell them that the guy I'm dating might be watching me from up there," she said to me. "So stop it!" So then I promised to not watch anymore, but...

Now, other than Jennifer occasionally coming over after these workouts to say hello, possibly change and shower, we really weren't seeing much of each other. It seemed that our schedules were always in conflict. So the promise we had made to train together for the marathon had slowly evaporated. We both noticed this but neither talked about it much.

The truth was I wasn't sure if she still held an interested in running in an upcoming marathon with me. Hell, I couldn't even tell if she was interested in me. It seemed that the newly blossomed romance had stalemated.

It was just something I'd have to accept.

Now as I was about to leave my apartment to meet her in the park she called me.

"There will be other runs," she said, cancelling once again. "I spent all evening working on a project."

I couldn't stand it anymore. I had to say something.

"I don't care about the lack of training we've done together, I just want to see you. It's been weeks!" I noticed my voice had a touch of anger in it. Apparently she did too.

"Paul, what do you want me to do? I'm working a lot of hours lately. Between my own training and my work schedule I'm exhausted."

She said a cold goodbye.

Well there goes that relationship, I thought. The strange thing is that as great as we initially hit it off there really was no "relationship." We hadn't spent enough time together to build one.

I couldn't decide if I was angry or hurt. I only knew that I'd blown it!

So now I was sitting around my apartment brooding over my misfortune. That "brooding" lay in my stomach breathing like hot coals in a fire. I couldn't think of anything other than the conversation we'd had. And suddenly nothing mattered to me: my job, Boston, anything! I called her three times that afternoon but she wasn't there.

In the early evening I finally went out for a run. Perhaps that would ease my burden, I thought.

But my imagination began to grow wild. She was seeing someone else, I thought. What else could it be? And if that *was* the case wasn't that all right? Reason should have told me that we had never agreed to see only each other. We had never actually discussed it. But, as I circled the park, I wasn't thinking of reason. I wasn't thinking logically.

I tore through the park as though I was racing. Anyone in front of me was fair game. Finally I exited the park not wanting to believe where I was heading, but fully aware that I was running in the direction of Jennifer's apartment

I had to find out!

This thirst for truth adhered to my every sense, violating my peace of mind like an enduring toothache.

I came to a stop on the street in front of her apartment. The lights weren't on, her car was nowhere to be seen. I gathered my breath and suddenly felt foolish. What am I doing here? Have I completely gone mad?

I turned to run back home. But in that instant I noticed Jenny's black Civic turning into the complex. I shielded my face. What a dumb thing to do, I thought. She saw me instantly.

Rolling down her window, "Paul, is that you?" She squinted in the shallow light. "What are you doing here?"

This looks real bad, I was thinking.

I tripped over my words in an attempt to sound sensible and sane. "I, I was just in the area and thought..." But my words trailed off as I looked at the situation from her point of view. I was soaked in sweat. I probably had a crazed expression on my face. "Actually, I was nowhere in the area," I confessed.

A rumbling echoed across the sky. I could smell rain somewhere close by.

"You look miserable," she said. "Come inside and we'll talk."

She immediately apologized for the conversation we had earlier in the morning. But I told her it wasn't her fault, that I was the one to blame. Again, we were at a stalemate. But at least this time we laughed.

Suddenly my words flowed freely. It seemed that a dam had given way and anything--everything--that I had longed to tell her spilled from me. I coupled her hands in mine.

"I've fallen in love with you," I told her.

She didn't back away as I feared she might. We kissed and she echoed my sentiments.

Outside the rain began to fall. The front was passing through. A flash of lightning lit the inside of the apartment. I drew her close to me and we kissed again.

*

It was late autumn. A foot of snow had already fallen on Denver. The landscape had since turned from a blazing sea of red, gold, and burnt orange leaves to a sullen flat gray. Two weeks earlier in the Halloween 5K in Washington Park I, dressed as Batman, had run down Superman with two hundred meters left and placed first in the totally-stupid division. And I thought I'd never have the chance to race anyone wearing a cape. But now the racing season had come to an abrupt end.

The sun now disappeared before the end of a typical work day. Time to stow the racing flats, reflect on the past season, and dream of the next. It was a time of change.

Much of the Toni's Thursday night group decided to meet at her home for a final run together to "officially" end the season.

Perhaps it was the spitting rain which seemed to be slowly changing over to snow, Jennifer thought. Or perhaps it was that she hadn't logged any miles under the warmth of the sun since daylight savings time went into effect. Possibly it was her boss, Janet Kurth, who had recently begun to grind on her nerves, constantly bitching about the quality of Jenny's work and her lack of dedication to her job. Or maybe it was the fact that since the Bolder Boulder she hadn't won any other races that year. For whatever reason she felt her spirits low and her energy drained.

Now, in the middle of a ten miler with the other women from track, she found herself absolutely bored and miserable. Jenny was aware that others in the group felt the same way.

Barbara Duff ran alongside of her and dumped heavily on her boyfriend, Mike. "He's been an ass lately," she said.

Ahead, Mel and the triathalete, Dee Smith, ran side by side. Mel's lack of coordination occasionally led her to bump Dee, who abruptly let her feelings be known: "Can't you keep a fucking straight line!" Mel had no idea how to respond and made a lame attempt to change the topic: "Isn't buffalo meat low in calories?"

Mel *has* lost her mind, thought Jennifer.

In front, Toni Jamison and Luz Diaz were bitching about how difficult it was going to be to stay in shape over the winter. "I just know I'll lose my sponsor in the spring," said Toni.

Apparently she has lost her damned mind too, thought Jennifer, who had recently seen Toni's name in a publication listing her as one of America's top female distance runners. The chance of Toni losing her sponsor was about as likely as a winter in Denver without snow.

The six threw themselves forward in an effort of habit and futility. There were no more quality races scheduled until the spring.

"This sucks," said Jennifer. Others agreed.

The cold, wet, dark and dreary conditions soon got the best of them. Forty minutes into the run Mel's big lips--which resembled the wax ones kids wear on Halloween--had turned purple, Luz complained about tight hamstrings, Barbara began to sneeze, Dee twice nearly fell, Toni began to push the pace in an attempt to just get the damned thing over with, and Jennifer had stepped into a pot-hole filled with slush and now nursed a water-laden shoe. Tonight, there was no beauty in the process, as Paul talked about, she thought. There was only the wanting to finish and seek warmth and comfort. No one said a word for the final two miles.

The women finished back at Toni's house. Somewhere along the route they had dropped Mel. Or at least they thought so until Luz pointed across the street where Mel had just pulled up her black Lycra tights next to Mrs. Wiler's rose garden.

"What in the hell was that all about?" asked Toni, a little perplexed at why Mel didn't just wait thirty seconds to use the bathroom in her house.

"Sorry, I couldn't wait," Mel explained. "I had E.D!"

Toni looked at Luz who threw up her arms, perplexed. Barb looked at Jennifer and Jennifer looked at Dee. No one knew what she was talking about, as usual.

"E.D?" questioned Toni.

"Yeah," answered Mel. "Explosive diarrhea!"

Some thought it funny and others were in total disgust, but everyone more or less laughed. If nothing else, Mel was always amusing in some way.

I hope Mrs. Wiler doesn't blame Lucy for that, Toni was thinking. Fortunately the garden might be buried under a fresh blanket of snow in the morning and Mrs. Wiler wouldn't notice the new and improved fertilizer.

"Hey I've got a great idea," Toni said. "I made a turkey big enough to last me through next year. I've got wine in the cellar. Anyone want to stick around?"

"You have a wine cellar?" Luz asked, skeptical.

Barbara: "You wouldn't believe..."

Dee declined the offer. So did Mel, who now complained about her upset stomach.

Luz, Barb and Jennifer accepted.

"Great," Toni said. "We'll get warm, fat and happy tonight."

Perhaps just warm and happy, thought Barbara.

*

The four exchanged stories and laughs while lounging in front of a raging fire in Toni's living room. Toni's Golden Retriever, Lucy, scurried from one petting hand to the next, loving every bit of attention thrown her way. No one seemed to notice that the earlier rain had indeed turned to snow and was now coming down hard and fast until Luz, high on good wine, holding a partially eaten turkey wing, spun from the window and announced slurredly, "It's a balalizzard out there!"

The three others sped to the window and looked outside. On the way Barb handed the rest of her turkey wing to Lucy. Jennifer tripped and nearly fell into the fire; she was too drunk to notice or care. The women pressed their faces against the glass, eyes wide, to get a better look at the raging storm.

"Stop breathing on the glass, Barbara, you're fogging up the window."

Like a thick sauce Barbara slid down the side of the wall, laughing the whole way. She looked up at Toni. "How many bedrooms did you say you have?"

Getting home, wine not withstanding, would be impossible now.

"So what do we do now?" asked Jennifer.

"I think we need to make another trip to the wine cellar," Luz said, displaying the large gap between her two front teeth. "I'll go get it!"

"Don't get lost."

That would be easy to do, thought Luz. Just the wine cellar, alone, was larger than the shack she grew up in Jaurez, Mexico. "Throw another log on the fire," she said.

Another bottle of wine, turkey leftovers, and several packs of Ring Dings later, the four faded happily asleep, each in her own upstairs bedroom, with the exception of Barbara, who wasn't moving from the sofa.

At six a.m. Toni walked in on Luz who had her head in the toilet. "Ain't goin'--*aaagh*--to work today."

"You couldn't even if you wanted to," replied Toni. "We're snowed in."

Toni walked downstairs. The kitchen was a mess. Apparently no one had remembered to put the turkey away. There was a good deal of it left when they had all retired for the night. But now the plate was empty and Lucy had a guilty look on her white, hairy face.

"You ate well last night," she said to the dog.

Nevertheless, Lucy stood over her bowl, whimpering, expecting to be fed.

At seven a.m. the scent of omelets rising to the second floor eventually woke Jennifer.

Jennifer slowly descended the stairs--a far cry from a sweeping grand entrance you might see at some gala occasion. She had both hands on one side of the railing, easing her way down. Her hair was tossed in a million directions. The skin under her eyes was puffy like mosquitos had nested there in her sleep. She held the same pained expression she had often seen on her hung-over friends back in college.

She stumbled on the last step and momentarily woke Barbara from her slumbered state on the sofa.

"What day is it?" Jennifer asked.

A voice from the kitchen answered: "Friday."

"Am I alive?"

The voice answered: "In what sense?"

Jennifer still hadn't placed the voice with the face. It might have been God's voice, for all she knew.

"I've got to get to work."

Finally, Toni walked out from the kitchen. "You're the only one," she said. "On account of the storm and all. Who wants to deal with it?" She looked at Barb who's eyes were coasting round and round beneath her closed lids. There was a glaze of dried, brown gravy smeared on her cheek.

"You'd think one of us would have told Barb about the gravy on her face."

"Barb barely ate a thing," said Jennifer.

"That's what I thought," said Toni. "Anyway, given her state, I think I can speak for her as well."

A minute later Jennifer called Janet Kurth's office hoping to get her voice mail. I'll just leave the dragon lady a message, she thought.

It was barely 7:10, yet Janet answered on the first ring, startling Jennifer.

"Who's this?" asked Janet.

Jennifer didn't say anything for a second, trying to gather her thoughts.

"I said, who is this? I can hear you breathing."

Jennifer hesitantly explained that she was very sick, "flu or something," and would not be coming in.

Janet poignantly explained that Jennifer was quite full of shit. "Look, this better not have anything to do with the snow! Work has not been called off today and if I can make it here you can too."

Jennifer read between the lines: if my life is miserable then yours better be too!

"We're presenting our findings on the low-level waste in storage tank thirteen this afternoon to the Mayor's aids.

Jennifer had completely forgotten.

"Get your ass in here or find a new job!"

The line went dead.

*

Three hours later Jennifer stumbled into her office smelling of alcohol. She had managed to look her best under the circumstances and greeted Sandy, Janet's secretary, with a pleasant hello.

Sandy was a short, plump woman in her fifties. Her hair was the exact same color and consistency of cotton-candy. She swore that working at the plant had caused it to thin. Had she ever considered all the dyes and oxides she'd tossed on it over the years? thought Jennifer.

Sandy had been employed as a receptionist in the Government for over twenty years. Her lack of education kept her from ever reaching a higher scale than GS9 which, in turn, provided to fuel her bitterness towards authoritative figures, especially ones who happened to be younger and better paid. She spoke only when spoken to, had perfected the "evil-eye" look, and offered absolutely no information willingly.

In Jennifer's eyes, Sandy was nothing more than dead weight in a system that needed to be drastically overhauled. Sandy expected a great deal from her employer but offered nothing in return.

Sandy responded to Jennifer's greeting by momentarily looking up from her computer screen and snidely remarking, "nice outfit."

Jenny looked down and saw what Sandy had already noticed. One shoe was blue, the other, black. She'd also forgotten to put on nylons.

"Where's Janet?" Jennifer asked, ignoring Sandy's remark.

"She's gone home," Sandy said flatly. "Flu or something."

Jennifer wanted to scream.

Sandy continued. "I'm supposed to tell you that you can handle it, whatever *it'* means."

Jennifer spent the next several hours locked in Janet's office going over the notes for the meeting. She carefully read them all. The entire time her head throbbed. I'll give the best damned presentation they've ever seen, she thought and hoped. Jenny had spearheaded the project during the past several months and knew that she could not only present the findings but also lecture on recommendations. With Janet gone this would prove a valuable experience; a moment to gain some respect and notoriety. She then found a solid black marker and colored her blue shoe black.

At three-thirty Jennifer walked into the conference room and found it completely empty. She waited twenty minutes, then stormed in to see Sandy, who was incessantly unloading a can of hair spray on her head.

"Where is everybody?"

"Who?"

"The Mayor's aids!" Jennifer said, duuh. "Where are they?"

"Didn't Janet tell you?" Sandy asked, guarded.

"Tell me what?"

"About the meeting?"

Jennifer felt a knot bunch up in her stomach. She already knew the answer before Sandy could say it.

"The meeting was cancelled first thing this morning because of the snow."

*

By the time Jennifer returned home it was past eight p.m. And getting home had been a chore. The streets had turned into a sheet of ice and the roads were clogged with incapable drivers. She called me immediately.

The conversation was a one-way bitch session. There was little I could say to make her feel better. Indeed, I held off telling her as long as possible that I had chosen in light of the storm to stay home and lounge on the couch, watching movies.

"...and I'm going to have to face the dragon-lady again tomorrow. I don't know how I'll act! I'm likely to tell her..."

Finally, I changed the subject. "Did I mention I saw Luz Diaz and Toni Jamison at Blockbuster today? Sounds like you all had one hell of an evening."

"And I paid for it all day long," Jennifer said.

"Did you know that Toni has asked Luz to move in with her?" I said.

"Her house is huge. She certainly has enough space."

Before the conversation ended I reluctantly reminded Jennifer of our date to run twenty miles on Sunday. The California International Marathon, where I would attempt to qualify for Boston, was only three weeks away.

TEN

I was riding in a noisy bus in the middle of the night. Looking at the other passengers, they could have passed for convicts in a movie scene--a hundred or so enslaved souls, bearing numbers on the front of their shirts, being driven off into the surrounding desert to be abandoned and made to find their way back by way of foot. Many looked underfed. Some were already perspiring.

Although these prisoners sported hundred dollar running shoes and clothing made of Lycra and other synthetic fabrics, white gloves and blister-free socks. Their gaunt faces revealed happy thoughts: months or years, miles and countless hours spent in training for the battle they were about to enter.

The same scene was played out on about twenty or so other busses that made the trip in front and in back of the one I was riding.

It wasn't quite five a.m.

The streets were silent. The city slept.

The sky was pitch black and the ride took on an eerie quality. A feeling of reserved excitement filled the air. Idle chit-chat could be heard throughout the bus but for the most part very few people talked with one another.

Jennifer sat next to me. My arm was draped across her legs.

"I'm glad you changed your mind," I said. "I know this wasn't in your plans but you've--"

"Done the training," she finished.

Next to her sat a man who was listening to a Sony Walkman. The volume was turned up loudly and even though he had the headphones nicely anchored in his ears I could still hear a pronounced beat and an occasional lyric. He appeared to be about my age and had a jittery manner about him that sent him rocking back and forth in his seat in an exaggerated manner to the beat of the music. Jennifer commented to me that he was annoying her. She thought he might be slightly insane.

At one point he removed his headphones and said something to a very fit, gray haired man who appeared to be in his fifties.

Jennifer whispered in my ears, "he just told that man if he felt he could break two-twenty he'd finish, otherwise he'd drop out."

I took another look at the man who appeared to be much taller than myself, awkwardly so, I was thinking. He'd have to be the quickest big-man in the sport. Knowing that an athlete would have to average close to a five-twenty per mile pace to finish in under 2:20 I quickly dismissed him. Talented big men in the sport of marathoning is an anomaly. "There's a lot of bullshit artists out here," I replied.

When we exited the bus he stared straight at Jennifer and me and proclaimed, "time to rock and roll!"

"Rock and roll," I repeated, humoring him. Didn't want to piss off a crazy man.

We found out later that he wasn't crazy or kidding.

At the awards ceremony Jennifer and I stared in disbelief as we watched him walk to the front of the room and accept prize money and a trophy for having placed third overall in just over two hours and thirteen minutes. He turned out to be Peter Maher, one of Canada's premier marathoners.

I remembered that Barbara Duff had once pointed out the irony of how even the greatest runners can virtually walk down a street and go unnoticed in our society. I was embarrassed that this one had just sat next to me on a bus for more than thirty minutes and that I had no idea who he was and that my only thought was that he was full of shit. As a runner who takes this sport seriously, I should have recognized him. Furthermore, the older man that Peter had spoken to on the bus turned out to be the Publisher of Runner's World magazine, George Hirsch. Again, a very influential man in the sport, yet possibly not noticed by anyone on the bus.

I was humbled to say the least.

So was Jennifer.

*

In the months preceding the marathon my training had gone particularly well. Since I had spilled my heart out to her she had made it a point to get back on track with her promise to help me train. So much so that she more often than not accompanied me on these runs which often went for more than twenty miles at a time. It was then that her talent at distance running became evident to me.

She was tireless and could maintain a quick pace like no other runner I had ever run with. Each week getting stronger and stronger.

"The marathon is your distance," I'd said to her.

"I know," she replied. "But I was hoping you wouldn't notice."

"How come?"

"It's the blue-collar sport of running," she said. "Little if any recognition comes with it. The public is blind to it."

"Yeah, but--"

"I know, I wouldn't do it for the publicity."

"That's good," I'd said. "Because unless you come in first or are part of human interest story that the press feels obligated to show you'll never get any."

"Unless I finish with bloody knees, crawling to the finish line."

"That would help."

"The networks love that kind of shit," she laughed.

"So, if you're ok with all of that what else bothers you?"

"Marathoning is brutal," she said. "No one wants to run it, including me."

"That's not true," I said. "A lot of people want to run it."

"A lot of people *do* run it," she corrected me. "But I, I just don't know."

"I thought you said you had a dream about qualifying and running in the Trials."

"I did?"

"Yeah, over a bottle of wine. Remember?"

"It must have slipped out."

"Nonetheless, it's true, isn't it?

"Yeah."

"So then, you've got a talent at running long distances. You should be happy."

"Why can't my talent rest in the hundred meters?" she joked. "They barely have time enough to breathe in a race. They can't possibly break a sweat. On the other hand, a marathon racer beats himself to death for two, three hours at a time--and that's not including the training."

"Life's unfair."

"It sure is," she'd said. "And even if we have a great race come marathon day we're rewarded afterwards with months of sore and dead muscles."

"Like I said."

"Yeah, just a cycle of training, I suppose."

"Speaking of training," I'd said. "Why don't you run Sacramento with me? You've done the training and you're in great shape."

She replied that she didn't have the interest now.

I pressed the issue. In retrospect, even though things turned out well, I should have never tried to coax her into running something with the magnitude of a marathon against her wishes. Even then I knew that going into a marathon without your head in the game is a sure cry for disaster; a poor time, the least of which. Still, I was so impressed with her during the training runs I let my emotions take over and wished her to run with me.

When she finally gave me a definite "no" I presented her a plane ticket anyway. "Well then," I'd said. "Would you be interested in at least coming out to support me. A few days in the California sun isn't a bad way to take the chill off a Denverite in December."

Well, it might have been the magic of holding the ticket in her hand. Or perhaps it was my endless pointing out that she was in great shape and could run well in the marathon. Whichever, she made the decision to run it at that moment, just a week prior to the marathon.

Now on the bus, I held her close to me and drifted into thought about how all-consuming the process to raise my fitness level had been.

In the weeks leading up to the event, I had unknowingly fallen to the other side of the line I knew represented obsession. I was so obsessed with race strategy--pace, split times, etc.--that I had sat through entire meetings with my boss and listened selectively with the marathon foremost on my mind.

I had no respect for the topics at hand.

"Paul, we can't discuss the Cooper account with --" my boss was saying.

If I take it easy in the beginning I won't blow up later on, I was thinking.

"We wouldn't want to violate any anti-trust laws," he kept on.

"No, of course not, Jack." I'd said, my mind a million miles away thinking of the race course. *I'll go through the five mile mark in thirty-five minutes just to be on the safe side. I'll stay in control and just do what I need to do to qualify for Boston.*

"Just waiting for approval," he was saying.

And through the half way point in, let me see. I scribbled one thirty-one on a sheet of paper.

My boss had seen it. 1-31. "What? You expect approval by January thirty-first?" he asked.

Suddenly I was alert. He'd seen my scribble! "Yes, Jack, the ADA is submitting their requirements to the Building Department sometime early next week. Licenses and approvals should be done by the end of January." I really had no idea.

Well, that was then and this was now.

Eighteen miles into the marathon I realized that my plan to go out slowly had gone straight to hell. Hoards of runners began to pass me, including George Hirsch. Just before he passed me I heard another man say to him, "see that person in front of you? He won't break three hours today. You will!"

Well, that person in front of George was me. *Great motivation for George, I thought, but thanks for tearing my heart out!* But that's all right, I concluded. I was out there to qualify for Boston. I just need to sneak in under 3:10. I could still hold it together and do that.

But I knew it wasn't going to be easy. I had made the ultimate rookie mistake. I had let my emotions get in the way of reason and jumped off the starting line too fast. The early miles sped by so fast that I flat out didn't believe my splits until the 10K mark when a race official had called out "thirty-seven-twenty." What should have been a clear warning to slow my pace only proved to spur me on. I'm running great, I had thought. It feels so easy! What I should have been thinking was; I'm running too fast. It's going to get ugly soon enough.

Yet ten miles into the race I still sped along thinking that this was my day and I would not be denied a fantastic time. I'd PR for sure!

At that point I could still see Jennifer who was running about thirty seconds in front of me. I was ecstatic for her. As I had anticipated, she was running well."

Then after the half way point I had lost contact with her. I was slowing down!

Twenty miles into the race I couldn't help but think of the opening sentence from A Tale of Two Cities: It was the best of times, it was the worst of times. What started out so promising was now turning into nothing short of a nightmare. My legs were hostage to the crippling effects of lactic acid. My stride grew short and tight, like I was trying to open a bear-trap that kept snapping shut.

Then, twenty-two miles into the race I felt a twinge in my right knee which reduced me to a walk.

"So, this is how it's going to end," I said to myself. All the time and effort, the months in preparation, and I'm going to walk away injured and not even finish the race, much less qualify to run Boston. I wanted to cry.

The irony of the situation was that my lungs were fine. It was my legs that betrayed me.

On-lookers called out their support: "Three more miles! You can do it! Two more miles! You're looking great!"

How could I be looking great? I wondered. I was walking!

Nevertheless, I chose not to not give up without a fight. I began to run again at a slow pace, denying the pain that shot through my knee, the cramping that turned my gait into that of an old man's.

I wanted to see Jennifer, to hold her in my arms and apologize for letting her down by not qualifying; that I was sorry I'd wasted her time on the weekends leading up to this.

Of course, perhaps I didn't. Perhaps there was a bright side to all of this. Perhaps she was up ahead somewhere having a great race. I was suddenly anxious to know how she finished, assuming she had. She had looked so good early on. But then, so did I.

When I crossed the finish line I looked up and saw the clock which read: 3:09:06. I smiled, thanked God, and was immediately greeted by an ecstatic Jennifer.

"You did it!" she screamed, happy for me.

I fell into her arms and was vaguely aware that her small frame didn't collapse under my weight.

I gathered my strength and pulled back, looking deep into her eyes for want and need. I read her thoughts easily--I'd seen the look before. For underneath a pained and weary expression was a distinct glow of exuberance. She had run an excellent race.

We held each other for several minutes. She told me that she'd run a two fifty-one. It's a time that is only a minute shy of the qualifying standard for the women's Olympic marathon trials.

It would surely raise some eyebrows back home in Denver.

Behind us hundreds of finishers were now walking through the chutes. Most looked exasperated. It's an emotional moment for all. A young man, perhaps having finished his first marathon, hung on the supportive shoulders of his girlfriend, balling his brains out.

ELEVEN

It turned out that Janet Kurth had been telling the truth the day she went home with the "flu or something." Later that night she had been taken to the hospital and treated for pneumonia.

Jennifer guessed that Janet had left work that day in some sort of odd display of power. She had fully expected to see her back at work the following day, sitting behind her desk, barking out orders and grievances. Sandy had informed her otherwise.

Janet's health only declined from there. Upon returning from Sacramento Jennifer had been notified that Janet had come down with Shingles, a disease which attacks the nervous system and causes severe pain and nausea. It was possible that Janet might not be able to return to work for months. Maybe she'd take this opportunity to retire, thought Jennifer.

Unfortunately, she had mixed feelings about that. She relished the thought of not having to put up with Janet's sour moods and demanding nature day after day. A promotion would loom closer in the horizon as well. Yet, she was already working fifty hours a week. Since the Sacramento trip she worked even more, filling in for Janet's absence. She couldn't fathom the notion of carrying more responsibility at this point.

Now as she was sitting at her desk she questioned whether she really wanted the extra work load. Do I really want to turn into my boss? She asked herself.

"Miss Ledge?" said a voice from her speaker phone. "There's a Mr. Ed Cooley on line four."

"Take a message, Sandy." The name was unfamiliar to Jennifer. Later, she would simply forget to return the call.

*

Jennifer and I exchanged gifts at her apartment under an inexpensive aluminum Christmas tree adorned with a few of our race medals. Harry Connick Jr. was giving his rendition of Sleigh Ride in the background.

It was the twenty-third of December. We would each go our own way for the actual holiday. Jennifer would leave in the morning and spend Christmas with her parents in New York. I'd planned to fly to Phoenix to do the same.

"Look at all the Christmas cards you've received," I said, envious.

Jennifer took the opportunity to tease me.

"Wait, there's more," she replied. "I haven't had time to open them."

"I was able to open all of mine while I toasted a piece of bread," I said. "But women tend to be more thoughtful than men and thus better at sending cards. You must know more women than me."

"Uh, hum." She wasn't listening. Or wasn't buying.

Jennifer threw a stack of about ten cards on the tinsel-littered carpet. "This one's from my Aunt Grace. She's senile and has no idea who I am." She picked up another one. "This looks like it's from my college roommate." Jennifer tossed it back in the pile.

"What did you do that for?" I asked.

"She thinks I owe her money," Jenny laughed. "She just wants me to think it's a Christmas card so that I'll open it, but I know it's going to be a request for payment."

"That's terrible."

Jennifer picked up another card. She gave it a quizzical look.

"A stranger?" I asked.

It didn't have a return address on it and she didn't recognize the handwriting.

"Could be," she said.

Jennifer opened the envelope and inside was a Christmas card with Santa on the front. He was wearing a pair of running shoes and he'd left a set of tracks in a deep snow.

"How cute," she said.

"He'd be better off flying those stupid reindeer," I said. "Who's it from?"

Jennifer opened the card. Written inside--under a caption that read: Glad I tracked you down; have a Merry Christmass--was a little note that said:

Congratulations on your marathon. You're a very talented runner. I've talked with some of my friends and nobody seems to know who you are. Call me if you'd like to be somebody and make a name for yourself. Best of luck, Ed Cooley, Head Coach, RMUCC.

"Ooooh," I said. "It looks like you've got an admirer."

"You're the only admirer I'm interested in," said Jennifer.

"You sure about that?"

"I want to show you something." Jenny jumped up off the floor and returned with a handwritten note. On it was a list. "I'll be taking this back with me to show my family," she said.

"What is it?"

"My family has a tradition where, at the end of the year, each person writes down all the good things that happened in his or her life during the course of the year. And for those things we give thanks."

Jennifer handed me the list.

My name was written at the very top.

*

Christmas time in Arizona is quite different from anywhere else. Christmas lights are strung up on Saguaro cacti, "snowmen" are built with the round carcasses from dead, thorny bushes, and racing season is in full swing.

I participated in a small, little publicized 10K in Scottsdale called the Reindeer Dash. It was a pleasant seventy degrees out and I wore shorts and a tank top. Other runners I ran next to weren't even wearing shirts. I felt a little guilty that Jennifer was in upstate New York, probably out doing her miles in tights and a jacket made for cold weather running. She was probably having to avoid patches of ice. I was busy avoiding an occasional pothole.

Late in the race I heard someone running just off my shoulder. Who ever it was had an even, efficient stride. I could barely hear the runner's feet strike the ground. I could barely hear the runner breathe. I, on the other hand, was huffing and puffing like a mad man, trying to just hang on. I was having a great race and didn't want to lose the third place spot I was running in. Yet I knew it was only a matter of time before this person would pass me. Who ever it was seemed at play with the pace. I was totally intimidated. Finally the runner pulled up along side of me and started to pass. Out of the corner of my eye I saw a flash of wavy, red hair. It was a woman. But just as she started to pass she backed off and I never saw her again.

I was so exhausted when I ran through the chute at the finish line that I forgot to look behind me to see who it had been. For the next half an hour I couldn't think of anything else. I'd swear to God it was Toni Jamison. But at the awards ceremony the race director called out someone by the name of Lucy Canine. Who ever *that* was she hadn't stuck around to claim her trophy.

*

After the holidays Jennifer called up Toni to inquire about Ed Cooley. She explained how Ed had repeatedly tried to contact her.

"How were your holidays?" asked Jennifer.

"Great," said Toni. "Went down to Phoenix to get out of the cold weather."

"Paul was down there."

"I wish I would have known."

"He said he thought he saw you at the Reindeer Dash."

"The what dash?"

"Reindeer Dash."

"I didn't race," said Toni.

"Well, I'm sure he was mistaken then."

"So, what's up Jenny?"

"You ever heard of an Ed Cooley?"

"Yeah."

"So you know who he is?"

"Sure," said Toni. "He coaches cross-country at Rocky Mountain U."

"Anything else?"

"All I know is that he had a great reputation coming in at RMU. But I don't think his teams have done well over the past few years."

"...and you've met him?"

Toni explained that on occasion she saw him at the races. She described him as a nice looking man, about fifty years old, with silver hair and black eyes."

"Black eyes?" Jenny repeated, trying to picture it.

"As black as a shark's," said Toni. "People even call him 'Sharky', but I think it has more to do with his drive than anything else."

"How so?"

"He seems a little intense," Toni said. "Always keeping a stern face like he's playing a chess match or something."

"Well, who needs that in their life?"

"Don't give up on him that easily," Toni said. "You had a great race in Sacramento. You really should consider bringing on a coach to take you to the next level."

"What about your coach?" Jennifer asked.

"Mine is in Texas," she said. "Used to date the guy until he got a job as an athletic trainer with the football team down there. Now the coaching is done over the phone and through letters."

Toni laughed. "Look, go see Ed. I wasn't even aware he was coaching outside of the university. If you like him let me know. Perhaps I'd be interested."

Just then Lucy began to loudly bark in the foyer.

"Jennifer, could you hold on for a second? Someone's at my door."

Barbara Duff had a small overnight bag in her hand. The smeared eye-liner and washed out look on her face was evidence of how she'd spent the past few hours. Behind her, parked on the street, was her '81

Ford Escort; dented, scraped and generally falling to pieces. Toni saw that it was packed with Barbara's belongings.

"Do you think I can crash here tonight?" She asked sheepishly. "Mike just kicked me out."

"I thought that was your house?"

"Just a rental," replied Barb. "He signed the lease too."

Toni felt terrible for her. "Please come in," she said. "You can stay here for as long as you'd like."

The neighbors will love seeing Barb's car parked out front, she thought.

By the end of the day Barbara was Toni's second tenant.

*

It was more than twenty years ago in a remote area in Southern Utah which was listed as "primitive" by the Bureau of Land Management. No official mapping existed.

He had spent months planning the backpacking expedition to Dark Canyon with his brother who was to fly in from Chicago. The day before the trip his brother cancelled. Ed chose to go ahead anyway. The stress from his job had gotten the best of him.

He was more miserable in his petty life than he had ever imagined possible. His blood pressure was high, and at only five-six weighed two hundred pounds. Even at just thirty years old he hadn't had a date in over a year. The last one had told him, just as he tried to kiss her good-night, that he was the most repulsive man she had ever met before slamming the door in his face. The most pleasing thought in the world to him was getting out in the wide open spaces and not having to speak, see, or hear another soul. In a sense he was glad his brother cancelled.

He drove out I-70 in a '68 Jeepster and turned left at State Route 191. He passed through Moab, then a small and isolated town of less than a thousand people--the world hadn't discovered mountain biking yet, which years later would account for much of Moab's boom in popularity. From there it was possible that he might not see another human for the entire duration of his vacation. Sixty miles south of Moab he turned right onto County Road 211. He had almost missed the sign, which was nothing more than a wooden railroad tie sticking vertically from the ground. He followed CR211 for twenty miles until it turned into a dirt -- road? Ed wasn't sure. It wasn't on the map and he could barely make out the tracks left by past vehicles. He followed that road for another twenty miles before parking his Jeepster and heading out on foot.

Dark Canyon is actually a series of deep, interconnecting canyons, spread out over more than a thousand square miles of arid landscape. Petrified Navajo sandstone make up the canyon walls that in places rise to over a thousand feet above the basins. Other than what many might call a stark beauty to the area there is little that separates the look of one canyon from the next. There are few landmarks. Few trees other than sparsely scattered pinons. There is little sense of direction. "Hundreds of miles from the closest town, a million years apart." That's how the Ranger had described the canyon when Ed had inquired about a permit to camp in the area.

Once he'd seen this part of the country from the air while flying from Denver to L.A. It had been a spectacularly clear morning and angled light scraped the rugged, red sandstone cliffs sending mile-long shadows westward. Everything below him stood out in relief. The canyon country was nothing short of an impossible maze. It teased his imagination. Ed knew he'd be back on foot someday.

The Ranger had also sent him information on its geological make-up, rough maps, and a brief history of the area. Anasazi pictographs were common sights in the canyons. The fine grain of the sandstone, a hundred and fifty million years old, made it easy for past cultures to carve their history into the walls. Ed could expect to see many of these pictographs during his trip.

The most common ones were of Kokopelli; the God of Fertility and Rain Maker. It was said that married women would embrace this God while unmarried women would run from him--for obvious reasons. There were also many drawings of Shaman; teachers of religion and harmonious existence between mankind and the Earth.

There were Anasazi artifacts spread about in the canyon as well. Ed was told if he ran across any to leave them alone and report the location of the sighting to the Ranger. "Nothing to see anyway," said the Ranger, "but a bunch of broken pottery."

It was late afternoon, time for thunderheads to rise above the pastel colored landscape in the West. The hot, turbulent wind blew in from the south, whipping sand across the canyon floor, blinding Ed's vision. He'd spent two days in the canyon already. He'd photographed dozens of pictographs, jumped over several rattle snakes, and held his breath when he'd heard a wild pig outside his tent in the middle of the night. But now, for the first time he was frightened beyond his own admission. The sandstorm had turned him around. It had come out of nowhere and in a plight to take cover in a deep crevice of a rockface he'd dropped his compass.

Nothing looked familiar to him when the storm was over. His compass was lost, buried in a blanket of sand somewhere. He walked a half mile west. Then east. Then in a circle. The canyons all looked alike.

That night he barely slept at all. His hopes were high that when the sun rose things would look familiar. But the sun did rise and everything looked the same; giant slabs of salmon colored sandstone rising from the desert floor all around him. Exactly what he had seen yesterday. The new day was no help.

He walked in circles.

The following day was spent in similar fashion.

His lack of conditioning wore on him. At some point during the fifth day he found it impossible to carry the weight of his backpack. It was sucking him dry of energy. The art of reasoning had long since vanished, typical of a person in state of panic. He laid the backpack to ground and walked away from it, bringing with him only a final quart of water.

The ensuing night was spent under the simple protection of an overhanging cliff. He fell asleep certain that he'd seen his last sunset.

The next day he woke and saw something shimmering in the glow of the morning sun. He'd spent the night next to an ancient Anasazi dwelling and there were broken chips of pottery all around him.

Just a piece of pottery, he thought. But pottery doesn't shimmer in the sun!

He made his way over to the object and saw that it was a bracelet made of silver and gold. Ed rubbed it clean and saw that on it was an etching of a bear. In Native American culture the bear symbolizes courage, strength, and introspect. He placed it around his wrist.

Drained of all rational thought he smiled, splitting the crusted dirt in the corners of his mouth. *It looked...good.*

Two hours later he walked out of the canyon. He had no memory of his trek.

A Ranger was parked next to his vehicle. He was a large, well tanned man, who talked as slowly as the time moved in this part of the country. "I've been looking all over for you! You were supposed to check in with me in Moab."

Ed had just stared at him and said nothing.

"You're lucky I spotted your Jeep," with two dirty fingers he worked a sliver of jerky free from between his teeth and flicked it airborne. Then continued, "otherwise I wouldn't have known you had even shown up." The Ranger looked up at the cloudless sky. He continued talking, aware that Ed had barely acknowledged him. "I only come by here once every other week you know. A man could get lost out here." Still not a word from Ed. "Hey, what's wrong with you anyway? You look like you've just been given a gift from God or something."

Exactly, thought Ed.

Now, Ed was sitting in his living room, turning the bear bracelet in circles around his wrist. He'd never removed it since that day. Perhaps it *had* been a gift from God. Ed was certain that it had saved his life. The bear was sacred in the Anasazi culture and somehow it had shown him the way out of the canyon.

He had driven back to Denver with a new outlook on life. He was going to change things for certain. He was going to be somebody.

He remembered how helpless he felt having to leave his backpack behind because he didn't have the strength to carry it any further. That had almost cost him his life. He resolved to get in shape.

In the mornings he ran. In the evenings he lifted weights. Before the end of the year he had lost fifty pounds.

The following year he entered races and ran surprisingly well enough to bring home an occasional award. His self-esteem rocketed. Within a year of robbing the dwelling of the ancient artifact he was dating on a regular basis, had quit his dead-end job as a Postal Clerk and began a teaching career in political science at Fieldcrest High School. In the afternoons he coached cross-country running. Ed had developed a charismatic personality that seemed to inspire his runners. Over a span of eight years, five of his teams won the state championship.

It wasn't long after that that he landed a position at the university, coaching the cross-country team. In his first few seasons his teams did well, but then his enthusiasm began to hollow and his teams began to finish farther back at the meets. Something was missing from his life and he was fairly certain of what that was: the collegiates whom he coached were all young and seemed incapable of putting in the type of training he believed necessary to succeed at the top of their sport. Often, it seemed to him that all they really wanted to do was drink and screw. On occasion he was the recipient of such an interest, always amazed at how some of the young women he coached trusted him so, listened intently to his bullshit stories, fell so passionately for a man of wisdom twice their age. Or perhaps they'd only been interested in keeping their scholarship, which was probably the case. At any rate, he longed to take another step forward--to coach professionals and maybe, one day, an Olympian.

As he sat on his eight-way-hand-tied-Italian-leather sofa and played with the bracelet he was in awe of himself. *Nothing's too good for my ass to sit on, he thought. I've come a long way since I found the bracelet.*

He never felt a twinge of guilt for not reporting the bracelet. God wouldn't have allowed me to find it if he didn't intend for me to keep it, he thought. And now, he sincerely believed that it was his God-given duty to make something out of himself; to be somebody. Anyone whom he paid any attention to would surely enjoy the same.

He'd seen Jennifer run through the tape at the Bolder Boulder. She had impressive stamina and a pain threshold he'd rarely seen before. As the summer wore on he'd kept an eye on her, sometimes seeing her results in the paper the morning after a race. For an uncoached runner her times impressed him. So it came as no surprise when he read that she had run a two fifty-one in Sacramento.

He kicked back lazily on the sofa, melting in it. He picked up a bottle of Becks beer and took a long swallow from it. "No domestic crap passes these lips," he said to himself. He followed that thought with, "And that Jennifer girl, by God, has potential. She could be somebody." He took another swallow of beer. "With me as her coach, of course."

The phone rang. He sat up high in his sofa and smiled.

"Ed Cooley? This is Jennifer Ledge."

Bingo.

TWELVE

Mrs. Wiler brushed back the curtain swags of her living room window and looked outside. "They're doing it again!"

Dr. Wiler had just polished off his third Tanqueray and tonic of the afternoon. He wiggled his way free from the Lazy Boy which seemed to have an magnetic grip on his ass and made his way over to the window. Sure enough, Toni and her two new roommates were clad in running attire, stretching on the thick green lawn. Within minutes they'd set off on a run.

Damn, they're great to look at, he thought. With a quick glance down at his wife's dimpled, gravity-laden ass he asked, "why have you grown so interested in them?"

From behind, the two looked like giant pears sun-drying in the window.

*

It was an unusually warm day in January; warm enough to sit outside and drink a soda.

"You're a very talented runner," Ed Cooley said.

Jennifer lazily swung back and forth in a hanging chair on the porch of Ed Cooley's red brick Bungalow home. She was interested in what he had to say but uncertain if she wanted or needed a coach at this time. A coach meant responsibilities, expectations, pressures and the like. And her job was already providing her more than she wanted. I'd like to just run for the sake of pleasing myself, she thought.

But there-in lay the problem. What exactly might please her? She had run well in Sacramento, better than she or anyone had anticipated. And now, the Olympic marathon trials qualifying standard of 2:50 hung in front of her like a carrot on a stick, teasing her to come after it. I've raised the ante, she thought.

If she went under the standard it wound mean a trip to Columbia, South Carolina and a chance to line up with the best women runners in the country, an opportunity to be labeled as one of them. Still, it will be a formidable task to take on.

She wasn't blind to the pressures that evolve from expectations. They come with the territory of being good at what you do. But now, she contemplated throwing herself head first into this arena. It's time to fold my cards or play on, she thought.

The answer was obvious. She wouldn't have even shown up to speak with Ed had she not known that. Of course she would bring him on as her coach. He would work to strengthen her, to quicken her, and she in return would be expected to perform.

Ed spoke in a very assured yet serene manner, like he was telling you he's about to take your queen with his bishop in three moves and there's absolutely nothing you can do about it. His eyes really were black and his hair shiny silver--just as Toni had described. Jennifer noticed the ornate piece of jewelry he was wearing around his wrist. He was a man of average build and lesser height but he cast a full, resonant voice when he spoke which commanded Jenny's attention.

He's a good communicator, Jenny thought. He stopped and listened whenever it appeared she had something to say.

Then out of nowhere he said something that surprised her.

"From what you've told me it sounds like you've been running without a purpose," he offered.

"I don't feel that's true," Jenny replied.

"How so?"

"I want to take my running skills to the next level. If I didn't I wouldn't have called you."

"That's a given," Ed said. "But what I mean is that, while I feel you know where you want to get, you don't really know how to get there."

Jennifer couldn't deny that. She ran nearly every day, but lacked the experience of knowing the cause and effect of her routine.

Ed continued. "The purpose I'm referring to is that of a plan. You've been running most of your life. Recently you've improved a great deal and show promise at the marathon distance. I take it that's where you'd like to set your goals?"

Jennifer nodded her head yes.

"That's good," Ed said. "That's where I too see your talent, but you're kidding yourself if you believe that a weekly speed session with Toni and her friends will be the constitution of your future success."

"Go on."

"What are you doing the other six days of the week?"

"I'm throwing in a long run each weekend. After work I usually go for a quickie around the park or somewhere." Jennifer thought she knew where the conversation was heading.

Ed explained that up until now her training had indeed been fine, otherwise she wouldn't have made the jump that she had. "But if you want to take it to the next step you're going to have to get serious."

"I am serious," she said, taking slight offense.

Ed began to preach sacrifice.

Just as I suspected, she thought. It's going to be a dose of the old sweat and blood story. Jennifer was unimpressed.

But then Ed added a new element which she hadn't expected. He began to talk about Jennifer's part in the coach-athlete relationship, should she decide to pursue it. "I'm not interested in just your body," he laughed. "I like to hear feedback from my runners and know what they think about the training. I promise that you'll have equal say in any decisions."

"You mean that?"

"Of course I do," he said. "You drive the car, Jennifer, I just want to occasionally steer it. Fair enough?"

She couldn't pass. "So what now?" she asked, fully expecting Ed to immediately take her out on a long run.

"Now?" he repeated after her. "Hell, I don't know. It's January and cold. Go out and have some fun."

"Excuse me?" Jenny said in disbelief. "What happened to all that talk about sacrifice?"

"Your training is fine for now. We'll analyze it better next month."

"All of that preaching and you don't want to change a thing?" Still bewildered.

"Actually, I do want to change one thing."

"And what might that be?"

"I'm not particularly fond of how you look?"

"Hey, if it's my hair forget it," Jennifer laughed.

"It's not your hair," Ed laughed too. "It's that damned thing on your wrist. Take the watch off and give it to me."

"You have a strange way of asking for things," Jenny said. The tone was light between them.

It was a common digital runner's watch, allowing one to see split times and over-all lapsed time. Ed shoved it in his pocket.

"I'll give it back to you in the spring," he said. "I don't want you to be concerned about trivial things like how fast you're running around the park." Ed stood up and began to walk toward his front door. The meeting had come to an end. "And one more thing," he said, turning toward Jennifer. "If you're logging your mileage right now, don't."

"What do you want me to do?" Jennifer asked.

"Just run," he told her. "Just run."

Later that day and the rest of the month that was exactly what Jennifer did. Without having the handicap of a watch to influence her appreciation of a particular run she ran as far, as easy, or as hard as she wanted. She deviated from her normal routes, finding new paths and areas to explore.

She had envisioned such a terrible web of pressure upon taking on a coach. Weren't coaches supposed to push you, make your life a living hell and constantly remind you it's for your own good? But it seemed the opposite had happened. Weeks passed and Ed continued to tell her, "just run."

And again, she did. For the first time in a long time she appreciated the simplicity of the run; of feeling the wind in her hair, the road under her feet, the ability to travel great distances under her own power. She understood what it meant to see the run as a beautiful thing. *Beauty in the process and not just in the product.*

I had often mentioned this notion to her, but it was Ed who had actually given it to her; given her the freedom to enjoy the run.

I felt a little jealous because of this. Perhaps I should have been the one to take her watch from her. But I'd never even thought of that! Who knows? In any case, I was glad to see her discover the other side of the run, no matter who had opened the door for her.

But I felt a little apprehensive about Ed. There were many questions I had that only time would answer. Is he too demanding? Is he not demanding enough? Will he care about Jennifer's well-being? Or is he in it for just himself? And how will all of this impact Jennifer's and my relationship? Ed was a new entity. And like any new entity he would command a certain amount of her time. Which, of course, meant a certain amount of *our* time. She would have to give it to him and I would have to understand. Ultimately, his tutelage would directly effect both of us. There was a certain amount of danger in that.

Additionally, there was also the letting go of responsibility that I had to deal with. In the short time that Jennifer and I had dated I had become increasingly more and more interested in her workouts. Up until then I was offering her advice. In essence, I was filling the role of coach. It was a responsibility that I bestowed upon myself. It was neither wanted or solicited by Jennifer. And it was a role which was doomed from the beginning. My advice to her lacked foundation. But like any good-intentioned person I only took on this role out of caring.

Which was exactly why it should have been an easy thing to let go. But it wasn't. Letting go suggested failure, right? Passing the baton to another is just one way of saying I give up, you take it, run with it.

Shortly after Ed began to coach Jennifer I think she sensed my apprehension in this matter. She told me that she felt Ed had strengthened our relationship since she felt I no longer pressured her to perform well.

Indeed the role of both coach and lover can prove difficult; the line between criticism and caring too thin. After all, at this point our relationship was still in its infant stages. We had only been dating for less than a year. We were still feeling each other out, understanding which buttons to push, which ones to leave alone. Our life together wasn't yet capable of embodying both criticism and love in the same breath. So after some time I resigned to the fact that I was no longer going to offer her advice on running. That was going to be Ed's job now. Instead, I would play a support role, in good times and bad.

Jennifer was right. Ed's involvement, his taking of responsibility, turned out to be a great relief on our relationship for the time being. After I swallowed my pride I soon became Ed's second biggest fan.

But even after this I still felt a bit jealous at times. I thought of how he had gained her trust so quickly by not pressuring her. I can only guess that he must have sensed her apprehension to bring him on during their first meeting because he was totally lax in his handling of her. Then, when he finally began to really coach her he knew how to reach her, of finding her hot spots, of knowing when to back off, of knowing when to criticize or when to applaud her. Areas where I had anticipated failing if my coaching had continued. I reminded myself that that was his job; he was experienced at dealing with motivation and an athlete's psyche. He was her coach; a position of power. I was her companion; a position of sharing. Or perhaps he was just a better salesman than myself. Perhaps he had a better pitch. Who knows?

As I said, in the beginning Ed was so lax at coaching Jenny that there were moments when I wondered if he was even in the picture at all.

One evening, Jenny and I were sitting next to each other watching TV.

"What do you think about Ed?" I asked her.

"Ed's great," she replied. "He never even calls me."

Is it just me, or does that sound a little strange? I thought.

"Well, what exactly then is he doing for you?" I asked.

"He's just letting me enjoy myself for now," she said. "You should know. You preach about it all the time--about simply enjoying the run in its most basic way."

"Yes, but don't you think--"

Jenny was a little perturbed with me questioning Ed's advice. I sensed it in her voice. "I'm sure Ed will start working me harder soon enough," she said too quickly. "Besides, who's coaching me anyway, you or him?"

I could hear the gravel in her voice and decided not to push it. I said nothing.

However, more time passed and Ed continued to keep her on the same "easy" routine. We were all ready into March. The racing season loomed on the horizon. By now even Jennifer began to question her workouts, or lack of them.

Still, she said nothing to him.

The Boston Marathon was coming up as well. I had presumed all along that Jennifer would run it.

"What does Ed say about Boston?" I asked.

"Boston?" As if she'd never heard of it.

"Yeah, Boston," I said. "You know, that little race in April we've been training for since the dawn of time."

She said flatly, "Ed doesn't know."

I couldn't believe that Jennifer hadn't mentioned Boston to Ed. My thoughts teetered on a razor's edge with rage on one side and dumbfoundedness on the other.

"You're telling me you haven't mentioned Boston to Ed?"

"I was planning on telling him."

"When? The day of the race?"

"Paul, please," she said.

"He's your coach," I reminded her, unnecessarily. "Why haven't you told him?"

She stumbled over her next words. "Because I don't think he'll want me to run it."

"Why do you feel that way?" I asked.

"Because every time I ask him about competing he changes the subject." Which was more or less the truth. The actual truth was that she had said something to him on a couple of occasions: the first time she had mentioned Runnin' of the Green, a 7K on Saint Patricks day. "Libby Johnson will be there." "You won't see her after the gun sounds," he'd replied. A week later there was a cross-country race in Boulder. "Gwen Coogan will be there. I'd love to toe the line with her." "Why? You'll only get crushed," he'd told her. "Yeah, but just for fun," she'd replied. "Trust me," he shot back, "and stick to your training regimen for now."

"Jenny, I know you hate it when I question Ed, but--"

I know," she said. "I've been questioning him lately myself. It's racing season. I really do want to run Boston. But he won't even put me on the track yet, much less let me race."

That was true. Ed had told Jennifer to hold off for a while and not run with Toni's Thursday night group.

In retrospect, I think that's exactly how Ed wanted her to feel: hungry, eager for speed, eager to race. I think he was counting the days when she would come to him literally begging him to let her race.

And when she finally went to him and asked if she could run Boston he nearly blew his stack. His sullen black eyes ignited. Jennifer witnessed a maddening chaos played out in them.

Which was probably an act too. He'd been waiting for this moment, knowing it would come about soon enough.

"The hell you're running Boston!"

"But it's Boston!" she pleaded. "My qualifying time in Sacramento will ensure me a high seed, high enough to line up close to Uta Pippig, with all of them! It's my dream, my opportunity!"

"Not this year," he said.

"You said I could drive, you'd steer," she reminded him. "You said we'd have a fifty-fifty relationship."

"And I meant it," he said. "I'm just not going to steer you in that direction just yet."

"Why?"

"Because you're not ready."

"What exactly am I ready for?" she asked. "To run around the park, chase squirrels and look at the pretty birds? It's all been nice and easy up to this point, but you haven't told me anything. You haven't shared any of the God-given wisdom you say you have pent up in your head. Don't you think it's time you give me back my watch and let me race?"

"Oh, so you want some coaching then?"

"Well, that's what I hired you for."

"Tell me, Jennifer." Ed's voice was calmer now. "How have your runs been going?"

"Fine, I guess."

"Have you been enjoying them?"

"Should I be?" asked Jennifer. "I don't see how enjoying them is going to make me a faster runner."

"Have you?" he persisted.

"Yes."

"And on average," Ed continued, "would you say you've spent more or less time on your training runs?"

"What are you getting at?" She was tired of being led in this conversation.

"More or less?"

"I don't know." Jennifer said, annoyed. "You've got my watch, remember?"

Ed ignored the comment. "I would venture to say you've spent a great more time on the roads than you ever have in your life."

"What's your point, Ed?"

"You're probably running a third more than you were when you came to me. This whole time I've only been trying to do one thing. That of course is to increase your mileage by not getting you injured." Ed looked hot under the collar. "A blind person could see that!"

Jennifer felt a little ridiculous now.

"The first thing we need to do is train you to get from point A to point B; to make the marathon distance a given," he continued. "Then, when I'm satisfied you can do that, I'll worry about getting you from point A to point B fast!"

Jennifer said nothing.

"The only thing I can teach you now is to have patience," he said. "One thing at a time. Forget about Boston."

"Yes, but--" with a fading glimmer of hope.

"But what?" he mocked her by finishing her sentence, "but you'll have a chance to match strides with the top women in the country--the world? but you'll get your ego fed with a seeded number? All that sounds great until you consider the consequences."

"What are you talking about?" Jennifer was nearly in tears.

Ed reached out to her but she pulled away.

"You're not ready, Jennifer. You'll stand on the starting line and have your ego fed for a brief moment. You'll look at Uta Pippig, you'll see other great ones as well, but once the gun goes off you won't be able to stay with them for a block."

"If you mean to crush me you're doing a great job of it," said Jennifer, unable to fend off the tears which were now trickling down her face, carrying with them her dreams.

"I know how difficult it is to swallow this pill but it's better you know now than later." Ed was smooth in his delivery, not deviating from the script he had clearly thought out. "I have no doubt that you would run a fine race and possibly even eclipse the time you ran in Sacramento. But what's that going to prove? You'll come home rewarded with a plastic medal and dead legs. You'll put your training at risk for months afterwards. Don't sell yourself short, Jenny. I've got bigger and better plans for you."

"Ok then, I won't run," she agreed. "Now leave me alone!"

Jennifer began to walk away.

"Trust me on this, Jenny," he said. "And wait, there's one other thing."

Jenny looked back at him. Ed was smiling.

"What are you smiling about? You just ripped me to shreds!"

"No I haven't," he said. "In fact, just this morning I praised you like no other. I know what you're made of."

"What are you talking about?"

"I've landed you a sponsor," he said, pleased with himself. *God, I'm great,* he thought, spinning his bracelet in circles around his wrist. "From now on all your races, running attire and shoes, will be paid for."

Jennifer immediately lit up.

"All except for Boston," Ed laughed.

"All except for Boston," Jenny repeated. She managed to laugh as well.

Although the sponsor was only from a local running store it was a step in the right direction and a moment that Jennifer had only dreamed about a year ago. A sponsor! And this man, whom only minutes ago she doubted could ever take her anywhere, had secured it for her.

"Ed, you're the greatest," she said as she left.

THIRTEEN

"I have nothing to offer but blood, toil, tears and sweat."

-- Winston Churchill

I was seated at my desk when I looked up at the calendar. Ten days until Boston! A melancholy feeling washed over me. And why shouldn't it? I was emotionally spun. My dream of running Boston would soon come true.

I fumbled for a piece of paper and began to scribble some thoughts:

...A year and a half ago I crammed all my possessions into my black Nissan and drove East on I-10, leaving behind a city I loved and a handful of good friends. Outwardly I told everyone that I was leaving because of a job change. That was true, in part. But really I just needed a change, period. I'd become too obsessed in my passion for running, too uncaring of my job. Oddly enough it was the thing I'd trained so hard for in the first place, the thing I wanted most, the performance in San Diego which brought it all to a head. I could have taken a stand in Tucson, tried to start anew, to put some balance in my life but I knew that a total change in venue would better serve me. The opportunity in Denver would provide me with that.

And provide it did. While I still live the run I can say that I do not obsess about it as I once did. My life seems so much more complete. Jenny is now at my side and I value my career. And the run has taken its place in my life as just one piece of the larger pie.

Jenny has been another piece of that pie. She's been everything I ever dreamed about.

I'm saddened that she will not run Boston. But Ed is right. There will be other races and by doing so she could hamper the rest of her season. She will be there with me however. She may even run the final ten miles with me to offer emotional support when the going gets tough. Illegal? So what. I can't imagine a better way to finish Boston than to have Jennifer close by.

Our relationship has grown strong in a short period of time. It is one of balance. I enjoy her youth, the fact that her eyes are wide with anticipation and expectation. She reminds me that when you put your mind to something no object is a barrier, unmoving. However, it is this impatience she shows which produces a level of intolerance in her that even baffles me. It is in these moments when she turns to me. I'm quick to point out that everything worth having comes in time, that she's the most resilient, confident person I've ever known, and that her fortitude and drive go unmatched.

We play well off each other.

*

When a runner hears the name Boston he doesn't think of the Celtics, the Tea Party, the Red Sox or the Kennedys. When a runner hears the name Boston only one thing comes to mind: the Marathon.

Boston is the epiphany of a classic. It's the oldest consecutively run marathon in the world--its lore simply unmatched. Runners go to bed at night dreaming of taking part in it.

An age group qualifying standard is employed for both men and women which makes this race a terrific goal for some and a tantalizing fantasy for many more. Naturally, this is so because standards act as barriers and it's human nature to overcome them. When you place one in front of an athlete it's like pulling a skeet at a shooting range; runners obsess about shooting for it. For being invited to run Boston is something one can be proud of for the rest of his or her life.

But more than the qualifying standard I believe that runners come to Boston to take part in the making of history, to be a part of something they know will be forever storybooked and passed on to future generations.

Before the trip I talked with a lot of runners who had run Boston. One friend described it in awe, talking a lot about the expected million or so spectators: "some places they're ten deep!" I couldn't fathom it. The only attention I'm used to getting while racing is when I get in the way of a passing car and the driver screams out his window for me to move my ass. "You mean people actually cheer for you?" I asked.

"Unless you can't make the distance, then they berate you," he answered.

"That doesn't sound very hospitable."

"Well, perhaps just in front of Boston College." The race is run on Patriots Day, a holiday in the state of Massachusetts. "Beer tends to flow freely at the colleges and drunk students can be vicious."

Yes, Boston conjured up visions.

I'd never even visited the city before. I really had no idea what to expect. Perhaps, when I touched down, I'd see an Emerald City and a million little Munchkin people who look like Michael Dukakis cheering me along a yellow brick road. (Aaaah, a twinge of guilt here. I shouldn't pick on Mike knowing that he is, after all, a veteran of the

Boston Marathon having clocked a 3:31 back in 1951.) But--perhaps a wizard at the end of the course would drape a medal around my neck. And perhaps he'd look like Ted Kennedy. And perhaps I'd look up at him and say, referring to my race, "I bet you ran faster than that after you dumped that car and woman into the river many years ago."

All of these things might have come true if Boston was just a dream. But Boston is real. I hadn't seen it yet, experienced its flavor, but I knew it was out there; its lore so powerful that the thought of running it had manifested in me until I knew it was my destiny to reach it.

Oddly enough, my Boston experience *did* have a fairy-tail beginning to it.

Jennifer couldn't get on my flight. But she managed to get on an earlier one and would meet me there at Logan International Airport. I was sad that the trip had gotten off to an unexpected start.

But as it turned out I had plenty of good company.

The time came for me to board my flight. I walked on the plane directly behind Frank Shorter. I couldn't believe my eyes! Here I was on my way to fulfilling my dream of running in the greatest marathon ever, following *the* most accomplished American marathoner ever. This has to be a good omen, I was thinking. The funny thing is that I'm not usually star struck, but hey, this was the man that almost single-handedly launched the running boom in this country!

He was wearing a sweatshirt which had Boston written across the chest.

A bubbly, blonde flight attendant saw the shirt and asked him if he was planning on running in it. I reacted two-fold at hearing this. I was both slightly pissed off and slightly amused when I saw that she really had no idea who he was. Once again, I thought how sad it is that the most decorated runners in our country receive no recognition from most of society. But I suppose it was a fair enough question that she asked. At least she'd noticed the shirt and was able to associate it with the marathon. After all, she could have said something like, Boston--what a coincidence, we're flying there. Frank said something kind to her and then took his seat in first class. I couldn't resist whispering to her that "that's Frank Shorter, an Olympic gold medalist!"

When I passed by Frank I asked him if he was planning on commentating since he wasn't going to be running.

"Yes, I'll be very busy."

Read between the lines here, Paul. He was *already* busy and didn't want to be bothered by every star struck, wet-behind-the-ears runner he saw. I suddenly felt stupid for bothering him. So I was surprised when he continued the short exchange.

"Are you running?" he asked.

"Yes, It's my first Boston," I replied.

"Well, don't go out too fast," he said. "The first half is really deceptive."

Looking back I wish I would have taken his advice.

Just before take-off I looked around at the other passengers. The plane was full. A strange feeling, one of wanting, washed over me. How many others on board were going there to tackle the marathon? I got the feeling there were more on board than just a few. I looked for the thin ones, the ones with gaunt faces and a look in their eyes that expressed excitement, wonder and wanting. I was certain that I spotted several and that they'd spotted me. Among all the passengers on this flight we had a certain secret, a silent comradery and purpose in mind. We knew with a simple look in our eyes who each other was.

I felt good knowing I was in fine company. No, I felt better than good--I felt great.

*

I was in the Hopkinton High School gym. It was going to be my first memory of this memorable day, I was thinking. The gym is a waiting area that many runners flock to prior to the start of the Boston Marathon. I looked at my watch. It was only nine o'clock. The race wouldn't start for another three hours.

I secured a spot on the hard-wood basketball floor and tried to relax. Just me and about two-thousand of my closest friends. The musty odor of nervous athletes, sports-cream ointments, and the ghosts of past marathoners filled the air. Under most circumstances I'd describe the smell as awful. But now I lay there, flat on my back, staring up at the ceiling thinking it was the sweetest smell in the world: the smell of success.

"This is it!" I said to myself. "This is Boston!"

But from that point on things really didn't go the way I anticipated.

In retrospect, Boston was a let down. In all fairness, how could it have not been? How can anything live up to the incredible hype that's bestowed upon it? That I bestowed upon it?

I lined up in my qualifying section, about a third of the way back from the start. It was the most crowded feeling I'd ever experienced at a race. Yet, I anticipated that and was fine with that. But for whatever reason I panicked when the horn blew and my entire wave didn't so much as take a step forward. Gridlock City! It took me over two minutes to even make it to the starting line. Things didn't get much better after that. It took me ten minutes to reach the first mile mark. And eighteen minutes to reach mile two.

When things did begin to thin and I was able to run freely I tried to make up the time too fast. I began to run at a six minute per mile pace, which is nearly as fast as my usual 10K pace. Consequently, I'd foolishly committed suicide before I even reached the ten mile mark.

I blew up early. By the time Jennifer met me at the seventeen mile mark I was nearly a goner. I walked much of the last nine miles, stopping occasionally, trying to hold back tears that I was sure would eventually come. At one point I was sure I was finished and came to a complete stop.

I took refuge near the side of the road and saw the look of concern on Jennifer's face. I cast my eyes downward, ashamed. I wanted to walk off the course but the crowd was thick at that point. It would mean having to push my way through them and I didn't have the energy. Jennifer begged me to keep going. If she hadn't I might have taken a seat right then and there. She handed me an orange slice and a cup of water. Just then, a woman who saw me grieving bothered to look up my number in a race program (which I didn't even know existed). "Paul Jeffries from Denver Colorado! You can do it!"

There was a pleading tone in her voice as if *her* life depended on it! As if I was the vehicle that held her dreams too. I looked up and quickly located her in the crowd. There were tears in her eyes! The funny thing is that in previous marathons similar words of encouragement had often seemed so trivial, but in that moment of need nothing ever proved so powerful to spurn me onward. Somehow this total stranger and I connected on a roadside in the town of Newton, Massachusetts, two thousand miles from my home. Let me tell you, it was very motivational.

Then I remember the struggle to finish. It was literally all-encompassing. I'd never run this far back in the pack before. Indeed, I was running in the mainstream now and there were hundreds of runners within a stone's throw of me, pushing themselves forward in a battle of will, a battle of need. The battle to finish was much more evident than what I am used to seeing by virtue of the shear number of runners. Every time I turned my head I caught a glimpse of someone coughing, spitting, or tripping. Christ, do I look that bad? I thought. Of course, I knew the answer.

Jennifer did everything she could to keep me going. I didn't have enough energy to veer from side to side to take on water so she would bring it to me. I was in an emaciated state. I don't even think I was running. It was more like I was falling forward and happened to catch myself each time by sticking out a leg. Even my mind was shot. I have very few memories of the final miles. Those that I have are, self admittedly, odd.

We passed Cleveland Circle and the smell of freshly baked donuts permeated the course from the nearby Dunkin Donuts. I could nearly taste the sugar in my mouth. I would have stopped if I had any money. So I ran on. I remember the crowd noise. It was deafening in places. I wasn't sure who was crazier; the spectators or us? And I remember looking off into the distance and seeing the giant red triangle on the Citgo sign which comes at the twenty-five mile mark. I was aware that I'd been looking up at it for the better part of a half an hour. It was huge and bright and loomed in the distance, teasing me, beckoning me like it was the star of Bethlehem--although I was certainly no wise man. Finally I passed it.

I came to the last mile of the course. It was like the scene from Gone With the Wind after Atlanta had fallen to the Yankees. There were wearied bodies everywhere I looked, struggling to survive. I tried to avoid a fallen runner but clipped her shoulder with my foot, nearly causing me to fall too. On my left was a fellow runner standing on one leg with the other one sticking missile-straight before him like it was in a splint or something. It had cramped up badly and he was franticly trying to massage life back into it. Even in my pain I took pity on him.

Then the finish was within sight. I didn't have the energy to even appreciate the moment. Many runners thanked the crowd by waving and clapping. But I simply threw my body forward.

When I crossed the finish line a kind, old-lady volunteer--not a wizard!--placed a "finisher" medal around my neck and congratulated me. I thanked her at least twelve times. "I've done it!" I tried to shout, but my voice was hoarse. It came out a whimper. Still, I knew my name would be forever placed in the archives of the Boston Marathon. And for that I was grateful.

Jennifer had not run through the chute with me, choosing instead to bail out a mile from the finish. When she finally found me in the crowded finish area she held me tightly and told me she loved me.

So even though the race unfolded in a far different way than I had fantasized about I will always carry with me a number of good memories about it as well. Certainly, many emotional ones.

Jennifer joked with me a half hour later. "Thank God you always talk about the beauty in the process and not the product because your better days were left in Denver. That was the ugliest finish I've ever seen."

That much was true. If I had looked at my final result I would have left Boston a bitter person. But I knew that my victory had been won before the race had even started. My victory had been in the cumulative effort of all the miles run in preparation for Boston. When I toed the line there I had all ready won. The race itself was merely icing on the cake. And so the icing melted. Big deal. The cake was still good.

On the plane ride back I sat next to a heavy set man in a dark, flannel suit. A salesman, I was thinking. Always looking for conversation.

Sure enough: "You from Boston?" he asked, hotdog breath.

"No, Denver," I replied.

"Oh, so just vacationing," he said. "Did you see much of our fine city?"

It took me a few seconds to answer.

Then I smiled; a leisurely, laggard smile. "A little over twenty-six miles of it," I said. Closed my eyes. Dreamed. Happy thoughts.

That, in a nut shell, was my Boston experience. I had a bad race but a great experience. Will I ever do it again? I hope so.

A while later I read something that I related to quite well:

"It took me a while to see that the best times at Boston aren't measured by hours, minutes, and seconds, but by just being there. By running Boston you become a part of history."--Joe Henderson, Runner's World Magazine.

FOURTEEN

A week later Jennifer told me she had a great time in Boston. Though, I suspected she was only telling me a half-truth. I knew she shared with me the pleasure I felt having completed the marathon, having achieved a long sought-after goal. However, the whole experience had been difficult for her in one particular way: Ed had kept her from racing. Or to be more accurate; he had strongly suggested that she not race. "You're not ready yet," he'd said.

Before that exchange Jennifer had gone as far as submitting her qualifying time and officially being entered. To add insult to injury, when we arrived in Boston she was given a seeded number based on that qualifying time. It meant that, had she chosen to run, she would have been ushered to the first several rows; an opportunity to rub elbows with some of the icons of the sport; women she'd only seen in magazines, and witness that still-photos actually come to life and move and breathe like the rest of us mere mortals. Yet, the morning of the race she held true to her word: she did not run.

She simply kissed me goodbye and wished me well. Later she would find me at the seventeen mile mark as I passed through the town of Newton and run with me to the finish.

I can only imagine what might have gone through her head, standing on the side of the road, blending in with the many spectators, watching the lead pack of women pass and knowing that she could have had the opportunity to have been somewhere in there, not too far behind. It's one thing to choose not to run because of an injury or illness; those are things that are easy to justify. You're saddened, but you feel comfortable with your decision. But to choose not to run because your coach says you're not fit enough, when you're already putting in high mileage, is altogether different. You're left feeling empty. You question the credibility of the decision and ultimately you question yourself. It left her rather frustrated.

Runners don't ask for much. But the opportunity to compete is essential. And willfully pulling out of a competition is one of the hardest decisions an athlete can ever make. Especially when the competition involves something of the magnitude of Boston. Jennifer had dreamed of the moment to toe the line with the greatest women runners in the world which, of course, Boston offered. Yet, she passed. I don't think too many athletes in her position could have made that decision.

So now I noticed her eyes were often cast downward. She seemed ambivalent to conversation.

I didn't know what to say to her.

"There will be other races," I tried. "Ones where you'll be better prepared." But even as I said this I was aware of how ridiculous it sounded. The girl was putting in about seventy miles a week. How better prepared could she have been?

"I know, I know, I know," she repeated, as if she had already circulated my comment in her head a million times.

I'd never seen her so frustrated. Though Boston was mostly to blame for this, the fact we were nearly into May and Ed hadn't put her on the track or allowed her to race yet added to this.

So, bottom line, Boston had succeeded in only acting as an insatiable tease.

I believe that Ed knew of the impression that Boston would leave on Jennifer. He had told her what a great idea it would be to go and support my effort in the race. "Go, and have a great time," he'd said. What he forgot to mention was that when she returned she'd want to race so badly that she'd tear her hair out with anticipation.

Finally in mid-May Ed started Jennifer on the track. Quite late in the season, I thought, but I was sure Ed had his reasons.

The first speed session offered Jennifer a release. It was the first time all year that she had the opportunity to wear racing flats, to hear the tatter of her feet laid quickly and rhythmically to ground and feel the spikes punish the rubberized track and spurn her forward. She ran with reckless abandonment from a delicious need for speed. Prior to the workout Ed asked her to go out and run intervals of 800's: twice around the track. He wanted each lap to be run evenly. But now she couldn't resist coming off the backstretch of the second lap and exploding into the final turn, letting it all hang out in the closing meters. Nothing ever felt so good. Screw Ed.

With the Bolder Boulder once again on the horizon she mentioned to Ed her desire to run it.

Ed thought it was a "splendid" idea.

"I knew you'd want to run it," he said. "In fact, I anticipated it. I've already signed you up."

Ed told her that he wouldn't be in town the day of the race because his cross-country team had a meet. He handed Jennifer a bib with a seeded number on it. "Here, you're in the elite field this year."

Jennifer couldn't believe her eyes. She felt a little weak in the knees. She thanked him several times.

"Good Luck," he said

"Ed, your the greatest."

Well, It turned out that Jennifer needed a little more than luck. She was beaten badly at Boulder. In a word: crushed.

I did my best to console her immediately after the race.

"Don't take it too hard," I said. "You don't have the leg speed this early in the season."

"Everyone else did!" she said. She cried hard.

I took her in my arms.

"Ed has had you on the track for less than a month," I offered. Jennifer and I are not oblivious to God-given talent, which was what most of the women in the elite field had, but she at least wanted to run at a competitive level. "You didn't stand a chance."

"I'll just have to try harder next time," she said.

It was a ridiculous statement but I didn't tell her so. It would only cause her more heartache.

Some time later I was thinking. *Try harder, she'd said.*

One cruel aspect about racing is that you can rarely, if ever, try harder while racing in the pit. There are no miracles there. It's not a boxing match where one lucky punch can drop the champion. It's not a basketball game where a shot from mid-court can put your team in the lead. It's a footrace; the most basic and oldest form of competition. Forget luck--you won't find it.

If you haven't trained properly you'll find out soon enough on race day. You'll do your best rendition of a death walk as if someone has stuck a hose in your mouth and spun a valve which reads: lactic acid. You'll tighten up and your stride will shorten. Your legs will feel like they've got bungee cords holding them together, snapping them shut when ever you try to stride out. You'll get dizzy and swear you have cataracts as your vision is reduced to a narrow slit, a white haze washing over your eyes.

But even if you *have* trained properly you're still subjected to simply being outclassed. And this is more cruel than anything I know. Because in a distance race you are not merely beaten; you are beaten slowly and into submission as you watch your competitor(s) slowly fade away into the horizon. Boxers that have been knocked out often talk about the punch that they never saw, but in foot-racing you not only see the "punch" but you see it delivered from a long way off. You are made to swallow your own ineptness and left to stare at someone's ass for the remainder of the race. In distance running that can be a very long time to ponder thoughts of mortality. Because in foot-racing there's no such thing as giving it a hundred and one percent. You give it your all and if that leaves you two lousy feet per mile behind your competitor than that's how it is. Pure and simple. It's a hard pill to swallow.

For a nunrunner it's a very frustrating thing to witness. It's difficult to imagine that a thirty yard lead with a mile to go might be insurmountable. It's difficult to understand when a TV commentator concedes a race to someone who has just surged and not been answered with perhaps miles left in a race. But put yourself in the chaser's shoes. You've spent all race looking at this person's behind and you're not getting any closer; perhaps you're two feet further back than you were a mile ago. Your body and soul are completely taxed as you're giving it your all. Soon you're made to recognize your limitations; knowing you're not as strong or swift as your competitor and that on this particular day you've been bought--and possibly owned for a long time if beaten badly enough. And in that case, you might as well have been crated up and shipped down river because it will be a long time before you come back, ready to battle again.

*

By the time Ed returned to Denver Jennifer had outwardly accepted her defeat. She pretended not to care. But I knew otherwise.

I knew that the defeat had been a rude awakening and a blow to her confidence. Once again, she was as low as I'd ever seen her. And even though I was quick to point out that her finishing time would have placed her third in the citizen's race it didn't seem to appease her. She'd never experienced a deluge of absolute defeat before at the hands of so many women. She never even saw the lead pack after the first turn. Toni's bright red hair disappeared with them. And chasing the middle pack proved equally as difficult; she might as well have been chasing the noon sun as it drifted west over the Flatirons and the Continental Divide.

Another week passed and I could tell she still suffered. I reminded her that half the women in the race had shoe contracts with major companies, many of whom were flown in from other states and countries specifically to run the race. *Paid Assassins I like to call them*. I also pointed out that she *had* beaten most of the amateurs in the elite race. "You had a fine performance," I told her. "Nothing to hang your head about."

But none of this worked.

She wouldn't even look me in the eyes, as though she was ashamed or something. She only told me that she was fine and that she wanted to forget about the race.

So, for the second time in as many months she seemed distraught and distant. She acted indifferently to everything I said. "Jennifer, I've got tickets to Phantom." "That's nice," she flatly replied. "Jennifer, let's go to Aspen for the 4'th of July." "Sure," she said as if she had nothing better to do. If I had asked her to go outside and stare at the sun she probably would have done it. If I had told her that the world was coming to an end she might have said ok.

All of this isn't to suggest that she wasn't focused on her running during this time. Indeed, she trained diligently. Yet it was obvious to me that something was missing. She was void of enthusiasm. When I questioned her about her workouts, particularly the runs which I knew were her favorites, she simply stated that they went fine and that she didn't have anything else to say about them.

I felt that she was severely breaking down. Not in a physical sense, but mentally. Quite possibly she was questioning her identity; the reasons why she ran, why she bothered with it at all. Like I said, I've always imagined it much more difficult for someone who runs at an elite level, someone who runs on the edge, to pursue their dreams than it is for an average club runner like myself. The expectations are so great. The highs are exceptional; the lows equally the same.

When Jennifer stepped into the arena with the professionals at Boulder she put her very being at risk. With her first step she walked a high-wire with fulfillment on one side and emptiness on the other. And now that she had fallen to the side of the latter she was really nothing more than a shell of flesh wrapped around a self-made machine that fed on the need to run and race. She instinctively ran to, well, simply survive. She knew nothing more than the need to protect the machine, to feed it often, to sustain its form and function, even if she no longer knew why.

Runners talk a lot about the synergy of the mind and body, the need for them to act as one. For Jennifer, no two things could have been farther apart at this time. Given the choice I think she might have given up the run for a while, if not forever. But there was no choice--not really anyway. Running was ingrained in her. She had turned to the run in times of joy and sorrow and now she could only hope that in time this feeling of worthlessness would pass. So she trained hard despite everything. Though I knew, as she did too, that she was just going through the motions. To appease her coach? Perhaps. To appease her sponsor? Her family? Myself? She didn't know.

I wanted to tell her to back off. It didn't matter that much. I loved her with all my heart whether she ran or not. But I knew what she was going through wasn't about me. It was about her. It was internal and she'd have to work it out for herself.

She went as far as to avoid the popular running spots, like Washington Park and the Cherry Creek bike path. She didn't want to be noticed as the girl in the Bolder Boulder who got her ass whooped.

As if anyone would notice or care. Of course I didn't want to bother trying to convince her of that either. In her mind it was real. In her mind everyone was staring, pointing, laughing.

Obviously I had never been so concerned for her.

I thought about talking her situation over with Ed, just in case he hadn't noticed. I was aware that he hadn't talked with her much since the race.

That was when something else began to bother me; something that I couldn't quite put my finger on until I remembered what I had said to Jenny just after the race. I'd tried to console her by telling her she hadn't developed the leg speed this early in the season, that she hadn't spent enough time on the track. No, specifically that Ed had not put her on the track until weeks prior to the race!

I guess Ed did have his reasons after all!

It suddenly became apparent that Ed knew all along that she'd get crushed at Boulder. He let her run anyway. No, he had actually signed her up for the elite wave! He more than knew that she would get crushed--he wanted it!

Jennifer had not seen this ploy because she stood too close to the fire. Her emotions had taken over when Ed had given her a seeded number; when he had wished her good luck. Why would she question him? There was no reason. She simply wanted to please her new coach by performing well at the race. And when she failed she knew of no one to blame but herself.

But I, on the other hand, should have seen it coming. How could I have been so blind as to let him do this to her? Perhaps I had let my emotions take over as well. I have to admit that I was excited for her. How could I not have been? It was her first shot at the elite. But knowing this didn't take the sting away.

I suppose the next question I asked myself was: why in the world would he do such a thing? Knowing that Jennifer would take a sound beating he risked losing her for a great length of time, if not forever. But I was sure I knew the answer to that as well.

Ed had shown a need to control Jennifer from the beginning. He obviously didn't feel that a simple lecture on why she shouldn't run Boston was good enough. He wanted to drive the point home. As they say, a picture--or in this case, the undertaking--is worth a thousand words. So there it was, I knew. It was a lesson--nothing more.

And the reason why he hadn't talked with her much since then was because he'd been sitting idly by waiting to see how she'd respond; which way she'd pop up. Head first? Not at all?

Sure, he'd wanted her to run Boulder. He had wanted it more than anything at the time so he could say: "See, I told you so!"

But Ed wasn't stupid. Having her run in the elite field at Boulder was an easy way to shake her awareness without getting her injured or hamper her training; as might have been the case if he'd allowed her to run Boston. It was just a little push on her psyche.

It was a sick game that Ed played.

From that day on I despised him.

This left me with a terrible dilemma. I didn't know what to say to Jennifer, if anything. She was going through a terrible time as it was. Did I really need to plant the idea in her head that her coach was a ruthless prick? What could I say? *Ed's mean. Ed's evil.* Anything I might have wanted to tell her would only sound ridiculous and further upset her. Besides, I had no proof of Ed's intentions. It was all just a hunch.

And what if my hunch was right? Didn't a coach have the right to go beyond the physical aspect of training and mentally preparing a runner for time spent in the pit? Sure, it was a sickening game. But hell, I'd never coached. I barely understood an elite athlete's psyche. Ed Cooley had coached for years and years. Maybe this was acceptable practice in the wonderful world of coaching. I really had no idea. And like I said, I really had no proof.

So I thought it wise to not drive a wedge between coach and athlete--but only for Jennifer's sake. I'd give Ed the benefit of the doubt this time and not rock the boat with my unfounded suspicions. Jennifer had accepted his coaching practices by now and the two had formed a palpable bond. Jennifer liked to call it a "love-hate" relationship.

From this point on I witnessed Jennifer go behind Ed's back on only one occasion.

It was a month after Boulder. We decided that a weekend in the mountains would do us good. Just our luck we ran into a member of Spiridon, Gordon Scherbinski, who informed us of a low-key 10K that was to be held the following morning.

Gordon suggested that we run it. His charm was overwhelming. I do believe that he could sell a Hawaiian pineapples. We were no match.

"What the hell," said Jennifer.

We ran it.

Jennifer completely obliterated the women's field. And even though it was a small race I knew that she enjoyed the win immensely; she hadn't won a race in a long time.

To top it off she was awarded twenty dollars for her victory. It was the first time she'd ever won money for a win. We laughed at the size of the purse but were really quite delighted since we hadn't expected anything at all.

That afternoon we had lunch on the patio of The Hole In The Wall restaurant, in Conifer, drinking beers and eating sloppy burgers.

"Don't quit your day job," I said, referring to the prize money.

She responded by asking me if I had a five. "The twenty doesn't cover the tab."

That day did a lot to lift her spirits. For the first time in a while she had something to laugh about.

I jokingly called her a professional. "Perhaps the lowest money earner on the circuit," I said. "But nonetheless, a paid athlete."

Weeks went by and she never admitted to Ed about having run the race. Since it was such a low-key race she doubted that he would ever find out.

And I don't know if Ed ever did. Although, one night after a brutal speed session on the track, Ed winked at her and jokingly said, "don't forget, I get ten percent."

The following day he walked outside his house and found twenty dimes neatly stacked on his porch.

Ed wasn't stupid. He knew when to back off and let bygones be bygones. And perhaps he felt the mountain race had been a good thing for her. He'd seen--and liked--how she'd "popped up."

FIFTEEN

"Be careful what you wish for, you just might get it."

My parents said stupid things like that when I was growing up. Now, as an adult and having insight to what those adages mean I often find myself repeating their words.

I only bring this up to offer a suggestion as to what might have swept through Jennifer's mind as she went into the next season.

Like so many things in life we enter into a new realm thinking ourselves to be wise and understanding, only to discover along the way how naive, ignorant, and fallible we were in the beginning. "Aaah, to be old and wise is a virtue."

For Jennifer, the new year promised many good things. She eagerly awaited the challenge before her.

She and Ed had seemingly worked out their differences. Although Ed insisted on racing her infrequently to keep her "hungry" and to not deviate from her training routine Jennifer had run exceptionally well in the fall. She was able to cap off the season with a second place finish to Toni "Torch" Jamison in a highly tauted race. She had earned five hundred dollars for her efforts but more importantly gained a tremendous amount of confidence in doing so. While Toni went on to cruise to victory Jennifer had actually clipped her heals well into that race.

Jenny and I spent much of the early winter anticipating the upcoming season.

We both thought that as long as she rode the wave she was currently on and maintained her enthusiasm and rigid running schedule she would surely make the jump to the next level.

Ed saw it entirely different: the status quo of the present would only equal itself in the next season. *"She'll have to step it up a notch, and I'm just the man to ensure it,"* he thought.

I talked once of my discovery of the run, how I crawled inside a cocoon in my mid twenties; soft and unaware, and emerged years later as a runner; hardened and wiser. In 1995 Jennifer went through a similar transition, although having twelve years of running experience behind her, the transition that she experienced would take place on a much higher plane than I had or will ever experience.

It started innocently enough.

*

Jennifer and I were out on a run in Washington Park. It was January and every night for the past week I'd watched the weatherman on TV refuse to take away a large "L" which appeared over the city. So now, with the air collapsed all around us, the snow came down thick and wet. Fortunately the cloud cover acted as an insulator and actually kept the temperature from dropping too low. "It must be a tropical ten out her," Jennifer commented.

I wanted to laugh but when I tried my cheeks were so frozen they wouldn't accommodate a smile. What's next? I wondered. Will my lips refuse to part on account of frozen spit and sweat?

In spite of the weather there were many runners in the park that night. Most of whom were covered from head to foot, layered in cold-weather tops and tights, masks and hats. Just faceless bodies wrapped in dark attire passing by. Then I heard someone coming up from behind us. Occasionally, we might get passed in the park by someone going our way but it was almost always some talentless runner who was looking at us like competition, someone who sprinted by us gasping for breath who we just knew was going to turn the corner at some point ahead of us and turn blue and die. But who ever was passing us now sounded fine; the breathing rhythmic and easy. We were just obstacles in this person's way.

Despite all the clothing she had on it was easy to recognize her. Bright red hair stuck out from the top of an ear-warmer.

"Hey Toni," Jennifer said.

Toni didn't recognize us as easily. A second or two passed before she responded.

Jennifer and Toni hadn't seen each other in a couple of months and there was some initial catching up to do. The conversation eventually led to Toni's new living situation, with Barbara and Luz now as tenants.

"What's it like?" I butted in.

"What?" answered Toni between breaths.

"Three competitive runners living together."

"It's working out fine," she said. "Obviously we all have common interests and goals. Besides, I was getting lonely living alone for so many years."

That much I could understand. I didn't have to be reminded of the size of her estate. I had been over a couple of times when Jenny and I had met Barbara for a run. Jennifer voiced my thoughts.

"I don't think I could live alone in a house that large either," she said.

Toni's next comment was directed at Jennifer. "You live alone, don't you?"

"Yes," unsure if the question was meant to lead anywhere.

"What would you think about moving in? I've still got two bedrooms to fill."

Jennifer didn't know what to say. The question startled her.

"You don't have to answer now," Toni continued. "Think it over. We're all having a blast living together."

Really there was little to think over. The real estate market in Denver was booming and, as it did, rents followed. Besides, her lease was up at the end of the month. "Sure, I'd love to."

I couldn't help but be a wise-ass and ask about the fifth bedroom. "You said you have two bedrooms to fill," I said, trying to move my frozen lips into a curl.

Jennifer jokingly punched me in the shoulder and mentioned there would be too much estrogen in one household for me to handle.

"Besides," Toni added, reaching out an smacking me in the head, "you wouldn't want to be the slow one of the bunch. This could be the fastest household this side of anywhere."

I agreed. "Frightening thought, isn't it? By the way, that hurt!"

"Exciting thought," Jennifer corrected me.

*

It was really none of my business but I felt like it was something Jennifer might want to talk over with me. I questioned her about the decision later in the evening. Besides the fact that her rent would be cut nearly in half she told me that it just felt right. And that was that.

She moved in at the end of the month, as planned.

To my surprise even Ed responded positively when Jenny told him she was moving in with Toni. About the only comment he made was "stick to your own schedule and never mind what the others are doing." After last year's lesson learned Ed's comment could have went without saying. Although during the winter the schedule really didn't consist of much more than building base mileage for the upcoming season. No speed. Certainly no racing.

One night about a month after Jenny's move we were out having dinner at Josephinas. It was the first time since the move that Jenny and I had had a chance to be alone and enjoy each other's company.

We were seated in a quiet, dark corner of the restaurant, an orange candle-flame licked the air between us casting breaths of light on Jenny's shadowed face.

Sometimes, when there are no distractions and we are attentive to only each other, I find myself looking at her for what seems like an eternity, memorizing the contours of her face, studying the subtleties of her expressions, admiring the slow curl of her lips just before she breaks into a smile. Tonight, was one of those times.

I sat across from her listening to her every word, appreciating the moment, acutely aware that my love for her had grown stronger with each passing month, and accepting the possibility that one day we might share much more than an evening out on the town. Times like these I feel drunk in her presence. I turn into a fumbling idiot, often spilling my drink, or dropping my flatware, or stubbing my big toe. She does it to me! She can look in my eyes and suddenly I am thirteen years old; proprietor of an impossible crush and ambiguous emotions.

I suspect that Jennifer can lay claim to the same symptoms. On our very first date she knocked over a glass of wine. However, as our relationship grew she became increasingly comfortable with me and incidents like hers grew farther apart, whereas, mine now happened frequently. She later explained that the more comfortable she felt with me the more confidence she had in herself. On the other hand, my anxiety rested on the stark realization that I had fallen in love--and in my feeble attempts to control it.

Even before the appetizer was served I found myself having to steady a water glass with both hands upon setting it down.

"Good catch," she said. "That was headed right for my lap."

"Can't seem to get a grip tonight," I responded. I really couldn't!

My eyes were fixed on her. She wore a beige, herringbone sweater that exposed the long line of her neck. I could already feel the softness of her skin on my fingertips. Her hair fell freely and slightly bunched at the touch of her shoulders. I was acutely aware of the candle-flame which was mirrored in her eyes.

"Jenny, you look beautiful tonight," I told her. It wasn't the first time I had told her that night and it wouldn't be the last.

She was slightly modest but otherwise appreciative.

"Paul, really, I'm just wearing jeans and a sweater."

"It's a nice sweater."

"It's not even mine," she said. "I borrowed it from Luz."

"So now I understand why you wanted to move in," I baited her.

"What, so I can borrow sweaters?"

"Actually, you never told me why you wanted to move in with Toni."

"Don't look too deep," she said. "It's a chance to be a little closer into town and the rent is cheap."

"That's it?" I asked.

"Well, it's closer to you too," she said, knowing I'd appreciate being humored.

"So, how are things working out between the four of you?" I asked. "I'm still a little surprised that you accepted Toni's invitation. Four runners under one roof."

"You've seen the size of her house. If I want my space I just lock myself in my bedroom. It's quiet. I'd have a hard time hearing a party downstairs." A puzzled expression crossed Jenny's face. "But you're not really referring to that, are you?"

"Perhaps not," I admitted.

One thing that I'd picked up from time to time was that Jenny often didn't like talking about running when she wasn't actually doing it. She never came out and said so but I think it caused her to feel pressure about future expectations. On one occasion we met Barbara for lunch. Barbara talked about nearly every aspect of running for nearly an hour straight, particularly her own experiences, the whole time her linguine dangled from her fork. I don't think she ever got around to even putting it in her mouth. Anyway, when she was done she--almost as a second thought--asked Jennifer about her running. "What's to say, " said Jennifer. "It's just running. It's boring." Jennifer's voice had a tone of annoyance in it. There was an uncomfortable silence that followed. I'd even say that as time went by and the better she got the more unlikely she was to talk about it. As I've said before, the better one becomes the greater the expectations are that follow. Responsibilities often equate to pressures. So I could appreciate her feelings. My pressures only existed at work, where I liked to leave them at the end of the day. So it came as no surprise to me that Jennifer often preferred to leave the pressures she associated with running at the track. Jenny understood exactly what I was getting at.

"So far it hasn't been too bad," she said. "Although Barbara can and does talk endlessly about running."

"And that doesn't bother you?"

"Sure it does, but I just retreat elsewhere if it gets to be too much."

"That's nice."

"And I never even see Luz. She's been spending a lot of time at work. She's been given a promotion of some sort. As for Toni, she's pretty cool. So far we talk a lot about her dog, Lucy."

"And--"

"And if I don't feel like getting into it with someone I just go to my room," she said. "But you're right in thinking that a house full of runners will ultimately end up talking about running in nearly every conversation."

"Sounds like a sure way to burn out fast," I commented.

"Or to stay focused," she suggested.

"That's good," I said. "Nice to hear you're looking at the bright side."

Jennifer paused for a second while a waiter tipped the bottle of chardoney in her glass.

"Although Barbara pissed me off just this morning."

I was surprised. If anyone angered Jenny I wouldn't expect it to be Barbara.

"What'd she say?"

"She asked to borrow my calculator."

"And that pissed you off?"

"Not exactly. When I gave it to her I said something about 'doing bills?' She responded by saying, 'No, I've got to add up my weekly mileage'."

My mouth opened in disbelief. "She needs a calculator to add up her mileage?" I said, nearly spitting out a mouthful of wine.

"Apparently so."

"Perhaps she flunked math," I joked.

"And perhaps she just wants to let the world know how motivated she is," said Jennifer, unamused.

"That is a little odd," I commented. "But don't let it bother you."

"I'm not," she insisted. "But it struck me as a competitive gesture."

*

Later that night Jennifer crossed the foyer and quietly walked up the winding oak staircase in Toni's house hoping not to wake anyone. She stepped slowly and hoped the stairs wouldn't creek under her weight. Fortunately they didn't. When she got to the top of the stairs she turned right, heading in the direction of her bedroom. She was exhausted and desperately wanted to brush her teeth and go to sleep. When she approached the bathroom that she shared with Barbara she didn't notice the thin sliver of light that breached the hallway from under the door.

Jennifer walked in and saw Barbara on her knees with her head over the toilet. She backed out quickly, softly shutting the door. Jenny was embarrassed and shocked. Then she heard the unmistakable gagging sounds of Barbara vomiting. *Poor girl, she thought, if she's sick she may need my help.* She decided to give it a minute before lightly knocking.

"Barbara, you all right?

Just then Barbara opened the door and walked out.

"Of course I'm all right," she said. "Just had to pee."

What she said nearly floored Jennifer. Obviously Barbara hadn't seen her open the door and never knew she was standing outside the door listening.

Jennifer didn't know what to say. "So...then...you're ok?"

"Of course I'm all right," insisted Barbara, smiling. "How about a run in the morning. I was thinking of a trail run. We'll head up..."

"Sure, sure," Jennifer said, confused. She hadn't heard the last part of Barbara's sentence.

"Great, lets sleep in and we'll take off about nine." Barbara smiled again and patted Jennifer on the shoulder as she walked by her and down the hall.

The next day Jennifer called me.

"I'm worried about Barbara," she confessed.

"How so?"

"I caught her with her head in the toilet last night," she said.

She told me everything that happened.

"I'm afraid she's hiding something," she added.

"Jenny, it's possible that she might have just been sick and embarrassed about having vomited," I said. "Has this kind of thing ever happened before?"

"No, but--"

"What?"

"Doesn't she seem slightly obsessed about eating?"

"Perhaps a little," I said.

"Have you ever actually seen her eat anything?

"You mean like the time she twirled her pasta around on her fork until it was time to go?"

"Yeah, like that."

"I suppose it's a little strange," I said. "But the last thing you want to do is confront her about an eating disorder. If it turns out that she was indeed just sick and didn't feel like telling you then it might be an embarrassing situation for the both of you."

"I suppose," she said.

"Just keep an eye on her."

*

Janet Kurth had not returned to work the same woman. Her illness had severely compromised her dedication to the job. Even though Jennifer had slowly grown to despise the woman one thing she had to admit and admire was that Janet seemed like the one person in the Department of Energy who actually cared about the matters at hand, often taking proactive stands on things.

Now Janet showed up to work, obviously not feeling well, sitting behind her desk most of the day with her head cupped in her hands.

The end result of this being that Janet had poured an even greater work-load than usual on Jennifer.

For example, once a week Jennifer was "asked" to attend after-hour meetings as a liaison between the Rocky Flats Plant and concerned neighborhood citizens. Of course, when dealing with issues on radioactive waste the "neighborhood" could mean just about anyone from the entire state of Colorado.

For decades the plant had manufactured plutonium. It had since stopped this manufacturing of the weapons grade material but there was literally tons of radioactive waste that sat in barrels and in storage tanks on plant site that nobody knew what to do with. Issues ranged from ground water contamination to particles becoming airborne, mobilization of the waste, to incinerating it.

Each citizen was given time to express his concern about one thing or another in regards to the plant. At a meeting I attended I listened to some moron try to sell his idea of building and putting the waste in a giant pyramid, similar to the ones in Egypt. "It's been thousands of years since them there things were constructed," he argued, "and they be still standin." Unfortunately, it was a professional forum and each idea, no matter how sound or ridiculous it was, had to be addressed and answered. If an answer was not readily available to satisfy the complaint or suggestion then research would have to be conducted until one became available. Sometimes Jennifer would spend days researching a specific topic so that she would have a satisfactory answer available for the next meeting.

"Why even have those meetings?" I asked her.

"It's a gesture of goodwill towards the community," she answered.

"It's a joke," is what I said. "Any concerned citizen who shows up for those meetings already has his mind made up that the government is trying to hide something."

"We're trying to educate the public so that they won't be fearful of the going's-on at the plant," she rebutted.

"You can't educate the general public on the complexities and dealings with of nuclear waste," I argued. "The general public can barely tie their shoes."

"I suppose," she said.

"It's a futile effort."

Well, that comment didn't sit well with her.

"So then, your suggestion would be to just keep them in the dark," she said. It wasn't a question.

"All I'm saying is that it's not a simple subject and there are no clear answers. You'll beat yourself to death trying to convince the public that Rocky Flats really gives a shit about their well-being."

"Do you really think so?"

"Hell yes," I said. "You might as well be attending a lynch mob. I don't think all the sincerity in the world could convince them. The damage has been done long before you arrived."

"I've thought of that," she said.

Rocky Flats has a poor history of being truthful with the public. Countless numbers of violations and a poor safety record added fuel to the flame as well. Sixty-Minutes called one of their storage tanks, 13, the most dangerous building in America.

"So then, tell me this?" she asked.

"What?"

"When I'm standing up there at the podium at those meetings do you believe what I'm telling you?"

"Of course," I said. "But that's because I know and trust you."

"Well, if you believe me then I'll have to find a way to convince everyone else."

"Jennifer--"

"Paul, I don't really have a choice in this matter, do I?" She was visibly upset now. Folds appeared on her forehead and her eyes looked empty. "They're grooming me for Public Relations Director. I can't very well just walk in one day and say, 'I give up, let's scrap the whole campaign!' I'll have to find a way."

But this was not a simple matter. I didn't want to let it go.

"And get killed in the process," I added. "You're dealing with a highly sensitive subject: nuclear waste. You're likely to get some crazy in there who doesn't like one of your responses, pulls out a gun and shoots you in the head."

Thinking back, that probably wasn't the kindest thing I could have said to her. She was clearly shaken by my words. Perhaps, because as frightening as they sounded there was likely some truth behind them. There wasn't even so much as a security guard at those meetings. The discussions often became heated. The meetings sincerely left me scared for her.

One day Jennifer walked in Janet's office and saw a faint smile on the woman's lips.

"Well, they've done it," Janet said.

"Done what?"

"Given me my early retirement," she answered. "I'll be leaving in May."

It was less than three months away.

Jennifer knew this moment would eventually come and had no idea how it might make her feel when it did. But now she did: nauseous. Her stomach turned, not from excitement, but from fear.

"What about your replacement?" she asked.

"Could take a while," Janet said, seeing the fear sweep across Jenny's face. "Look, Jennifer. They're not going to throw you into the fire on this one."

Jennifer looked a little relieved.

Janet continued. "A replacement will be sent here soon enough. You might have to work a little harder in the mean time."

"How long?" asked Jennifer.

"Six months, a year tops," said Janet.

In government language that meant 'till death do her part. Jenny felt ill. She was already struggling to keep her head above water. There would be no way she'd be able to handle an even greater work-load.

"Well, I'll hate to see you go," Jennifer said--and meant it.

"You're a sweet girl," said Janet. Better you than me, she thought.

"Excuse me." Jennifer held back tears as she left Janet's office.

She could see the problem facing her now. She'd have to put off her running career for the time being. *It's just the way it is, she thought. Ed will have to understand. Paul will be supportive. There's just no other way.*

SIXTEEN

Luz Diaz spun herself full circle in the black leather chair. It was a well cushioned one with a head-rest. When she came to a stop she leaned back in it and threw her feet up on the cherry-laminated, oval desk where a picture of her mother sat.

The black and white photograph was badly worn. There were folds in it that Luz hadn't been able to get out after she'd carried in her pocket for several weeks as a child. Still, its condition made no difference to Luz. It was the only picture she'd ever seen of her mother. Quite possibly the only one that existed, she thought. And it proved that at one time her mother had been a beautiful woman, much different than Luz's last memory of her.

"You look just like her," Derrick Ralls, the owner of Ralls Advertising, commented. Derrick was tall and attractive and his even, confident voice was soothing to one's ears when he spoke.

But the words startled Luz, who had not seen him walk into her office.

"Do you really think so?"

He picked up the photograph and studied it for a second. "Yes indeed," he added. "She was a beautiful woman."

"Derrick, really now."

"What?" He handed the photo to Luz. "I'm sure you wanted an honest answer. She was beautiful."

Luz stared at the photo for a second. "So she was," she said, smiling. She then turned her attention to Derrick. "Well now, what can I do for you?"

"Nothing. I just wanted to drop by and see how your new office was working out?"

"I love it," she said sincerely. The office had been a storage room for years before Derrick had it cleaned and converted. The day Derrick had placed her name and title on the door and given her the keys to it was one of the happiest days of Luz's life.

"I know it's not what you expected," he'd said, referring to the make-shift space. "Just tolerate it until I get the lease worked out on the other building."

The company had been expanding for the past several years, thanks in part to Luz. Three years earlier Luz had competed in a race an hour's drive west of Denver in the mountains. The race director, a balding man named Jeremy, had promised prize money to the winners of the men's and women's races. Luz won her race. Unfortunately, only fifteen people had shown up to run. The race director apologized profusely to the participants. One, for lack of competition. Second, because he had planned on using the other entry fees to pay the winners. "I can't even come close to paying my own expenses," he'd said, "I can't possibly pay you." It really wasn't any big deal to Luz or the men's winner. But the race director was so distraught about the situation that he couldn't stop talking about it. "I used a small advertising firm in Denver," he'd said. "They'd never advertised a race before, but they said they'd do a great job anyway. And look what they've done!"

Well, that was right up Luz's alley. It was an easy sale. Luz was one of the most respected runners in the entire state of Colorado and had just been hired as a receptionist for Ralls Advertising. "Don't worry about the prize money," she told him. "Just give me a call next year if you decide to give this event another shot. I'd like to have a shot at your business."

"You can count on it," Jeremy said.

Luz had the resources and knowledge to spearhead the project. The following year the race was a complete success. So much so that Jeremy quickly spread Luz's name around to other race directors in the area. Within the year, Ralls Advertising was promoting twelve races. Luz was promoted to an account executive. A year later that total grew to over fifty. Luz was respectfully given all the credit and promoted to Senior Account Executive.

At that point her work-load increased to the point where her little cubical with the three by five desk could no longer accommodate her. "I need more room," she'd told Derrick. "Where am going to put you?" he asked. "In the closet?"

Hell, the closet was no ordinary closet. It was huge. "Sure," she said.

So now Derrick apologized for having to convert a closet to accommodate her. "Every time I walk by I still have the tendency to open this door and look for the Lysol or something."

"Derrick, don't worry about it," Luz said. "I love it."

Or at least the idea of it, she thought. Her own office! She'd come so far. But not just in work. In life all together! Which was exactly the reason why she neglected to tell him about the little headaches she often experienced. She was too grateful to complain about something so trivial. A change in the lighting would probably make a world of difference, she thought.

"Good," Derrick said, looking at his watch. "Well, it's time to wrap it up for the day. You want to grab a drink or something?" It was a friendly invitation, nothing more.

It was the first Thursday in March and thus the first track session of the new season. She'd have to decline.

"Derrick, you know I would but I've got track tonight."

"That time of the year again, huh?" he said. "Well then, tear 'em up!"

"I'll try," she said.

"And ask your friends if they know of any new races that we could promote," he added, smiling, before he left her office.

Luz turned her attention once again to the photograph of her mother. It pleased her when others commented that she resembled her so. Luz's hair was straight and black and shimmered like lava fields under a summer sun. She had been blessed with soft, honey-brown skin and a chiseled jaw line. Overall she was attractive, but far from perfect. Her cheek bones sunk low making the area below her eyes look hollow. The large gap between her two front teeth was something she'd often been teased about. But soon she planned on having her back molars removed which, she was told, would make her cheekbones look a little higher.

She wasn't as thin as most of the talented runners she knew. She was aware that she possessed a few more curves. "Your figure make-a my work look sooo good," a tailer once told her.

She laughed with the memory of that.

"If you could see me now, Mother," she said to the image in the frame.

Luz's earliest memories of growing up were those she had of her neighborhood in Jaurez, Mexico. It wasn't really a neighborhood at all, she reminded herself. There were no streets, no grass lawns, no electricity, no sewer system--unless one referred to the Rio Grande which carried away most of the garbage and waste from her home and the surrounding homes.

The shack she referred to as home sat on the side of a small, polluted hill overlooking the river and the city of El Paso, Texas. It was a small adobe structure that housed her mother, her brother and herself along with countless numbers of scorpions and centipedes. At night when she closed her eyes she could hear them crawling on the floors.

As a child she had no concept of nations or boundaries or governments and the like. She didn't understand why the homes on the other side of the river were so big and clean. She was fascinated with the sparkling lights that lit them. So much so that her mother nicknamed her "Luz" early on. (Luz means "light" in Spanish.) When Luz asked why their house couldn't sparkle like the ones across the river, her mother said," no electricity, my Sweet." But that didn't really answer Luz's question since she had no idea what electricity was.

She also had no idea what the word "whore" meant either. The bigger children on the hillside called her mother that.

Finally, one day she asked her. "Mother, what's a whore?" Luz's eyes were innocent and wide.

"My Sweet, " she said, aghast. "Where did you hear that word?"

"The other kids call you that."

The question had taken her by surprise. Nonetheless she recovered well and answered. "A whore is someone who has lost her husband." She could feel tears well up in her eyes immediately. She stroked her daughter's hair.

Luz saw the pain in her mother's face.

"Well, I lost Daddy too," said the innocent eight year old, feeling her mother's sorrow. "Can I be a whore like you?"

"Please, my Sweet, go to bed," she answered.

That same night Luz and her four year old brother, Xavier, slept as usual; curled up next to each other with Luz's protective arm draped over him. In the middle of the night a strange voice awoke her. It came from the only other room in the house. It was a man's voice and it sounded angry. She stood up and slowly walked across the room-- hoping not to step on anything that might be crawling on the floor-- and put her ear to the door. Someone was saying all kinds of things that didn't make any sense to little Luz. Her eyes were wide and reflected the light of moon that shot through the bedroom window.

Luz opened the door just a crack, and in the dim light of a gas lantern witnessed a man on top of her mother. His pants bunched up down around his ankles and his naked rear-end rose and fell as he continued to say things to her mother that made no sense.

"You're hurting my Mommy!" Luz screamed. "You're hurting my Mommy!" Luz sprung open the door, ran to him and jumped on his back.

He spun around and with one hand discarded her as if she'd been a rat that had suddenly dropped from the ceiling. He didn't stop "hurting" her mother either. But now she heard her mother saying something as well: she was screaming for him to get off her, to get out of the house.

Luz remained in a corner where she had been flung. The man did indeed get off her mother. He pulled up his pants and looked at little Luz. He was a very dirty looking character and seemed to be about ten feet tall. Even from where he stood Luz could smell the foulness of his breath.

"I'll have you one day too!" he said, scowling, blood-shot eyes.

Luz's mother threw an open bottle of Tequila wildly in his direction. "Get out!" she screamed. The bottle smashing against the wall behind him, spraying him with glass and alcohol.

But the man stood undaunted, peering down at the young girl. "You'll be pretty, unlike your ugly mother."

Then he left.

The following week her mother gave her a small purse containing some money and the photograph that Luz now had on her desk, and sent her and Xavier north across the river. "You're going to the land of bright lights," she told them. Luz pleaded not to go, but her mother insisted on it, saying that she would follow soon.

The world was small to Luz. "The land of bright lights" consisted of nothing more than the city across the river. "I'll wave to you from across the river each night until you come," Luz said to her. It was the last thing Luz would ever say to her.

A white man, who spoke Spanish in broken words, then hid Luz and her little brother under a fake wooden floor in the rear of a large truck. There were others in there besides herself and Xavier. The air was hot. The others smelled foul. No one spoke a word and when she began to cry someone put a hand over her mouth to hush her.

She was frightened! But the lights on the other side of the river were so close. She was sure the ride would only last minutes, perhaps an hour at the very most.

What Luz didn't know was that her mother had told the man to take them far away, "so that they won't know how to come back." She had saved for years to do this; to give them a chance at life and happiness in a new land. Of course she would not follow. She was broken and weak and would live out her days as an aging whore on a dying, dusty hillside.

Now sitting at her desk, proud owner of a big title, Luz remembered her mother in only a fond sense. As a teenager she'd felt a bitterness towards her from having been abandoned as a child, but that feeling had long since faded, given way to an understanding of circumstance and intention. The love her mother felt for her and her brother must have been deeper than any love she might ever wish to know. How could one give up the only happiness in her life--her children--so that they might find a better life away from her? And surely, her mother must have also known that future contact would be improbable, if not impossible.

One time, when Luz was twenty, she and Xavier returned to Jaurez in an attempt to find her. The two located the hill easily enough, but the few shacks which still stood had since been abandoned. The one they believed to have been theirs had been leveled. In the end the search had proved futile. Neither Luz or Xavier could even remember their mother's first name. As young children it hadn't been important.

*

Jennifer could feel the butterflies swirling in her stomach. The first track session of the new season always reminded her of the first school-day when she was growing up in New York. It didn't matter that she'd been through it before. Nor did it matter that she knew everyone there. An excitement filled the air as each of the women in Toni's invited club exchanged stories of how they'd spent their winter and of the impending race season. And now that Toni, Luz, Barbara and herself were all living together the other women were interested in knowing how things were working out.

The group was a little smaller this year. Only eight girls had shown. Still, Mel was there, running her mouth faster than her legs.

Dee Smith, the talented triathlete, was there too, looking fit and intimidating as always. Jenny hadn't spoken two words to hear since Dee's smart-ass comment as she passed her towards the end of the Cherry Creak Sneak two years earlier: *"wonderful race, wasn't it?"*

As the women circled the track an aura of silent curiosity filled the air. Though nobody wanted to admit it, each tested each other in the repeats. They were all competitors deep down, and while they were friends off the track, each fought for position *on* the track.

It soon became apparent that little had changed since last year. Toni continued to lead the pack through the workout. That much was a given. Jennifer hung closely on her shoulder, occasionally challenging her coming out of a turn but never actually taking the lead.

One noticeable change was that Barbara Duff seemed a bit more confident than last year. She was unusually solemn. Her weathered face taking on a stern look as if she was quite serious about the task at hand. Still, she finished each 800 repeat towards the back of the pack.

Curiously enough, Luz also finished each repeat consistently towards the back, often coming in behind Barbara. If nothing else, Luz was a strength runner, capable of turning quarters even faster than Toni. Jennifer could only figure that Luz had managed to fade into terrible shape over the winter.

Jennifer came over after the workout.
"Did you watch the workout?" she asked. She sounded upset.

123

"I caught a little of it," I admitted, guarded.

"I can't stand the thought of you looking on at us like you do!" Her voice was angry. She was definitely in a foul mood.

"What do you want me to do?" I asked. "Pull the shades?"

"You can watch TV or something. Go for a run. I don't know!"

"What's bothering you anyway?" I asked. "You looked great out there."

"It's too damn competitive. Everyone's just out there wanting to run each other into the ground."

"How's that different from any other week?"

"It's a track session! We're supposed to be working on even splits, quality intervals and the like. It's not supposed to be a race!"

Her point was obvious. I reminded her that it, being the first track session of the new year, was likely to be competitive. "Everyone's looking to test each other."

Then she said something that befuddled me.

"Well, I'm not going anymore!"

"It's Ed, isn't it?" I was taken aback. Surely Ed must have been behind Jennifer's aggravation. Jennifer had probably told him she wanted to do the Thursday night track sessions and Ed had probably told her not to. Last year he hadn't started her on the track until May.

"It has nothing to do with Ed." She looked away. "Ed actually thinks it's a good idea."

"He did?"

"Yeah, he told me it was time I stop chasing Toni and start beating her."

"You think that's realistic?" I asked.

"Of course not!"

"Did you tell him so?"

"No! The man's got these grand visions of me. Didn't want to blow his bubble just yet."

"So then, is that what's bothering you?" I asked.

"Hardly."

"Well Jennifer, what am I here? A mind-reader?" I wanted to help but she wouldn't come clean with me. "You've got to tell me what's bothering you."

She looked up at me and stumbled on her next words.

"What?" I asked. "What aren't you telling me?"

Jennifer's eyes were red and tearful. "You won't understand."

"Don't pull this on me," I said. I was getting upset now too. "Don't come over here pouting and not tell me what's bothering you."

Then she came straight. "Janet's leaving."

Her words threw me for a loop. It took me second to respond. "I, I thought that you hated her," I said. "I thought when the time came for her to leave we'd be celebrating."

"Does it look like I'm celebrating?"

"I still don't understand what all of this has to do with your not wanting to go back to track."

"It has everything to do with it," she said, her tone of voice demeaning. "How can I do the work of two people and still compete with everyone at track?"

I saw her point.

"Time to stop chasing Toni. Yeah right!" she said, letting out a long sigh.

"It's not fair for Ed to put that kind of pressure on you," I offered. "She's a professional. Surely he couldn't have meant it."

Silence.

"I'm not going to be able to do it all," she finally said. "Ed's already running me eighty miles a week!"

It was difficult for me to respond. I didn't know what to say. But it did seem like she was jumping the gun. "Jennifer," I said. "You're already counting yourself out. You don't know what DOE is going to throw at you. Janet's been ill and you've already been doing the work of two people. If they send in a good replacement your job might actually get easier. Just take things one day at a time and see what happens."

She didn't tell me that she had a bad feeling about a replacement being sent any time soon. She pretended to accept my words, only adding, "It's all just a little overwhelming."

SEVENTEEN

Shortly after Jennifer had confided in me about her hectic schedule I had to leave on a business trip. I headed north to Cheyenne and then west through southern Wyoming on my way to Salt Lake City. It was a full day's drive over a barren and dull landscape and offered me a great deal of time to relax and think. Unfortunately, the more I thought the more I found myself in a sour mood.

"Seventy, eighty miles a week," she had said. Such words can spill from a runner's mouth so evenly, so nonchalantly, that they often slide the ear of a nonrunner. *When there is no understanding how can there be an appreciation?*

I once had a conversation with a nonrunner about the high mileage I was putting in and about the energy expended in this commitment. He was unimpressed. My mistake had been in telling him that I ran about an hour or so every day. "Big deal," he said. "I spend hours every weekend golfing."

He obviously had no idea what running high mileage involved.

But I do. Which is exactly why I was upset. I had let her comment slide right by me, barely acknowledging it, offering exactly nothing in the way of support to Jennifer.

I glanced at the digital clock on the dashboard of my Nissan. It read: 8:30.

Jennifer's commitment to the run meant that she would have put in five or six miles this morning and was all ready thinking about going out again in the afternoon.

The commitment would ensure that she was up early to stretch, loosen tight muscles, cool down after the run, and then get ready for a long day at work. It meant that she would probably tire early and pass on going to a movie, a restaurant, or a baseball game with a friend. It meant that she would watch her diet and plan her meals around her run. Basically, it meant that everything she did in any given day or week would revolve around her running schedule.

Jennifer was now training with a specific marathon in mind. It meant that she would spend months focusing on that race, hoping to peak at just the right time. She'd increase the intensity and mileage every so often to reach that peak. She'd risk all of it to injury. That was the real kicker. Every time you increase your mileage or intensity you're adding that much more stress to your body and increasing the probability of injury. So the stakes are high and the game can be cruel, to say the least. The payoff--or lack of in the case of injury--being equal to the sum of input.

Up ahead a sign read: Laramie--20 miles.

Oh, and it meant that she would run something in the realm of twenty miles in a single shot on Saturday.

I was traveling at over sixty miles per hour. Twenty miles is a hell of a long way, even in a car.

It also meant that she might spend the evening sitting on an ice pack, tending to sore muscles, an inflamed tendon, doctoring a blackened toenail or a split callous, or any one of endless possibilities that can arise when the body is exposed to the punishment of flesh and bone striking the ground thousands of times with each workout. One day her foot swelled to the size of a grapefruit for no apparent reason. She took that day off. One of few days she would ever take off.

Because her dream to toe the line with the best women runners in the country would ensure that she'd get up and do it all again, each and every day. To run at the level she aspires to requires that much. Any athlete in search of the same has ultimately faced this inevitable test of his or her integrity. See, a well conditioned athlete and seasoned runner might not have a problem with any given single workout, but it is not the single effort that brings about difficulty and imposes the arduous lifestyle of that of a runner. The difficulty which I refer to is born from the cumulative effect of "living the run" day-in and day-out. Jennifer was running twenty miles on one day, running a speed session a couple days after that, racing from time to time, and finally adding up her mileage at the end of a given week and having to double check her addition as it raced skyward. Every Monday the whole process started over. When you run high mileage the run becomes all consuming in every aspect of your life. You literally live the run.

I never tried to explain this to my golfer friend. I figured my attempt would be futile. Some things just have to be experienced to be appreciated. Besides, I would never claim to understand the things he went through in preparation of the time spent golfing each weekend-- perhaps staying up late the night before to polish his six-iron?

I was suddenly consumed with the wanting to call Jennifer, to talk things out and tell her that I understood her situation. When I got to Laramie I stopped at a pay phone and dialed her number.

I'd reached her voice mail. *Damn!* How could I tell a machine I understood and loved it? I hung up and drove on.

It wasn't until later that evening when I finally reached her. My worst fears had come true. All day long I had envisioned her calling Ed. He would tell her to choose between a thankless job and a promising running career. "You're only young once," he would say.

127

"Go with your heart." At this stage Ed had a lot of influence over her. His argument would be convincing at least.

To my surprise she told me otherwise. She told me of their conversation.

"I don't think I'll be able to continue to run at this level," she'd confided in him.

"Have you mentioned this to Paul?" he'd asked.

"Yes."

"And what did he tell you?"

"To take things one day at a time," she'd answered.

"Well then," Ed had said. "That sounds like good advice to me."

I couldn't believe what I was hearing. Perhaps I'd been wrong about Ed. He was looking after her well-being, after all. And I, who had been so afraid that he would try and sell her on the idea of quitting her job, felt ridiculous.

Actually, I felt a gambit of emotions welled up inside. I was thrilled that Ed had backed my advice. It was likely that Jenny wouldn't view me as an uncaring ass now. Unfortunately, I was also bitter that the voice I heard coming through the other end of the line was warm and comfortable. Ed had "reached" her once again and settled her down. I hadn't succeeded in that. I tried to convince myself that it was merely the "seconding" of advice that had led to her levelness. But why had it been Ed who had settled her? Why not her parents, or Barbara, or anyone other? So I was a little jealous. Why shouldn't I have been? She had found understanding and compassion in Ed once again. I cursed myself for not being there. I was five hundred miles away in a cold hotel room in a town that Jennifer knew as only a dot on a map.

*

Luz Diaz enjoyed spinning herself full circle in her leather chair. She did it at the end of every work day as if to say "I'm on top of the world and I don't have a care." Except this time, after she'd steadied the chair, her head didn't stop spinning. Nauseousness overcame her. Out of fear she rose up and tried to gain the attention of Derrick Ralls who was in the next room.

She was unsuccessful at standing but quite successful at gaining Derrick's attention with the sound of her head hitting the floor--*Thud!*

*

A few weeks after I returned from my business trip to Salt Lake City I spoke with Jennifer over the phone. She confided in me that while she was taking things one day at a time she wished the *day* could be longer.

"It's not getting better?" I asked.

"It's getting worse."

She sounded exhausted.

"Any word on Janet's replacement?" I asked.

"Nothing. What's worse is that Janet has suddenly turned lame-duck."

"How so?"

"She's not doing anything! She's obsessed with planning her retirement. She's got brochures on every tourist trap from Texas to California. I think she's buying a Winnebego."

"Where does that leave you?" It was a stupid question that really didn't deserve an answer. Nonetheless, she enlightened me.

"It leaves me up the creek--"

"I know, I know," I said. "It hardly seems fair."

"What's worse is that I've got to attend another one of those public meetings next week."

"I thought you were feeling more comfortable with those," I said.

"I was until this morning."

"What happened?"

"Some anonymous man called our receptionist and said he was going to come down to the meeting, shoot and kill anyone who tried to sell him on the idea that Rocky Flats was looking out for the public's best interest."

"Jesus Christ," I said. "You shouldn't go!"

"I have no choice," she said. "Janet's arranged for a security guard this time."

"That's it?" I pictured Barney Fife sitting in a rocking chair with one bullet in his gun, eyes half shut.

"That's it," she said.

"Jenny, I know it's not much but I'll come with you to that meeting. These threats shouldn't be taken lightly."

"I know," she said. "I'm really beginning to hate this job."

"Well, don't do anything drastic," I said.

"Like quit?"

"Yeah, like that."

"Look, I've got to run," she said impatiently.

"I know, it's late," I said, understandingly. "Get some sleep. You sound tired."

"No. I mean I've literally got to run."

"What are you talking about? I thought you talked to Ed?"

"I did."

"I thought he was cutting back your schedule?"

"He increased it. I'm doing doubles on Wednesdays now."

"But--" I was furious.

"Ed said to take things one day at a time," she reminded me. "He never said anything about cutting back my schedule. In fact I'm racing on Saturday. You want to run?"

"Jenny you really shouldn't!"

"Do you want to come?"

"Sure." I said, defeated.

When I hung up the phone I immediately called Ed. I was polite but insistent that he understood and acknowledged the strain that was being placed on Jennifer.

"She's going to have to make a decision," Ed told me.

"That's not what you told her," I reminded him.

"You're right," he said. "I told her to take it one day at a time. Just like you did. It's just that one day she'll have to make a decision."

"That's ridiculous," I said. "There's a lot of elite runners I know that are able to juggle their running schedule around their professional careers."

"Most elite runners don't work sixty hours a week," he shot back at me.

"You're forgetting one thing," I said.

"What's that?"

"Jennifer is one hell of a runner," I said, "but hardly an *elite* runner!"

"Which validates my point even more!" he said, raising his voice. "She'll have to make a change if she ever wants to improve. The girl can't be worried about someone blowing her away at one of those damn public meetings while she's trying to take minutes off her marathon time."

Silence.

I wasn't happy about that thought either. It left me with nothing to say.

"She's not a dumb girl," Ed continued. "I'm sure she understands that she'll have to make a decision sooner or later."

"Well, it looks like you're helping her make it," I said, angrily.

"I'm just acting as her coach."

"A coach is supposed to be understanding, empathetic towards his athlete's problems," I said.

"A coach is supposed to do what he gets paid for," he spat back. "Jennifer wants to run faster. She wants to *be* somebody."

"She *is* somebody!"

He ignored my comment. "I'm just helping her get there."

"Look Ed. Something has *got* to give," I said. "It's obvious to everybody. And I don't want it to be her job!"

"Why not?" he asked candidly.

Sometimes it's the most obvious answers in the world that one stumbles to come up with.

"Because--" I began to say something but I couldn't get it out. Ed finished for me in a sarcastic nature.

"Because she loves her job so much and she sucks at running?" He actually laughed at me.

I wasn't about to answer this rhetoric. I took a different lead. "I've been there," I said. "I spent two years of my life obsessing about nothing other than the run. It's a dead end!"

"For you," he said. "You've got no talent."

That hit me like a pile of bricks. Not because it was an attack on my esteem. Indeed, it wasn't an attack on me at all. If it *had* been I would have thrown it aside easily enough. After all, I'm well aware of my talent level. But the comment had been said matter-of-factly to point out that Jennifer had more talent than I was able or willing to recognize and support. It stopped my train of thought and made me see his point. Jennifer is not of the same mold as me. She *has* talent! A few years ago I had been a runner locked up in a realm of fantasy, living a lie. Jennifer, on the other hand, could reach out and nearly touch success. She was that good. We both knew it. I was speechless.

Ed knew he'd delivered a good blow. "Look Paul," he said. "Why don't you just stay out of her running affairs and leave them up to me."

I started to remind him that she was my girlfriend and that I loved her with all my heart, that my only concern was for her well-being. But as soon as I was about to launch into it the line went dead. The asshole had hung up on me!

I fumed for hours afterwards. He had a lot of nerve telling me to mind my own business. Jennifer and I were in love. Anything that might effect her would ultimately effect me. In my mind her business *was* my business. Still, was he right? Was I too far behind the eight ball to see the pocket? Was I acting like the conservative, protective parent, frightened by the necessary sacrifices that awaited my loved one. Did I stand in the way of her success? It was quite possible that she *did* have a future in running and I was dismissing it because of my own little failure years ago. It was the first time that I ever stopped and thought, "*am I holding her back?*"

EIGHTEEN

The spring racing season was in full swing now. Yet Ed insisted that Jennifer not waste time with small, unimportant races. "Perhaps an occasional one," he told her. Indeed, he raced her infrequently, keeping her hungry for the next major event. He'd told her the weekends were too valuable for training purposes to throw away on unheralded races with little or no competition.

Given that, I should have known that Jennifer was not going to show up at a local race in Washington Park one Saturday morning.

Still, I expected to see her there offering her support to me as she had so often done in the past.

Barbara Duff, looking sternly serious this morning, and Luz Diaz had toed the starting line with me. I asked them if they knew where Jennifer was, but neither one did. Apparently, it had been days since either one had talked with her. "I heard her come in last night," said Barbara. And that was that.

When the gun sounded we jumped off the line heading north, in the direction of Toni's house. I didn't need any other enticement than that. "Screw this race," I said, minutes into it. I veered off the course when it changed direction and continued to run towards Toni's. Oddly enough I heard the patter of footsteps behind me. I turned and saw that I had a few mindless sheep in tow. Within seconds they noticed their error and sped back toward the course, swearing as they went. I would have laughed if I hadn't felt a veritable need to investigate Jennifer's absence.

I arrived at Toni's some ten minutes later, bathed in sweat and feeling flush. There was no one home. Toni had flown to California for the weekend to compete in an invitational meet. That much I knew. But where was Jennifer?

I paced back and forth across the rich, green lawn and deliberated my options. I could just wait here all day or go home and call later. When I noticed a blue haired lady staring at me from behind a window from across the street I decided it was probably time to leave. That must be Mrs. Wiler, I decided, having heard about how nosey Toni's neighbors were.

Just then Ed's yellow pickup truck pulled up in front of the house. Jennifer was riding in the passenger seat.

A twinge of jealousy gripped me and my heart dropped as I imagined the possibilities.

But upon seeing me Jenny flashed a bright smile and I knew my thoughts were erroneous. She stepped out of the truck wearing running attire and carrying a small athletic bag. She'd been out on a training run!

Ed waved hello or goodbye--I'm not sure which. Then he drove away.

"How did your race go?" she asked.

"Great, I made it here in about ten minutes," I said, unable to look her in the eyes.

She could sense the concern in my voice and understood immediately what I was driving at. "Ed called last night, left me a message that he wanted to do repeats on Ruby Hill this morning. By the time I got the message it was too late to call you." She paused and added. "I'm sorry I screwed up your race."

Mine and the fools who followed me off course for those few seconds, I thought briefly, a wry smile appearing on my face. Then I lifted my head, searching her eyes.

It wasn't an act. Her voice was soft. A pouty expression washed over her face that I couldn't ignore. She was truly sorry. I swear, Jenny could tell me she just shot the President when she looked this way and I would forgive her. If she confessed she just shot Ed Cooley I would have applauded her.

"I can't tell you how frightening it was to see you drive up with Ed at nine o'clock on a Saturday morning." I decided to unveil my insecurities. "I thought I'd lost you to him."

"Gross!" she said, amused by my jealousy. She held an expression like she had just sucked on a lemon.

"I know," I said. "I should give you more credit than that. So remember, if you ever drop me promise it won't be for Ed."

"Oh, but Ed is so romantic!" she joked back, baiting me in a silly tone. "Imagine this, Darling. Me, charging up Ruby Hill, sweat dripping from my brow, a lurid moan escaping my lips as I beg him to let me do another. And he screams back, 'Yes my love, you're not leaving until you break a minute thirty!'."

Jenny reached around and goosed me and I chased her across the lawn. She was quick as a cat. I couldn't turn fast enough to catch her.

In a state of exhausted laughter Jenny finally stopped and fell to the grass. I picked her up and threw her over my shoulders. She continued to mock me, "... and Ed kept saying, 'use your arms, pump those legs, you sexy thing!'."

I grabbed the keys from her and carried her inside. Lucy greeted us by jumping on me. I lost my footing and I dropped Jenny on the hard marble floor in the foyer. No damage. Jenny ran up the staircase and reminded me that we had the place to ourselves.

Across the street Mrs. Wiler had franticly tried to gain the attention of her husband who was sitting, as usual, in front of the TV watching Cory Pavin sink a thirty foot birdy. "Come here!" she shouted. "I think he's going to kill her. He caught her with another man and chased her down and dragged her inside!" "That's nice, Dear," the good doctor said, turning up the volume on the TV.

Some time later Barbara and Luz returned from the race. Jennifer and I were out back lounging in the sun on the veranda.

Barbara was beaming. She carried a foot-high statue.

"I won!" she shouted.

My ears still ringing, my heart still jumping. "You certainly did," I commented, looking closely at the statue.

"Must have been those four pounds I lost," she said. Then she immediately launched into the details of her race. Five minutes later it seemed as if she still had enough breath to run another.

"And how did Luz do?" Jennifer interrupted.

"Oh, she dropped out. Then I..." And her story went on.

"Is everything all right?" asked Jennifer.

"Sure! I did great! Weren't you listening?"

"No, I mean with Luz. Is she sick?"

"I don't think so. She's just gone upstairs to lay down a bit."

"I'll go check on her," Jennifer said.

"I've got to call everybody!" Barbara said, excitedly. "Everyone will be so proud."

Barb dashed inside before Jennifer had gotten up out of the chaise.

I was happy for Barbara, don't get me wrong, but her excitement exceeded nausea.

"When did she become so inflated?" I asked.

"Toni says it's gotten worse ever since she moved in the house." Jenny added, "racing seems to really bring it out in her."

"I'll say."

"Being the slowest one in the house doesn't help either. She's totally obsessed with bringing her times down."

"Well, she sure wasn't the slowest one today," I said. "What's up with Luz?"

"What do you mean?"

"You know. She's running terribly lately."

Luz said she felt fine now that she was lying down. "It's probably just a bug or something."

But Jennifer could see the sweat on her brow and her flushed expression. "You stay here on the bed and try to relax," she told her. "I'm sure Toni has an ice-pack somewhere around here."

She went downstairs and searched the kitchen, checking the freezer twice. Nothing. *Toni had been nursing a sore ankle lately, Jenny thought. Perhaps she'd have a dry-pack in her bedroom that I could fill with ice.*

Jennifer made her way to Toni's room. There was an old chest at the foot of her bed. Seemed like a good place to search. When she opened it up she saw that it contained trophies and ribbons and old race bibs. The chest was literally bursting with them. "Not in here," she said to herself. Just as she was about to close the chest she spotted an old race bib that had a little reindeer on it.

Something about it jarred her memory. She reached down and picked it up.

Just then, something cold and wet touched the back of her arm, startling her. Jenny turned to see that it was only Lucy, Toni's dog. "Hey, you crazy canine," she said, "you scared me half to death."

That's when it hit her.

She took a closer look at the bib which had REINDEER DASH printed boldly across it. On it was a handwritten name. It wasn't Toni's name but it *was* her handwriting: LUCY CANINE. AGE GROUP: 30-35. FEMALE. There were at least a dozen more bibs in the chest under the same name.

*

The following Monday Luz was at work. She had since softened the lighting in her office hoping it would ease her dizziness and headaches. But she had another fainting spell that day.

Derrick Ralls was convinced her headaches were being caused by a greater workload due to her promotion. It wouldn't be long before the company would move into a new location and he would be able to hire Luz a secretary to help ease the burden. Until then he offered up some lame excuses as to the cause of her headaches. The first time she had fainted he mentioned how *he* often got dizzy when he stood up too fast. "Stand up slower," he'd said. When she complained that she couldn't breathe well he'd told her, "There's a brown cloud over the city. Leaves everyone short of breath."

Derrick didn't know what to say this time. He leaned over her holding a cold towel on her head. Concern riddled his usually calm face. Concern shook his usually serene voice.

"I didn't stand up too fast and it's not a brown cloud," she told him. "I'm going to the hospital as soon as I can stand."

*

That same week Jennifer worked over fifty hours and ran over eighty miles. "One day at a time," she told herself over and over. *One day until I don't have any hair left!* She wondered how she'd look with Sandy-the-secretary's blown-cotton, pink hair. Suddenly it was all too real of a thought. Another meeting with the Mayor's staff was scheduled for next week. So was her annual review--to be given by Janet's Boss, Tim Rosen, the Plant Manager. Stacks of paper cluttered her desk. And Janet had passed along most of her phone calls to Jenny. "I'm leaving and won't be able to follow up on this, however my assistant Jennifer can blah blah blah..." Janet had repeated time and again.

Jenny made three different lists and, labeled them: Urgent, Important, and Stupid Shit. She picked up a report citing ground water contamination in nearby Westminster. The press were hot on that issue. *Damage control.* There were at least ten immediate call-backs she needed to make by the noon deadline to ensure the newspapers couldn't slam Rocky Flats and the Public Relations Department for having no comment. Jenny posted this as "urgent." There were rumors that the Plant guards, employed by an independent contractor, were planning on striking at the end of the month. Again, more correspondence with the press. She marked that one, "important." It could wait--barely.

For the fifteenth time in one week she'd received a message from the man with the pyramid waste-storage idea wanting a better and clearer understanding of why pyramiding the waste wouldn't work. His message said something about a brother-in-law, general contractor, a plan, and a price. "Why do I get all the crazies?" she asked herself. She filed that one under "Stupid Shit." Nonetheless, eventually she would have to call him; every question coming in would have to be dealt with respectively. Jenny's "scream meter" was pushing 10.

On Friday I called Jenny and asked her about running with me on Saturday.

"Can't," she said. "Ed's got me going up Ruby Hill again today."

"Well, how about a movie in the evening?"

"Can't, my review is on Monday. I haven't begun to prepare."

Ed felt the pinch as well.

After the repeats up Ruby Hill he talked about doing a long run the next day.

"Can't," she told him. "I've got a meeting with the Mayor's staff on Tuesday. I need to prepare some charts."

"Do it after," he said.

"It's an all-day job," she responded. "Besides, I'd be too tired to think."

"You can't afford to cut out your long runs!" he said, hastily.

"I can't afford to not collect a paycheck, either," she rebutted.

"Fine," Ed said, coal for eyes. "You're compromising yourself, Jenny."

NINETEEN

It was soon after the conversation with Ed that I began to look at Jennifer in a new light.

I was never blind to the fact that Jennifer had exceptional talent and I had none, but Ed had pointed this out with such frankness that this knowledge festered to the extent that whenever I saw her it was foremost on my mind.

A wedge had been driven between us.

She became a study in physics--or rocket science, perhaps. If we were together and she turned away my eyes fastened on her hips. They were narrow, barely wider than her waist. She could slice through air like a dart in a wind-tunnel.

If my arm was draped around her shoulders I could sense the quickness of her movements, the lightness in her feet. If she was even slightly excited it was like holding a fish out of water; eventually she would just wiggle her way free--deliberately or not.

If I gave her a massage I might work her calves and notice that they were high and tight like two springboards; capable of launching her yards ahead with every step.

And, of course, the more I studied her the more I became critical of myself. One night I stood naked before a mirror looking at a different animal altogether. The man staring back at me was stocky with large bones, wide hips and low calves. I wasn't built to run. My bloodline probably spent time pulling the tonnages of stone that eventually made up the ancient, Egyptian pyramids.

Now don't get me wrong here. The wedge I refer to was not born from envy or jealousy or anything the like--as I've said, I had long since accepted my role in the hierarchy of running.

It's just that now we were no longer two runners who could share the simple act of a run through the park or up the side of a mountain. She had her agenda and I had mine and the two were worlds apart. She was chasing the bear. I was looking at the clouds. *Oil and Water.*

So, something we took for granted, something so basic as throwing one foot in front of the other, was suddenly more complicated, uncomfortable.

And it was Ed who had planted the seed in my head that made it so. Suddenly I was asking for approval or validation on every run we went on. Consequently, I asked less and less.

"Let's run Mt. Falcon," I'd say.

"Sure," she'd reply.

"You think Ed would mind?" I'd reply back.

...Another time...
"Let's go for an easy five," I'd say.
"Ed has me doing repeats on Ruby Hill later," she'd respond.
The next day I wouldn't ask.
And there it was--*the wedge.*

*

Jenny was called in to Janet Kurth's office at four o'clock on a Tuesday afternoon.

"I've been out of work so long it seems impossible to catch up," said her boss, fumbling through a stack of papers. "The Mayor himself is going to be here and I don't know how I'll be able to--"

"Don't worry, Janet," said Jenny, well aware of the task about to be handed to her. "I threw most of this presentation together. I'll be glad to present the findings next week."

"I don't know how to thank you enough," Janet said.

"It's nothing," Jennifer offered.

"Of course, you know the meeting has been moved up to tomorrow morning at eight?" Janet added.

Jenny felt a little weak in the knees. "No, I didn't. You never said a word to me about that."

"That's all right Dear," Janet said evenly, handing her the disheveled pile of papers and manila envelopes. "I'm sure you'll do a fine job."

It would mean that Jennifer would have to spend the evening preparing for the meeting. She had a twelve miler scheduled; eight of them were to be run at a moderately fast pace over rolling hills. But she'd have to cancel it and run another time. The meeting took priority.

But when she arrived home Toni was waiting for her dressed in running attire. "I thought I'd run with you tonight," she said. "We haven't run together in so long."

It was true. Other than Thursday night track the two hadn't run together since Jennifer had moved in. What the hell. The run might let off some steam.

And then some...

Toni pushed the pace hard, seemingly testing Jenny. However it wasn't an obvious test, nothing that Jennifer might accuse her of. It was the subtle shifting of gears, the constant shoulder-in-front approach. The friendly "how-you-doing?" every so often just to pretend they were running slow enough to converse. And when it ended Jennifer was exhausted.

She'd just go upstairs and lay down for twenty minutes. Time enough to freshen her thoughts so she could prepare for the meeting.

She woke with terror in her eyes. The clock read: 8:15--*a.m.!*
She'd slept through the night.

Over the phone, Janet went off. "I knew I couldn't count on you!....You'll never be Director here....I'm writing you up on this one..."

I don't know how to thank you enough.

Jennifer's hands were shaking so badly that she could barely hold the phone to her ear.

Janet was known for ending the conversation by getting in the last word then slamming down the phone. This time was no exception. "Do you know how hard it will be to reschedule?" *Click.*

*

The meeting was rescheduled for three weeks later. One painstakingly slow word at a time Janet said, "the--May-yor--made--it---ver-ry--clear--not--to--stand--him--up--a-gain."

Jennifer put in a great many hours during those three weeks and paid little attention to me or her running.

She ignored Ed.

He twice called me looking for her and asking why she hadn't returned his phone calls.

"She's very busy," I told him. "Although we both knew she wasn't returning his calls because she wasn't doing all the workouts.

"It will get better after this meeting," she finally told him after he'd called her at work.

Ed doubted it. And he was tired of beating around the bush. He swung for the fences.

"Why don't you just quit." It wasn't a question. "You're only young once. You've got this God-given talent that others would die for--"

"Ed, this really isn't the time or place--"

But Ed jumped all over her. The conversation moved fast.

"It's a thankless job--"

"I worked hard to get it."

"You'll get it back."

"They wouldn't take me back--"

"Then you'll get something else--"

"No! I was Cum Laude, Deans List, I'm not throwing away--"

"And you'll always have that!"

It was time for Jennifer to put her foot down and cap Ed's fantasies about her. "Ed, get real! I haven't accomplished much of anything yet. I'm unproven! All I have is a lot of desire and you who keeps telling me I can do it!"

"But you can!"

"Perhaps," she said. "But is it worth risking --"

Ed cut her off. "Why wait until you have a break-through? You're young. Go after it now!"

"No!"

"Why not?"

"Because eventually work will slow down. I'm not stupid! I can work a forty hour week and still train exceptionally hard."

"And when was the last time you had a forty hour week?"

Silence.

Ed continued. "Let me rephrase that," he said. "When will you *ever* have just a forty hour week?"

Jennifer couldn't underscore what Ed was saying. There was a lot of truth behind his words.

"But what would my parents say?" she said.

"It's your life."

"It was their money partly that put me through."

"They'd understand."

"Ed, my mother thinks the Kenyans will be running in the U.S. Olympic marathon trials! I seriously doubt that they'll understand my leaving my job because I want to run. Besides, what would I do?"

"I can get you on as an assistant coach here at the university. I can do it for you!"

Jennifer's ears perked up. She'd always wanted to coach.

Ed knew he'd hit on something. Jennifer was silent on the other end of the line.

"It wouldn't pay much, but it would cover your expenses. You can concentrate on running. If you make the jump to the next level you'll start earning money on a regular basis."

It all sounded too good somehow. "Ed, I just don't know..."

*

I was openly scared for Jennifer's well-being upon hearing about the conversation. Inwardly, I was frightened about any change that might somehow affect our relationship.

Ed had managed to gain total control of her running--to the point where I didn't even feel comfortable running with her anymore. But I had accepted that. After all, he was her coach and I suppose he had a right to set her agenda and expect her to follow it.

But now he threatened to hold the purse strings too.

"You know," I said to her. "If you accept the position of Assistant Coach you'll be financially dependant on him. I don't think it's a smart move."

I pointed out all the negatives and reiterated what she had told me about her working too hard in school to just give up a great job. I went on and on. "How could you even think about leaving?"

"You're right," she said. "It's a stupid idea."

And the subject was dropped.

Still, I knew that Ed would have his turn.

Later that night I lay in bed, eyes fixed on the ceiling, deeply troubled.

Call it insecurity. Call it jealousy. Call it anything you'd like. But I clearly saw the trend: Ed was becoming increasingly more important to Jennifer.

She was dependant on him for her running. If she ever accepted his invitation to coach at the university she would be dependant on him for her income too. Where would it end? And where would I fit in? Worse yet, would he ever make a play for her? If so, what would I have to combat it? It seemed like Ed had all the answers, held all the cards.

I dropped by to see him the next day.

"This is becoming a sad habit, isn't it?" he said, upon seeing me. "You and I talking about Jennifer's future like she doesn't have a say in it."

He didn't invite me inside, nor did he come out. He stood in the doorway of his house, a rickety screen door separating us. It didn't take a genius to figure out why I was there.

Suddenly, aware that Ed might be viewing me as hostile, I placed my hands in my pockets to look disarming. I just wanted to talk.

"You shouldn't suggest that she quit," I told him as calmly as I could.

"I'm just offering her choices. She hates her job."

"Well, you know the reasons why she shouldn't quit."

"I know the reasons why she *should*."

"You'll ruin her life," I said, a bit too fast.

"That's ridiculous. Your overreacting," he said. "She's an adult. Let her make her own decisions."

That upset me.

"I thought you prided yourself on making her decisions for her," I lashed out.

"What's that supposed to mean?"

I decided to tell him of my suspicions about how he'd set Jennifer up to fail by sticking her in the elite wave at Boulder.

"She wasn't ready for Boulder," I said, accusingly.

"That was a mistake on my part," he said. "I took full blame for that."

"You never told Jenny you did!"

"I might have, might not have. What does it matter? The bottom line is that we both learned a lesson after that!" Spit dribbled off his chin.

"I don't believe you," I said. "You set her up!"

Silence.

I had him.

"So what if I did?" he finally shot back at me, the screen between us getting wetter by the second. "The mind is like a muscle. It must be broken down first in order for it to grow and get stronger!"

"You're sick," I said. I turned and started to leave.

He shouted at me. "What doesn't kill you only makes you stronger!"

I stopped and faced him again. "And what other famous quotes do you want to throw my way?" I said. "Perhaps you know who said 'damaged people are the hardest to hurt?' Well, I know all about that crap--all those sayings. Don't even think about practicing them on Jennifer!"

"You sound like you know what you're talking about," he said. "You must believe in their validity!"

"I don't," I said. Yet I did. Sayings rarely become adages if there is no truth behind them. Yet, as with everything, circumstance surrounds the matters at hand. And there was no way I wanted to see him "hurt" or "damage" Jennifer in any way.

So when I said "I didn't" there must not have been any conviction in my voice. Ed knew that he had me on my heals.

I turned to leave again.

"You just let her make her own decisions," he said, back on track.

I had little else to say. Confronting him might have been a mistake. It left me more confused and upset than when I woke that morning.

I stopped in my tracks once more and turned to him. "Ed, you know as well as I do that a coach can be very influential. Especially if you start putting ideas in her head about turning pro."

"What?" he said astonished. "You don't think she can do it?"

"That's not the point--"

"Then what is? Look, why did you come here? To threaten me?"

"No, of course not!" I said. But in an odd sort of way I guess that's exactly what I was doing there. I felt ridiculous. "I just wanted to talk about this idea you're putting in her head."

"Like I said, she's an adult and well capable of making up her own mind." Ed began to close the door on me, then added. "And I don't think she'd appreciate knowing that you and I are having this conversation. If you tell her your crazy thoughts about me setting her up at Boulder I'll just deny them and you'll end up further upsetting her."

Ed was right. That's what pissed me off. He always seemed to be right about everything. Yet I didn't want to lose this exchange of words.

"You're going to burn her out," I said hastily, reaching for something, anything.

"I'm going to give her what she wants," he replied. "You just don't believe in her talents--your own girlfriend, the girl you claim to love-- and that's sad."

"I *do* believe in her happiness!"

"Then you'll believe that she won't be happy until she turns pro." Ed pointed a long finger in my face, hitting the screen door between us. "She's told me that, you know."

"I don't believe you," I said. But even as I said it I questioned whether or not that was true. She probably had said it to him. And in a strange way it saddened me; not so much because she never mentioned it to me but because I couldn't recall ever actually asking her. So then, why hadn't I asked her? Was I afraid of Jenny's success? What it might do to our relationship? And once again I questioned whether or not my conservative attitude was holding her back--even subconsciously. I was very confused.

"Then what?" he asked.

"I don't know. It's not that simple." And it wasn't either.

Ed had some good points. Ed always did.

TWENTY

Jennifer Ledge had something to prove. Every night for the past week she had spent sequestered in her bedroom working on the presentation to the Mayor.

Low-level radioactive waste was a hot topic. There was proof that the contaminates had penetrated the ground water and traces were now being found in nearby reservoirs. The Mayor insisted upon being brought up to date on future plans and current issues with the Plant.

Her presentation would include: a historical analysis of the Plant's operations, an education on the different types and grades of waste on site, Acts of Congress that either impeded or helped in the efforts to clean up the site, speculation on future activity, and a composite of recommendations from several sources. It was enough to keep her busy, to say the least.

But finally, the night before the presentation was to be given she lay back on her floral chintz comforter knowing that she was finally and fully prepared. The presentation would be so much more than expected from her. It would leave no doubt in her mind--or anyone elses--that she was more than competent to fill the position of Director of Public Relations.

They'll have to offer it to me after this, she thought. They won't have a choice.

The funny thing was that just days ago she'd been fearful of that very thought. But having put together a better presentation than she knew Janet was ever capable of she now relished the idea. It would make her parents very proud.

Jennifer sat up and looked around at the stacks of paper and graphs she had drawn to illustrate her topics. Bits and pieces of her presentation littered her room like confetti after a parade. Nothing was sacred from the mess--not even a poster of Uta Pippig in mid-stride, glancing over her shoulder at a pack of women she'd just left in her wake. A recent newspaper article slamming Rocky Flats for failing to share its findings with the public was tacked over Uta's chest. Jenny looked up at it and smiled. "Let's see how fast you can run with a newspaper strapped to you." Then she leaned back on the comforter once again and closed her eyes. She was mentally spent, but a feeling of accomplishment overwhelmed her. The only thing left was the actual presentation. She was sure it would go off without a hitch.

Just then Barbara knocked and opened the door. Lucy ran in first.

Unless Lucy eats my homework, she thought wryly. Fortunately, that only happens in the movies.

"Ed's on the phone," Barbara said, handing Jenny the portable.

Ed had been concerned at first that Jennifer was missing too many quality workouts, but after she'd told him she had no intention of quitting her job he'd seen things her way and was now sympathetic to her situation. "We'll get back on schedule after your big meeting," he'd assured her.

"Hi, Ed."

"I want to run Ruby Hill in the morning. Can you come?"

"Tomorrow's my presentation, sorry."

"I completely forgot," he lied. "What time are you giving it?"

"Ten o'clock."

"Feeling good about it?"

"I'll knock 'em dead," Jenny exclaimed. "I just finished up and I'm totally prepared."

Ed saw the opportunity.

"Well then, I can pick you up at six and have you home by eight," he said, feeling her out.

Jenny was amused with the bold proposition. "Ed, you never give up, do you?"

"Well, the run might make you feel at ease, you know. Loosen the nerves a bit before you meet with the Mayor."

He had a point. Besides, she was tired of handing him excuses.

"If you promise to have me back by eight."

"Promise."

The next morning the two were seated in Ed's yellow truck at the base of Ruby Hill. They'd just finished the workout.

The engine refused to turn over.

"I know how to fix this," he said. "Just give me a minute."

He popped the hood and disappeared beneath it.

"Ed, I've got to get home." *Concerned.*

"I think I flooded the engine," he said, a pained expression on his face. "It will just take a minute."

Ten minutes later nothing had changed. It was now just after eight.

"The meeting!" she bellowed. *Panicked.*

At twenty after the hour Jennifer hopped out of the truck and ran home; five miles. It was probably the fastest five miles that any runner in the Denver area would log that day.

*

146

"I've got a busy schedule," the Mayor said, leaving Rocky Flats. "Send your findings to my secretary. I'll review them."

Jennifer stood in disbelief. She was a half an hour late and the Mayor wasn't going to let her give the presentation.

"I'm so sorry," said Janet to the Mayor, behind Jenny's back. "I would have given the presentation myself but the girl insisted. I didn't have the heart to tell her no."

Janet turned to Jennifer. Her eyes were narrow slits. If she was "Superwoman" laser beams would have come from them and burned holes in Jenny.

Minutes later Jennifer and Janet were in the office of the Plant Manager, Tim Rosen, explaining the mishap.

Jennifer's thoughts were filled with possible excuses. But each thought was followed by her own admission of errablility. *I woke up extra early--but I went running on the biggest day of my professional career. I would have been here in plenty of time--except my coach's truck wouldn't start. I was so concerned about this meeting--I had to run a PR just to make it here at all!*

She knew there was nothing to say that would make them understand, to make them appreciate the fact that she had put so much time and effort into the presentation, that she was truly sorry. Everything would sound so trivial, so petty. She'd just sit there and take it on the chin.

"What do you have to say for yourself?" Tim Rosen finally said.

Jennifer looked at Janet, the next Mount St. Helens, then back at Tim, whose lips were tight and splitting. From outside the office, Janet's secretary had one ear to the wall, listening. Jennifer could see several inches of her pink hair spilling into the doorway.

I've got to get the hell out of this nut farm, she thought.

"Well, what do you have to say for yourself?" echoed Janet.

"Nothing," Jennifer said, looking Janet straight in the eyes. "I quit."

*

Prior to picking up Jennifer that morning, Ed had fired up his truck and then gave a nice yank to the ignition wire.

When he had tried to restart the engine after the workout it naturally failed. He had looked confused at just the right moment. Moments later concern had riddled his face in light of Jennifer's meeting. It was wonderful acting, and that pleased him. It's for her

147

own good, he thought. *I have a God-given right to do this for her, to make her somebody.*

After Jennifer had bolted from his truck he reattached the wire and drove home.

He called her that evening.

"I'm so sorry! I feel like it's my fault," he said, rolling his eyes, surfing the channels on his TV and sipping beer nearly in the same breath. "I just feel terrible!"

"Don't be ridiculous," she said, consoling him. "I should have known better. I'm always trying to do too much in too little time."

"Look Jenny, I hope you're not upset by my speculation, but I had a feeling that this might end it for you," he said. "I checked today and received permission to hire an assistant. The job is yours if you want it."

So there was a bright side to this miserable day after all, thought Jennifer. Ed had--once again--looked out for her benefit and come through for her.

"It must be fate," she said. "I've always wanted to coach."

"So then, you'll take it?"

"Of course!" she said, her smile coming through the phone.

"That's wonderful!" Ed said, excited also.

"Ed, your the greatest!"

"Ah shucks," he replied, actually blushing through the phone. *Tell me something I don't already know.*

*

Two days later. The dual engine, puddle-jumper circled once before being cleared to land. Cutting through a turbulent bed of clouds its left wing dipped long enough to allow Jennifer a brief glimpse of her old hometown. In a heavily treed valley of the Adirondacks, a lazy, wide river meandering through its center, lay Vestal, New York. She thought it funny that as a child Vestal seemed overwhelming in size, bulging with commerce and far too many people. But after living in Washington D.C., Las Vegas, and Denver, it appeared as a quiet town of modest homes with a few church steeples and a few three-story office buildings rising up between them. Rush hour was not likely to exist here, she thought, realizing just now that she grew up in something resembling a Norman Rockwell painting.

The airport was appropriately small as well, a single terminal with a few gates that weren't capable of offering door to door service. Passengers were required to step off the plane onto the tarmac and walk to their gate. Not that it mattered to Jennifer. She was hardly pressed for time and walked slowly behind the other passengers, carrying with her a small overnight bag which she'd overstuffed with a week's-long supply of clothing. There was no telling how long she might decide to stay. Depends on how things went, she thought. Depends on her mood, her parents mood.

The whole notion of returning home seemed overwhelming. Especially when the trip involved the bearing of disappointing, unacceptable news--such troubling news that Jennifer figured it would require a face to face delivery without so much as a phone call to announce her arrival. She'd just show up at the front door, a bag in hand, looking for acceptance, looking for comfort in the eyes of those who expected so much of her.

The gravity of the situation pulled her beneath reason. She walked through the terminal babbling to herself, rehearsing what she'd say.

When she hailed a taxi and stepped inside her thoughts were distant. She told the driver to take her home.

The driver looked over his right shoulder and smirked, "would that be your home or mine, honey?"

The bad joke didn't register. So lost in her thoughts, she said nothing.

"Miss...," the driver continued, making a circling motion with his hand, this time staring back at her in the dashboard mirror, "...the address?"

She rambled it off to him and sat back in her seat, quietly staring out the window. The drive wouldn't take longer than ten minutes, she figured, yet she knew that as the taxi meandered its way into town, speeding by various cornerstones of her childhood, she would awaken a thousand memories. There was the intersection of Elm and Main, where as a ten year old she'd fallen off her bike and scraped her knee, more ashamed than hurt. Her parents would be so disappointed in her. *Their daughter--the uncoordinated kid.*

Then there was the movie theater. Once, an usher had caught her sneaking in through the back door. He took Jenny into the manager's office and sat her down in front of the phone and insisted that she call and explain the situation to her parents--her disappointed parents, no doubt. *Their daughter--the criminal.*

The taxi continued its trek through town. It wouldn't be long now, she thought, looking south at a mountain ridge where her prom date had once kissed her and declared his ever-lasting love, a love so strong it lasted barely a week. She remembered coming home from school one day in tears, announcing her failed relationship with a boy her parents thought was "just perfect." Jenny could imagine their disappointment. *Their daughter--the dateless wonder.*

A half mile to the east of that ridge was the city park. It came into view as the taxi turned left on Old Vestal Road. There, in that clearing, high on the ridge, was a place of fond memories--the ones of Saturday morning cross-country meets in the fall where the addiction of proving herself--and improving herself--had flourished for four strong years. Always getting stronger, she thought. Each week finishing higher in the pack until one special day in her Junior year, she broke free and won for the first of many times. Her parents would not be disappointed. *Their daughter--the winner.*

She was overwhelmed with an abrupt thought.

"Turn left here," Jennifer shot at the driver.

"But the address you gave me--"

"Left!"

The driver took the turn hard, throwing Jennifer off balance and up against the door. Jenny didn't seem to care.

"There!" she said to him, pointing to a small, brick house at the end of the street. "I want you to stop there and wait for me."

Out in front of the house was a man wearing blue overalls and a Yankees baseball cap, tending to a bed of flowers. He looked up just as the taxi came to a stop, anticipating giving directions to a lost stranger.

Then, without warning, recognition struck him like a Tyson left-hook, sending his jaw open.

"If it isn't Jenny Ledge!" he said, beaming.

"Coach," she addressed him, happy to see this man who appeared to be a little older than she remembered, the lines on his face a bit more defined. Still, it was Coach, good old Coach.

"It's great to see you," she told him, reaching out and giving him a hug--something she'd never done before, but feeling good about it now. "I just had to see if you were still living here."

"Same old," he said.

"You still coaching?"

"Same time, same place," he said laughing. Then he removed his cap, took out a handkerchief and wiped his brow with it. "Now," he inquired, "I heard you ran a two fifty-one a while back. Tell me it's true so I can have some bragging rights."

How word traveled through the running community astonished Jenny. Even two thousand miles from her present home, that information had somehow crossed paths with her old coach.

"Yeah, something like that," she said, actually embarrassed. A 2:51 was a fine time but not one she would expect to travel on word of mouth.

"Well then, I must have taught you something back in school, he laughed. "Speaking of that, I've got a great group of kids this year. I think they'll make it to States!"

Their conversation was suddenly breached by an obnoxious honk from the taxi.

Jennifer motioned to the driver that she'd just be another minute.

This chance encounter with her high school coach would be short lived, she knew. She smiled and studied his eyes for a second too long.

"What is it, Jenny?"

"Nothing," she lied, then thought about it again. "It's just that--"

"What?"

"I--"

The honk came again.

Jenny was filled with the wanting to thank her old coach, but she knew the meaning would be watered down--perhaps even lost--in its delivery. She couldn't very well step out of a taxi, not having spoken to this man for seven years, and tell him point-blank how much he meant to her back in school, how she'd only recognized--perhaps this very moment--the magnitude of influence he wielded on her in those four years so long ago, helping to truly shape her identity. It wasn't possible to relay such a deep message with a simple thank you. Perhaps that's why she held his gaze a bit too long. Perhaps he'll just know it. Could a coach do that? Can he read my thoughts, she wondered, and take more out of this two minute encounter than a whimsical tour down memory lane with a runner by the name of Jennifer Ledge, a runner he once took to the side before a meet, looked deeply and appreciatively into her eyes and announced, "I have faith in you." Could he?

"I... I've got to go," was all that came out, frustrated.

He reached out and touched her arm. "Wait--"

"Yes?"

"Jenny, he said slowly. "Thanks for stopping by." He smiled assuredly and added, "it means a great deal to me."

He could!

A minute later she was back in the taxi speeding along Old Vestal Road, just minutes from her parents house. She wasn't ready.

"Take me back to Main Street," she told the driver.

"But that's the other dir--"

"I know where it is!" she shot at him.

Back on Main Street she found herself looking impassively at the row of small, dying businesses that had once been the backbone of this town, replaced now by corporate giants who's names ended with warehouse, or club, or superstore. Things had changed. And she wanted to care. Tried to find it in her heart to care. Oddly enough she felt nothing. Just the coldness a stranger might feel in a town that no longer belonged to her.

"You can take me home now," she said, exasperated.

Finally, a half an hour after she'd left the airport she pulled up in front of the house. It was a modest home, but impeccably taken care of, with neatly trimmed hedges and finely cropped grass.

Jenny handed the driver his fare and stepped out, taking in a deep breath, filling her senses with the smell of the old neighborhood, the definitive look of her old home. Behind her the cab shot away in a cloud of dust. Jennifer scarcely noticed.

She stood squarely facing the house, bag in hand, rehearsing once more what she would say to her parents. A lone figure, a stranger to most of the neighbors, neither here or there, having come home.

The screen door opened and from behind it came her mother, intuitively understanding the gravity of a situation yet unknown to her. Daughters don't just fly across the country and appear on your doorstep unannounced for no reason.

Jennifer was about to say something but her mother stopped her.

"We'll talk later, Dear," she said, "when your father comes home. You go upstairs and get some rest. You look tired."

Jenny spent the afternoon asleep in the bedroom she once thought to be the center of the universe.

When she awoke she lay there on her back, staring at the ceiling, looking at the same water spot where the roof once leaked during an afternoon cloudburst some ten years ago. Looking at the same window which a wild turkey had once flown through, spattering glass and blood on the wood floor. Looking at the mahogany corner dresser and remembering how, as a fifth grader, she had once taken a butter knife to its side, carving out a heart with her and her boyfriend's initials in it. Surely the engraving would still be there chipped in its side. The surroundings so familiar, streaks of sunlight spraying the room through the half-open blinds, lit particles of dust swimming in them. The stillness of her solitude intact, just as it always had been. Same sheets, the grain of them so soft against her skin. Same comforter, the loft of it so high, so yielding to her touch. Slipping out of bed the same floorboard flexed and creaked underneath the weight of her body, a sound she so associated with every waking day of her youth, yet one forgotten until now. And too was the leisure of being cared for, of having a parent in the next room, of an aroma of an oven roast permeating her room from the kitchen downstairs. Everything was in its place.

And how ironic, she thought, that even now, seven years since she last lay claim to this room, that she'd be leaving its comforts in a few minutes to shower her parents with disappointing news. Nothing ever changes.

Meanwhile, in the downstairs living room, her parents were expressing concern over their daughter's return, taking stabs at what the problem could be.

"She's got to be pregnant."

"No way! She's probably broken up with Paul and needs our support."

"Perhaps," Mrs. Ledge said, "but maybe she's decided to leave that waste-dump job of hers and move on to something she likes."

"That would be nice," her husband agreed. "I don't know how she's been able to put up with it as long as she's had."

"Yeah."

"But why she's come home to tell us in person is beyond me," Mrs. Ledge said. "Unless this is another one of those trying-not-to-disappoint-us things."

"Yeah, that's got old," her husband agreed. "I used to think it was amusing--even funny at times. I mean, all the kids these days out there trying to be rebels and all, and here was our own daughter frightened that she could never do enough to please us."

"Imagine that," Mrs. Ledge worked in.

"Yeah, I thought it was so funny I'd even tease her about it every now and then," a bit guilty.

"You didn't!"

"Yeah, I did," confessed her husband. "So I guess I'm partly to blame. Like the time she fell off her bike and I joked with her about being a klutz."

"You didn't!"

"Yeah, I did," he continued. "I never realized Jenny took things so serious."

"It's in the girl's nature," said Mrs. Ledge. "She's always been so competitive. When she fails at something she takes it too hard, takes it personal, thinks everyone is down on her."

"That's ridiculous."

"If that's the case we'll have to finally straighten her out."

"Jeez," Mr. Ledge said. "I just never thought it would come to this."

A while later in the dining room, Jennifer told them everything. Told them about Janet, the Hell-Bitch. Told them about the public meetings and the life-threatening phone call. Told them about the meeting with the Mayor that went belly-up. Told them about Sandy and her cotton-candy hairdo spilling into the doorway as she listened to Jenny's resignation, which would undoubtedly be circulated later on

153

as dirty laundry. Finally, she admitted to breaking under the pressure and quitting like a coward. She summed it up by asking them to understand and forgive her disappointment.

Her father looked sympathetic at first before breaking out in laughter. "What took you so long?" he asked. "Your mother and I would have been out of that dump long before you quit!"

"Really?" Jenny asked, surprised.

"Really," her mother assuredly said, laughing too.

Then, when the laughter finally died out, her mother added, "Now, lets discuss this asinine fear you have about disappointing us--"

"Yeah," Jenny's father interrupted, "the real issue here...."

TWENTY ONE

Ed was anything other than "great" in my opinion. So when I heard the news I was skeptical. It was difficult to believe that Ed's truck wouldn't start on the most important day of Jennifer's career.

But as usual I didn't have any proof to support my notion. And to accuse him of debacling Jennifer's career would likely be the end of one of us. Up to this point Ed had so successfully chiseled away at my self esteem that I didn't want to take that chance. In yet another run-in with him he had, once again, told me that I was bad news for her. He reminded me of the time I had persuaded Jennifer to run the marathon in Sacramento, when I had qualified for Boston. "You were an idiot to have talked her into running California International just a week prior to the race," he'd said. He'd then gone on to tell me that she hadn't been ready to run it and that I was lucky I didn't get her injured. At that point I hadn't even the fight left in me to give him an argument. So now without any proof and a look of defeat in my eyes I would, at the very least, look like a jealous, paranoid boyfriend if I was to accuse him of such a feat. So I refrained from saying anything.

Besides, Jennifer seemed relieved about leaving Rocky Flats. "I feel like I can run like the wind," she said, "now that I have the monkey off my back."

"That's good," I told her earnestly. "Your happiness is all that counts."

So give credit where credit is due, I decided. Aside from Ed's character--which I obviously despised--he had brought Jennifer a long way in just under two years. She was a much better runner than when I had seen her on the track that first Thursday night and seemed to be on the brink of parlaying that success.

Still, I couldn't help but feel that Jennifer was nothing more than an experiment for Ed. It was Biology 101 and Jennifer was the frog. If she died on the operating table Ed would simply toss her aside and grab another. Though I never expressed this to Jennifer--again, not wanting to spoil the coach-athlete relationship--I kept one eye on him and one on her.

So now, with all the extra time, the alleviated stress, she was able to run at will and follow Ed's workouts without interruption.

One cool, summer's evening Jenny and I walked along the grassy infield of Washington Park. I held her hand and we looked off to the East. Distant billowing clouds rose some forty thousand feet into the ashen-sky and promised to reek havoc on the plains later that night. A radio was playing nearby and we heard someone singing about a train that was *"a-comin' on down the path, a big fat locomotive gonna tear you in half. Jump sista, jump. Gotta run, run real fast, or darlin' this locomotive is gonna tear you in half."*

"Well, I've done it," she confessed. "I ran a hundred miles this week."

Higher mileage doesn't necessarily mean better results, I knew. But I congratulated her just the same.

"I feel strong," she commented.

She was. I held her close and could feel the lean, rippled muscles in her shoulders.

"Have you decided where you'd like to qualify for Trials?" I asked.

"No, but we've decided it will likely be in October."

We continued our walk. I was lost in my thoughts. *What's with this we stuff? I wondered. We this and we that.*

"You'll do great," I said after several seconds. *The both of you.*

Now there was one bright side to Jennifer having left her job and getting an assistant coaching position at the university. She now had more time on her hands and we were able to be together more often. (I guess I should have been thankful to Ed, given this new revelation. But I despised him even greater for it. It was just one more thing that *he* had done for her.)

One day she told me she felt our relationship had blossomed during the summer, ever since she began coaching. It was true. I have to admit that there was a short while after she'd quit her job that Jennifer and I had some of our finest times together. She seemed genuinely happy.

One time she accompanied me to a race and in a moment of light-heartedness, at my expense, she called out to me in the middle of the race, "Run Forrest, Run!" with all respect to the movie, Forrest Gump. Well, me and everyone I was competing with nearly busted a gut we were laughing so hard. Totally blew my race. But I didn't care. I was happy to see her smiling.

Another time, I had asked a friend of mine, an exceptional runner by the name of Robert Well, to pace me through a sub-five minute mile. It was a goal that had somehow eluded me up until now and I was dead-set on breaking the mark. So we met late one evening when we figured we'd have the track to ourselves. Sure enough, we did. There would be no fanfare, no medals, no crowd support, nothing really except the two of us with one purpose in mind; taking care of business under the dim lights surrounding the four hundred meter oval, and the knowledge that when this thing was over, if successful, I could stick a small feather in my cap.

We warmed up with a slow run, followed by a series of fifty meter striders. Other than a few nervous comments tossed back and forth we really didn't say much. The task I was about to undertake left little room for other topics of discussion. As we circled the track, still warming up, I glanced over at Rob and thought about how many times he had been where I was about to go: the venue of the sub-five minute mile. Probably *every* time. Even in distance races of up to a half-marathon, Rob had been known to throw in a sub-five late in a race and squash the spirit of anyone who might be on his heals.

So there we were. One of us, who had played with the sub-five pace more times than he could recount, and I, who was about to jump head-first into this dangerous pool for the first time, to swim in an unforgiving current that would surely suffocate me before its end. So, as to be expected, I was rather uptight.

That's when Jennifer showed up with a boombox and several long sticks in one hand. A large, canvas bag was draped over her shoulder. She just, nonchalantly, walked to the inside of the track and waved hello to us.

"Well, well, well," I said. "What have we got here?"

She set the box on a bench and hit the play button. Suddenly we were being treated to orchestrated version of the Star Spangled Banner. She simply looked up at us and smiled. Didn't say a word.

"Looks like she wants to make this official," Rob offered.

Then she reached into the shoulder bag and took out a banner which was about six feet in length when she unrolled it. To our amusement, she'd written on it in bold letters: THE ROBERT WELL INVITATIONAL MILE. On the infield of the track, she stuck two long sticks in the ground, about six feet apart from each other, and hung the banner on them.

"She's goofy," commented Rob. "Besides, I didn't invite you. You talked me into this," he laughed.

The National Anthem finally came to an end.

"That was nice," said Jenny. "Now get ready to run."

She reached into the shoulder bag and took out a nickel-plated starter's pistol. "Don't think Ed will miss this tonight," she said softly, as though to herself.

Rob and I threw a look of disbelief at each other.

"Runners take your mark."

We did. Rob on the inside. Me, just off his shoulder.

"Just remember one thing," she said to me.

"I know," I said. "I promise not to go out to fast." *Three 75 second quarters and kick it on the fourth, I thought to myself.*

"Oh, I'm not worried about that," she replied. "That's why Rob is here."

"Then, what?"

"I've got cold beer in my car after this is over. Sam Adams if you break five, Budweiser if you don't."

"Let's get on with it," said Rob. "I *know* what I'll be drinking."

Just then, Jenny fired the gun.

We were off.

Rob in front, taking me through a 74 second quarter. Perfect. Too easy, it seemed. But the first quarter of a mile race always feels easy. Pure adrenalin.

We passed by Jennifer who was on the inside of the track bouncing up and down to some hip-hop music which was now playing on the boombox. She commented as we ran by: "looking good." She sang it.

We ran the second quarter in 75 seconds. Still good--perhaps. Worried. I was beginning to hurt.

And there it went. Somewhere half way through the third quarter the bottom dropped out from under me. Suddenly I felt like I was running up the down escalator. A ten meter gap had opened between Rob and I. He looked back. As dryly as if he'd asked me to pass him the butter he said, "where'd you go? Get back up here."

I thought about how he must have been viewing me. The look of a hostile child no-less, unable to have what he wanted, a cold stare followed by an empty gaze, a tightness in my jaw, my skin a ruby hue of red. Then I thought about how many times Rob must have witnessed this very "look" I was offering up. I am sure he must have seen it hundreds of times in the middle of a race. Perhaps he'd glanced over his shoulder to find someone clinging to his heals, desperately trying to hang with him. If indeed that was the case Rob would have seen the "look" in this person's eyes that would, in turn, tell him to throw the hammer down now! leaving this dreamer in his wake, sliding him into oblivion.

Fortunately, for me, I would not have to witness this hammer being dropped. This, of course, was not a race--at least not for Rob. Otherwise, his racing instinct might have told him to deliver the blow now, to surge and watch me come unglued, watch my face reveal truths of ineptness, concessions. Rob simply looked back once more and said without the slightest hint of panic in his voice, "relax, think about your form and get it back." It must have been an odd sort of feeling for him: to say such a thing; to *not* surge once he saw the "look," to actually invite this straggler to come along for the ride. Much like sanding wood against the grain, I imagine.

Well, I did manage to bridge the gap and once again I was on his heals. Although the third quarter had severely damaged my shot at breaking five minutes. We had run it in 77 seconds. So now, even though the finish line was close, I took little comfort in this, knowing that I'd have to make up the lost time sometime soon, very soon if I was going to break the mark. I heard Jennifer shout to me to give it everything I have.

Finally, when I reached the homestretch I saw that she had strewn tape across the finish line. Rob saw this too and pulled aside to let me pass on the inside so that I could be the one to break the tape. I gave it my all in the closing meters. Fortunately, if I can attest to one running attribute it's that I am built more along the lines of a sprinter. I reached deep within myself and found another gear. Suddenly I was up on my toes, forward motion at its finest moment, motoring toward the tape. Just before reaching it I glanced at my watch which read: 4:57, and counting. Less than a second later I threw my arms up over my head and broke the tape. I'd done it!

"Cool running," Jenny commented.

I said nothing other than "yak." I was bent over and busy staring at my feet, wondering why they were fading into black, wondering why my whole world was spinning, wondering if someone had repeatedly kicked me in the gut in the last quarter.

When I was finally able to look up I saw Rob high-fiving Jenny. They were happy for me. Happy for themselves too. They knew they'd each played a role in helping me achieve this little pinnacle in my running saga.

And damn if Rob didn't look so fresh! He was just standing there, smiling at me, looking like he'd expended no more energy than if he'd just brushed his teeth.

"Well, how do you feel?" he asked.

"I've just got one thing to say," I was able to spit out.

"What's that?" answered Rob.

"It's Budweiser for you."

"But--"

"Hey, you didn't break five," I reminded him.

"Yeah, but I stepped to the side to let you--" He looked at Jennifer for support.

"Well," she said, "that *was* the agreement."

"But--"

"Budweiser for you!"

We all had a good laugh.

I turned to Jennifer. "Couldn't have done it without you," I said.

"Yes you could have."

"Doubtful." I looked at the banner she had gone to the trouble to make and then back at her. "What's gotten into you lately?" I asked, again, happy to see her smiling.

"Just happy, I suppose."

"That's nice," I said."

"You don't know what it's like to be rid of Rocky Flats," she continued.

"I'm truly happy for you," I said.

Then she had to ruin the moment.

"If it wasn't for Ed, I don't know what I would have done. He's the best, isn't he?"

I swallowed hard. "He's taken you for quite a ride," I said.

*

Now, because I saw Jennifer more often, naturally I spent more time at her house. It seemed that things had become noticeably more competitive around there than before.

All except for Luz, poor girl.

One afternoon Barbara came home to find Luz sitting outside on the brick steps of the porch dipping into a gallon of marble-fudge ice-cream. Luz was petting Lucy and seemed to be in a quiet, melancholy mood.

"What's wrong?" asked Barbara.

"They found out what's wrong with me." She didn't look up at Barbara; she just continued to pet Lucy. "I haven't been running well because I've damaged my lungs."

"Oh my God!" exclaimed Barbara, slack jawed.

"When I received my promotion Derrick converted a storage space into an office for me. To make a long story short, when they cleaned it they overfumigated it. I've been breathing toxins for six months now."

"You'll be better now that they've caught it, right?"

"It's affected my respiratory and nervous systems. It's going to require a great deal of treatment."

"But you'll be better?"

"I can run," she said. "Racing won't be the same."

Well, that hit Barbara like a ton of bricks. "Oh God! How awful!"

Well, Luz really didn't need to hear such a histrionic reaction. She looked up at Barbara, rather irritated. "It's not like I'm going to die, Barb."

"But you can't race," she pointed out.

"Oh, I forgot, living and racing go hand in hand with you."

"What's that supposed to mean?"

"It means you're driving me crazy! You're an obsessive-compulsive who would rather die than not run."

Barbara stood speechless.

"I've got a great job," continued Luz, letting off steam. "I grew up on a border town. My mother was a whore! When I closed my eyes at night I could hear mice on the floors. Sometimes scorpions would come out of the adobe walls in my room. My life is good now and I don't need you telling me that it sucks because I can no longer race!"

Luz whipped the spoon in her hand across the lawn and shoved the gallon container of ice-cream into Barbara's stomach.

"Why don't you eat some of this and gain a pound," she said nastily, "before a gust of wind comes along and blows you away to Kansas!"

Lucy scurried away with her tail tucked between her legs.

There was a lot of consoling to do after that exchange. Luz, for obvious reasons. Barbara, for having taken the brunt of Luz's agitation. I told Barb that she had just been at the wrong place at the wrong time. "Luz might have lashed out at any one of us given her state of mind at the time," I'd said. "You just happened to be the unfortunate one to have come across her first." Luz later apologized, but the damage had been done and things were forever different between them.

As I said, things really began to heat up in the house.

A week after that incident Barbara was caught sneaking a peak at Jennifer's training log. It was Toni who caught her. After an uncomfortable silence, Toni said, "I won't tell if you let me look."

One night, on the *seventh* day--the last day of a training week--I was driving home from a bar and saw Barbara out running at midnight. Earlier in the day I was there when Jennifer had mentioned to Barb how she'd run ninety-eight miles that week. Barbara was only at ninety-six. So I can only guess that she'd snuck out that night to run another three.

"Sneaking" miles became a standard practice in the house. Then, one night, Barbara and Toni passed each other under a full moon long after each had "retired" for the evening and supposedly had gone to bed. When the two crossed paths they had no choice but to laugh about it. The sneaking continued but from then on it was a running joke in the house--no pun intended.

*

A surreal quality filled Barbara Duff's world. She lay limp on the Italian marble floor in the kitchen, unable to fend off waves of nausea. Her head swam. Her eyes betrayed her. A feeling much like being submerged in water, she thought. The kitchen walls seemed to bow in the middle, the crimson and forest green stripes in the wallpaper melted unmethodically together, and the ceiling fan divided into four. She suddenly vomited, but expulsioned nothing. Her stomach was empty. She heaved a second time, more violently. Her abdominal muscles contracted forcefully, uncontrollably, sending waves of spasm through her jaded body. Then her world turned black.

Barbara remained on the floor for minutes after regaining consciousness. Her strength had abandoned her. She still felt weak and dizzy. But most of all she felt frightened. But for other reasons than you might expect.

See, Toni had just qualified for the Olympic trials and Jennifer had gone to the airport to pick her up. The two would be returning soon and she needed to pull herself together.

The twenty mile run was a common ritual on Sunday mornings. And it was also common to feel spent afterwards. But she had never passed out before. She thought she might be coming down with the flu. Or perhaps she should have eaten something before heading out this morning. Which ever the case, a dire need for food flooded her thoughts.

When she managed to stand her legs felt wobbly, so she steadied herself with one hand on the blue-tiled counter-top. A moment later she practically inhaled a bran muffin. Several pieces fell to the floor as she stuffed the entire thing into her mouth. Instantly she began to feel better. A long, even growl emanated from her stomach, which seemed to be pleading with her for more food. She snatched another muffin and ate it with the same expedient affliction as the first. *God, this is gooood!* A partially eaten deli sandwich, saved from the previous night, became the next item hastily grabbed and devoured.

She stood squarely facing the open refrigerator like Indiana Jones in the entrance of a newly found tomb, quickly plotting the value of the treasures inside and which to take first. Her eyes wide, her look intense. She grabbed a gallon of milk and drank until her lungs demanded air. A loud burp escaped her. Still, her hunger was intense, insatiable. She wanted more. She craved more. Needed more! Needed! Something quick, fast! Cereal: one bowl, then another, and one more. And still another. Her stomach ached and bulged several inches from its norm, distorting the proportion of her small frame. She reached inside the freezer and pulled out an unopened quart of chocolate ice-cream. *My favorite!* She ate it straight from the carton and when it was half empty she crumbled chocolate chip cookies on top and ate more.

Her stomach fought to accept any more. She walked like a duck to the bathroom.

When she came out she felt much better. She went back into the kitchen and ate the remaining amount of ice cream.

She threw the refrigerator door closed, disgusted, happy, sad, whatever. She couldn't understand exactly *what* she was feeling.

The phone rang.

"...this is Mel Johnson." Her voice was cheerful as usual. "I was wondering if you've run today because I'm looking for someone to go on a ten miler with me later this afternoon please tell me you haven't because I could really use the company and besides I haven't seen you in a while would you like to come....."

She really was insane, decided Barbara at that exact moment.

"Hold on a second," she told Mel. Barbara opened her running log and studied it. The whole time Mel was babbling incoherently on the other end of the line.

Including this morning's run, she calculated she'd run 81 miles for the week. Friday she had been called into work early and was unable to run at all. *Damn, Friday really screwed me up.*

"I'm glad you called," Barb said. "As a matter of fact I haven't run at all today. I'd love to join you."

After the call Barbara headed back to the bathroom.

When she came out Jennifer and Toni were standing in the kitchen looking at the mess Barb hadn't cleaned up yet, putting two and two together.

Barb had a look of terror in her eyes. There was chocolate smeared on her cheeks.

Jennifer thought back to the time when the girls had all gathered at Toni's house that first night after the 10 miler in the rotten weather. On that evening Barbara had passed out on the sofa. The following morning Toni and Jenny had stood over her and witnessed the dry crust of gravy smeared on her face. Suddenly it all made sense.

"I think we need to talk," said Jenny. "You need help."

TWENTY TWO

I own an autographed picture of Uta Pippig running through the winner's tape at the '94 Boston Marathon. She holds her arms out to her sides, slightly higher than her head, in victory. Her eyes are closed, suggesting a moment of inner-triumph. Her look is two-fold. The first time I looked at it I saw the joyous, electrifying expression one would expect to see on the face of a champion. Then, when I looked a little deeper, I witnessed a calmness in her face that suggested otherwise: it was a look of confident self-gratitude for a job well done. The kick-back-Saturday-in-the-park-sipping-a-lemonade look. *The payoff-equal-to-the-sum-of-input look.* Over head a digital clock reads: 2:21:45.

I don't know Uta personally but I don't think it would be wrong to suggest that she's quite proud of that moment--to say the least. She'd demolished the course record and run the third fastest woman's marathon in history in front of a million cheering spectators. She blew kisses and waved to them over the last mile in sincere appreciation of their support.

An exceptional moment.

An exceptional athlete.

An exceptional person.

Some time later in an interview with Runner's World she talked about wanting to make the marathon a "beautiful thing."

A beautiful thing. Quite inconceivable at one time.

When I look at that picture I am constantly reminded of how far the sport of marathoning has come in its short life; particularly women's marathoning.

I have an on-going fantasy of Uta running her 2:21 in the inaugural Boston Marathon, in 1897. Given the unlikely chance to participate, she would have easily beaten the all-men's field. But not by a few feet, or a few minutes, or even a mile. She would have won by about six miles! Unfortunately that's where my fantasy takes an ugly turn. Her feat would have been so incredible it would have conjured up certain images of wrong-doing. She might then have been responsible for a rebirth in Puritan rule and the practice of "witch-hunting", led immediately to the Commons and set ablaze. For that matter, Jennifer's 2:51 would have resulted in the same punishment.

Sometimes, when I think women have won this battle for credibility in sport, I am too often reminded of the ignorant attitudes that are still prevalent in our society.

One particular time was during the Summer of '94. Jenny and I had camped just outside Jackson Hole, Wyoming. On the first morning of the trip I woke just as the sun was rising. Our tent had a clear mesh lining and I was able to look through it quite easily. Well, I couldn't see the sun because it was low and off in the east but I saw the angled light from it touch the highest peaks of the Grand Tetons, a dusting of snow on them resonantly glowing in the morning light. Eventually the mountains were just swallowed up altogether. It was just about the prettiest sight I'd ever seen. I just lay there next to Jennifer the entire time, witnessing this miracle that we so often take for granted: the dawning of a new day. But back to my point...

A few hours later Jenny and I were about to embark on a trail run when a very overweight, beef-eating Texan approached us and warned us about the perils of the trail. "Yep, I just come from there," he said. "It's a Sumbich--as tuff as the Appalachian Trail." He looked at Jennifer and sized her up. "You're just a little thing. You ever hiked the Appalachian Trail?"

Here was Jennifer, with six percent body fat, a top athlete in the state, biting her lip. Her eyes were focused on the man's huge gut which spilled over his belt.

I knew I'd better say something to ease the tension. "Why no, Mister," I offered, mimicking his tar-and-feathered accent. "We're mighty frail folk and we don't get out too much. I hope we come back alive." I pinched Jennifer's arm. She burst out laughing and before we waited for a response from Tex we took off up the mountain trail.

Fortunately much of the world is finally ready for the "Utas." But, just barely. In fact, it wasn't until 1972 when women were allowed to officially enter the famed Boston Marathon. Just five years earlier, then Race Organizer, Jock Semple, had run onto the course and tried to physically remove Kathrine Switzer from the race. (She had obtained a race number by signing up only as 'K. Switzer', thus not revealing her gender.) "Get the hell out of my race and give me that number," he'd shouted. The infamous message was heard all around the country and succeeded only in inspiring more women to run the next year.

Nor was the marathon an option for women in the Olympics until 1984. The greatest woman marathoner this country has ever seen, Joan Benoit Samuelson, won the Gold that year. After seeing her at a seminar in St. Paul, Minnesota, I can't figure how she ever got so good. To paraphrase her: "When I was in high school women were not allowed to race distances greater than a mile because of a common belief that they would do harm to their reproductive systems." In fact, it wasn't until Title 9 passed in the early 80's that allowed women equal access to sport in public school, allowing them to compete in distance races.

The fallible thinking and ignorant minds prior to Title 9 shocks me. What did they think? Their uteruses might fall out the way a muffler might fall from a car? I can see it now: two women out on a morning jog when they hear a loud, clanking noise. "Hey, what was that?" one asks. "Just my uterus," answers the other. "Let's go back and get it."

Gender aside, the public has never known much about the marathon or the remarkable athletes who run them. Unlike mainstream sports, like tennis perhaps, where Steffi Graf and Monica Seles are televised regularly, runners--particularly marathoners-- receive little air time from the networks. Marathon racing is presented to the public in doses that rival children's aspirin.

And what the public does know isn't often "beautiful."

The image of the marathon has always suffered in the public's eye.

The long-run was labeled "marathon" during the times of Ancient Greece. Supposedly, a soldier-athlete named Pheidippides ran about twenty-three miles from the Battle of Marathon to Athens to declare that the Greeks had defeated the invading Persian army. It is said that he dropped dead immediately afterward. *An inauspicious beginning to an act--and later a sport--in search of beauty.*

With the stage of the first modern day Olympiad, held in Greece in 1896, the marathon gained credentials as a sport. But the beginnings of this sport were crude and raw. Runners wore stiff leather shoes, battled clouds of dust from accompanying vehicles, horses, and wagons. Athletes had no concept of how to train for a marathon since there was no precedent. Many would jump from the starting point in an all-out gait with no knowledge of the ill-effects of anaerobic running. (Anaerobic or aerobic or any variation of it had yet to become a word.) A year later, in Boston, spectators viewed the race fully expecting to see some of the competitors drop dead on the course. The effects of long distance running were not known at that time, and doctors of that era warned that such things might and probably would occur.

Even in recent times we are reminded of the cruelty and ugliness of the marathon. In the 1984 Olympiad, some time after Joan Benoit Samuelson had crossed the finish line, the frenzied stadium crowd was treated to the *other side* of victory as they watched in horror as Switzerland's Gabriele Anderson-Scheiss, overcome by heat prostration, hobbled into the Coliseum crippled from the effects of severe dehydration. Her body lurched forward and to the left in an incapacitated state. She dragged a nearly useless left leg behind her.

Her expression was blank and incoherent. A mix of saliva and salt pasted her face. It is a horrific site to witness a human being in this exhausted, emaciated state. To see a world class athlete like this is twice that. So horrible was the site that an official standing close to the track rushed towards her in a humanitarian effort to escort her from the track. But an athlete's will is something a nonathlete may never grasp. She swerved from his outstretched hands, somehow avoiding falling, and continued to hobble to the finish line, finishing in 37'th place. It was like watching your pet dog, Lucky, crawl off the highway after just being struck by a car with another one fast approaching. *That* incident was far from beautiful.

Nor was the 1995 Ironman Triathalon in Hawaii when eight time winner, Paula Newby Fraser did the box step with four hundred meters left to go in the marathon, the last leg of the three sport race. In her emaciated state her knees buckled and a moment later she was lying on the ground telling everyone around her that she was going to die. Again, one of the greatest athletes this world has ever, or will ever see, reduced to a level unimaginable, inconceivable, by most.

Marathon racing isn't a sport like figure skating: there are no rogue cheeks, perfect hair days, or designer dresses to appease the networks and their viewers. Marathoners don't prance onto the ice with coached smiles and perfected postures. Marathoning is a get-down-in-the-dirt kind of sport where the athlete's bodies are typically bathed in layers of crusted salt and sweat and physical intolerance is aptly revealed on their faces. Spitting is common--you won't see that from Katarina Witt on the ice. And lets get real; bodily function accidents have been known to happen.

Who can forget Greta Weitz, while leading the women's race in the New York City Marathon? She lost control of her bowels and defecated on herself just as the network cameras zoomed in on her. The commentators were left trying to explain the tragedy of the moment to the television audience. I'm sure she was quite embarrassed, but the only "tragedy" I saw was that the commentators were reduced to the task of having to remind viewers that humans do occasionally defecate, and that running twenty-six miles is no easy endeavor on the internal workings of the body, especially if you happen to be running at around a 5:30 pace, which she was. The networks must have panicked with the thought of viewers madly switching their dials in hope of finding something acceptable, more civilized, to watch--like Sly Stallone beating his competitor's face bleeding-purple in a boxing ring, or Chuck Norris launching a handgrenade into the middle of twenty "bad guys" disembodying them.

But defecation? Why, that's just down-right unacceptable. *Perhaps if she would have worn a bow in her hair...*

So I acknowledge the difficulty in seeing the beauty of the marathon.

Yet, it exists.

And anyone who has ever run one knows this.

If I ever get the chance to talk with Uta again I will tell her that I admire her for wanting to make the marathon a beautiful thing and that she all ready has in my and every other runner's eyes. But the task to make it a beautiful thing for the general public is a formidable one, at least.

How could the public understand the discipline and inner-fortitude it takes for the average marathoner to engage in a race of this magnitude, much less an elite athlete like herself? Sure, you see them on the side cheering and offering their support and for this we are all grateful, however do they really understand?

Marathon racing is an endeavor that launches the human spirit. It is corporeal and definitive and reveals truths about ourselves that may otherwise go unnoticed and buried. Dreams are both found and lost along the way. Limitation is recognized. Mortality is respected.

In this day of age when we've done the Earth--and the Earth's been done!--we can still look within ourselves for new discovery. Think about it--it seems like every hidden treasure has been found, every pristine white-sand beach has been walked upon, every mountain has been climbed. Computers have brought us information with the push of a button, travel brochures and television have brought us pictures from every exotic location on the face of this planet. In the not-to-distant future, products like Virtual Reality might make it possible to vacaction in the Bahamas while never leaving your living room. The wonderment of things like travel and technology are simply taken for granted. We can ride in a plane (flying metal no-less) thousands of miles above the earth, drink hot coffee and have a cellular phone conversation all at the same time. Something that no other generation in mankind's history can attest to. Something that should strike us in awe and excite us. And yet these are things that we've come to expect and yawn at. So much so that we're remarkably upset if our plane lands twenty minutes late! So what's next? Where does the excitement lie in the future? Well I believe it lies in the same place it's always been: within ourselves. And the marathon opens this door of self discovery.

Furthermore, racing a marathon conjures up images of heroism, adventure, exploration. One can talk of running a marathon and sailing the South Pacific in the same breath. Discovery awaits both pursuers. And I suppose that in this way the general public might sense a beauty in it. But sensing and understanding are still worlds apart.

Beauty lies in truth. And truths must be sought and experienced to be appreciated.

*

While the summer offered Jennifer a great release from the aggravation of working at Rocky Flats, allowing her more time to train, and more time to spend with me, I noticed that the closer she got to the fall marathon the more tense she became.

"What if I run poorly?" she asked.

"There will be others," I replied. "Even the greatest marathoners in the world run bad races. If you run enough of them you're bound to have your share of mishaps and disappointments. Maureen Custy-Roben blew up so bad in Boston that she began running in the wrong direction after having stopped for water! And she was one of the top ranked marathoners in the country at the time. Hey, it happens."

"I suppose it does," she said.

"Just remember, goals are targets, not obligations."

"My sponsor is an obligation. Ed is an obligation. The fact that I changed jobs to pursue running is an obligation," she said, wide eyed.

She had a point. She was an unproven talent in the sport. There was a lot riding on the upcoming race. I'd never thought of it on that level.

Sure, I had lived the run for several years; obsessed with it in every possible way. Yet, my lack of talent limited my scope of understanding.

Jennifer possessed feelings and worries that never crossed my mind. And it was now that I knew Jennifer's pursuit of the run had far outreached my appreciation.

Some things must be experienced....

So from this point on I truly felt like an outsider looking in.

Circumstantially, I could now only speculate on her inner-most feelings she experienced with each high and low that followed.

*

When Jennifer finally ran a marathon in the fall her questions were answered. She ran well and finished in 2:46; good enough to be invited to the Olympic trials in Columbia, South Carolina.

169

A runner carries a new PR the way a first-time mother carries a newborn; there is a certain honor in it that embroiders the heart.

Make no mistake about it: a PR is something tangible. Jennifer was the proud new holder of a 2:46.

For a week straight there was a smile permanently etched on her face.

I was thrilled for her.

Everyone was! Toni went so far as to bake Jennifer a cake. I was invited over to the house to share it and in a small celebration for her.

"Eat this," said Toni. "I don't want you catching me at the Trials."

"That's unlikely," said Jennifer, cutting and handing the first piece to Barbara.

Toni, Luz, and Jennifer all stared at Barb. "Eat it," they said in unison.

"Looks like I won't be getting any faster today," commented Barbara as she took her first bite.

"No, but think of how much happier you'll be," said Toni.

"What's it like, Toni?" asked Barbara.

"It's chocolate over chocolate," said Toni, "and the only thing in this world that's really worth living for."

"No!" Barbara said, a pathetic tone in her heavy voice. "Being good. Being fast. What's it like?"

Toni was taken aback. We all were. Jennifer's eyes got wide and she stared at me. Luz averted her eyes and reached under the table to pet Lucy, who was always close by. In all the years Toni had run nobody had ever asked her something so basic, so blatant. After an uncomfortable silence Toni answered.

"I'm not that fast," she said. "I get my ass kicked all the time."

"By other professionals!"

"Look Barb," Toni said, searching her own thoughts. "It's not all that it's cracked up to be. I started running because I enjoyed it, much like yourself. But I was successful and started winning."

"And what's so bad about that?"

"Half the time I'm out there I'm running not necessarily to win, but to avoid losing. Do you have any idea what my sponsor would say to me if I lost a step, if I began placing farther and farther back in the field?"

Barb either didn't want to see Toni's point or couldn't comprehend it. "Well, I wish someone would ask *me* to run for them," she simply said.

"Why?" said Toni. "You run for yourself. You're lucky. I run because others expect me to."

"You talk about your success as if it's a curse," said Barbara. "You're the one that's lucky. A million people would give anything to be in your shoes--pun intended!"

"And sometimes I'd give anything to be in a million other people's shoes!"

Jennifer and I were still looking at each other. I knew what she was thinking because I was thinking the same thing. We suddenly understood the reason why Toni had run the Reindeer Dash that year in Phoenix and had denied it when Jenny questioned her. Toni was a tragic figure. The thing she loved most caused her the most irrefutable anguish. Every time she toed the line she was expected to perform at a level that very few will ever know. She'd entered that race incognito for the simple reason of disposing the pressure that beset her--even for just a day. She'd chosen to run that race and *not* do her best. Hell, I remembered the moment I saw her pull up along side of me at the race. I had caught a glimpse of her shoes before I'd seen her red, wavy hair. She wasn't even wearing racing flats! She must have recognized me too as she pulled up next to me. That's why she didn't end up passing me. I might have blown her cover. Spoiled her fun.

Now, I sat there feeling sorry for her. Oddly enough, feeling sorry for an icon that I once longed to be.

Just then Jennifer interrupted, wanting to break an escalating conversation that was likely to go nowhere. "I don't think Toni meant to imply it was a curse," she said. "I think she's just trying to tell you the grass isn't always greener--"

"--on the other side," finished Barbara.

This time Luz spoke out. "This is supposed to be a celebration for Jennifer, let's drop this talk."

"Thank you," said Toni, relieved.

"I feel bad," Jennifer said, looking at Toni. "I didn't do anything this nice for you when you qualified."

Under the table Barbara was now holding a half eaten piece of cake in wait of Lucy. A moment on the lips, a lifetime on the hips, she was thinking.

"Well, as I was trying to tell Barb, everyone just kind of expected *me* to qualify."

With that comment the smile that Jennifer had *just* put back on her face quickly faded. Jenny didn't say anything but I could tell Toni's comment had upset her.

As had often been the case Toni had now said something so ambiguous that Jennifer read between the lines. Toni might as well have said: no one expected *Jennifer* to qualify!

The celebration had come to a quick halt before it had even began. Sure, everyone stayed. So in a physical sense we were all there. But mentally we'd all left the room, everyone's thoughts racing somewhere adrift.

I sensed that things were not at all well in the household. Barbara was envious. Luz was bitter. And Toni was--among other things-- paranoid.

And Jennifer? Well, she was on cloud nine.

A dangerous mix.

*

A few days later God showed up at the door disguised as a heavy-set, rosy cheeked, mailman. He delivered a white handbook with a personalized inscription of Jennifer's name printed on the front cover.

Inside, was a handwritten letter from a woman claiming to be Jennifer's personal liaison. The letter read: "Greetings from Columbia, South Carolina, host of the women's 1996 Olympic marathon trials. Congratulations on qualifying for the trials! My name is..."

Other letters of greeting were enclosed as well. Among them was one each from the Governor of South Carolina, the Mayor of Columbia, and the Chair of the USATF Woman's Long Distance Running.

Suddenly the weight of what she had accomplished fell on her. Butterflies swam in her stomach. Her knees shook. Jennifer's opportunity to run with the best women distance runners in the country--to be labeled as one of them--was now corporeal. The proof was in her hands.

Jennifer read the handbook from cover to cover. Anything and everything she might possibly want to know about the course and the event was included. There was even a course video available!

Well, Jennifer was never so happy.

And I'd never seen Ed so happy either. Of course, this was after he'd gotten over the disappointment of Jennifer's 2:46 qualifying time which had placed her in the "B" standard. (A 2:42 was needed for the "A" standard in which the Olympic Committee pays your expenses.) "You can do much better than a 2:46," he'd said. Nevertheless, Jennifer hadn't had the Trials handbook for more than a couple of days before Ed snatched it from her so that he could study it.

Ed had big plans for Jennifer.

Within three weeks she was back training hard: one hundred mile weeks filled with interval speed sessions, hill work, doubles, and an occasional triple. Jennifer was now asked to supply Ed a list of everything she ate for a few weeks so that he could analyze it and make recommendations.

I found this ridiculous, as did Jennifer, but Ed justified it, as usual. He scrutinized her every move and every action.

Finally one day I came right out and asked her, "don't you find it nauseating that Ed tells you how to run, is responsible for your job, and now wants to know what you eat?"

She looked up at me, a little surprised by this outburst. "I don't think it's unusual for a coach to scrutinize an athlete's diet."

"I suppose you're right," I said. "Perhaps I'm being a little hard on him."

Jennifer just sat there and stared straight ahead.

I continued to voice my thoughts.

"I mean, Ed's like to running what Bela Karolyi's like to gymnastics," I added. "His coaching is so damned militant and demanding."

Jennifer hated when I questioned Ed's coaching practices, but she didn't argue my point. Instead she engaged in a puzzled look. The lines in her forehead deepened and her eyes became narrow slits. "Yeah, he can be a real asshole!" She nearly spat the words out. The scorn in her tone surprised me.

I couldn't remember the last time, if there was ever one at all, that Jennifer had maliciously defamed him so.

But those words didn't change anything.

The thrill of the fall marathon was just a memory now and Jennifer's mind was enslaved to the task at hand.

And that, of course, was chasing the bear.

*

I refer to it as "chasing the bear" because I think it best describes any distance runner who aspires to the highest level of competition.

Most people never chase it for reasons that include a basic lack of interest, motivation, or fear.

But, of course, there are those who do pursue the bear. While each has a story to tell, most end in the same way: a recognition that they are ill-equipped for bear hunting. In other words, they lack the physical prowess to ever get close enough to take a shot. The lucky ones in this bunch recognize this impotence early on and take their physical limitations in stride, putting the run in perspective, and go on to enjoy additional pleasantries in life. However, there are those who live in denial for a great length of time until they wake up one day staring at the cold, hard fact that no matter how hard they train, no matter how much they obsess, no matter how many late night snacks they pass up, they might only get marginally better, if at all. In accounting it's called "diminishing returns." I know. I suffered them after the San Diego Marathon.

Furthermore, I know a man of lesser ability than myself who spends more time in training than many professionals. Years ago this obsession resulted in the loss of his job and fiance within months of each other. To this day he runs, bikes, and swims about six to eight hours a day. He's still trying to break a lousy forty-two minutes for a 10K. I think that somehow he wakes up each morning feeling a little empty inside.

Now don't get me wrong. All of us fantasize. I think that's healthy. All of us dream about the one magical day when we will call upon our inner strengths--the very soul we have molded with thousands of miles run--to come forward and break out of the genetic prison with which we are enslaved. I imagine a sixty year old runner dreams about running through the winner's tape equally the same as an inspiring young one. But fantasy is just that. The danger lies when we obsess and let it run our lives.

Now recognition of talent does come to the lucky few.

There are even those who's talent lies dormant until they are lucky enough to discover it; the late bloomers of the sport like Peter Maher, the six-foot five Canadian marathoner. Rumor has it that he used to be overweight and smoked cigarettes and was actually sitting in a bar drinking beer and watching the Boston Marathon on TV when he bet his friends that one day he would run it. Five years later he was not only running marathons but he'd joined the ranks of the elite. The term "sleeping giant" never seemed so fitting.

Now, let me tell you about Jenny. She seems as capable as any runner I've ever seen at chasing the bear. As long as I've known her she's possessed unbridled motivation. And physically speaking I look at her in awe. I've seen her run next to the top professionals and I swear I see no difference between them that would suggest one is physically superior to the other. For instance, at Race For The Cure, in Dallas, I stood near the finish line anticipating the arrival of the first woman. When she came into view I witnessed the graceful, yet powerful stride I'd seen so often seen from Jenny. I was ecstatic knowing that this was going to be a break-through performance on her part. Unfortunately, a few seconds later, I realized that it wasn't Jenny; it was Cathy O'Brian, the Olympian. Still, it was a moment in time I'll never forget because it was then that it struck me: Jennifer has the physical prowess it takes for the chase.

However, as Barbara put it, I am also aware of the "curse" which bestows her as well. The pressures that come from the territory of being good at what you do. Let's face it; if you're one of a few in town that possesses a gun you're likely to be expected to go bear hunting. In one way you're honored, but in another your scared. But you go anyway. Self gratification? Sure. To please others? Sure. So you start off on this trek. Your teeth rattle, your knees shake, and you're not sure why. Excitement or fright? Take your pick. But you're aware that the closer you get the more they rattle and shake. Still, you can't retreat. You've come too far. So, again you push onward, guns cocked and take aim. Then you sense the enormity of the bear. A little closer and you see its jagged teeth. You sense that it has tasted and spat out the bloodied bodies of hunters before you. A bit closer still and you feel its fury as it spins to take you down. *Time spent in the pit.*

Jennifer's first experience of this nature was when she ran in the elite wave at the Bolder Boulder and was badly beaten. She'd gone bear hunting without the right weapons; she wasn't physically or mentally prepared to compete at that level. That time she was lucky enough to have survived the encounter with the bear. She licked her wounds, got a little older, a bit wiser, stronger, and began the chase again.

And then there are the "Toni Jamison's" of the sport; the ones who have caught the bear and currently wrestle with it.

Beyond that are the athletes that have actually brought it down and ripped its neck. But that's another story. Those are the elite among the elite. Those are the Paid Assassins and Olympic medalists.

TWENTY FOUR

For the next month Jennifer trained harder than I'd ever seen her. It seemed that every waking moment was spent in preparation of her next run.

Unfortunately many sleeping moments were spent in a similar manner.

She confessed to me about a reoccurring dream she was having.

In it she is flying through the dense brush of a forest as though she is riding atop of a low-flying missile, narrowly avoiding trunks of trees, hanging branches. But when she looks down she sees that it isn't a missile at all that propels her, but the rapid motion of her legs pumping furiously. Perhaps one in five "steps" actually touches the ground. It's as if her spirit has suddenly vacated the weight of her body and whisks its way through the trees. *(A thinker's weight is in his thought, not in his tread. When he thinks freely his body weighs nothing.)*

And in this dream she is suddenly aware of a purpose. Up ahead is an animal, a large, woolly creature that speeds along with the agility to stay just out of reach. It quickly appears in front of her then veers to the right, disappearing in the thick brush. Jennifer follows after it. She is in the hunt.

She's a predator, a carnivorous animal, no doubt. Her incisor teeth, made for tearing meat, remind her of that. She momentarily feels their razor-like sharpness as her tongue sweeps across them. And like most predators, her eyesight is keen, able to judge the distance to her prey. They are fixed and wide.

In a clearing the beast appears again. Jennifer is almost upon it now. Just then the beast changes direction. And then once again. Each time Jennifer follows suit. The hunted and the hunter locked together in a dance of death. Finally she closes in and with a great reaching leap pounces onto its hairy back. She feels the coarseness of its hide just before she sinks her nails into its pink flesh.

Then with a quick yank of its head she reveals the sweet spot of the beast's neck where the carotic artery stands out in relief, wide and pulsating. In another second she would feel the warmness of its life drain into her. But the beast rises up mightily and throws her, thwarting the attack.

Jennifer woke up hungry every time.

"What do you think of that?" She asked me.

"I think you're a little crazy," I said, laughing.

"Still date me?"

"Sure," I told her. "You wouldn't believe some of the dreams and feelings I've had."

*

What is it about running that arouses such passion in the human heart? Bucky McMahon, in an article in Running Times magazine, describes the fearsome aggression one feels while racing in the pack during a one mile race: "...you get a strong sense that this is the speed at which our species once hunted on the plains, back when we were all damned fast and wouldn't, couldn't quit. In a flat-out mile some atavism must kick in, some bloody, joyous dream of pursuit. Forget finesse or technique; the flat-out mile is a honing and a harrowing of the hunter's heart in its most violent experience of exhaustion."

In the *Quotable Runner,* a runner out of Boulder, Colorado, Shawn Found, describes the running experience in a similar fashion, as a beautiful thing: "...when you experience the run, you regress back to the mandrill on the savannah eluding the enclosing pride of lions that is planning to take your very existence away. Not only that, but you relive the hunt. Running is about thirty miles of chasing prey that can outrun you in a sprint, and tracking it down and bringing life back to your village."

Once, on a run in a most desolate stretch of the Nevada desert, I was overcome by the desire to rip off my clothing and run as fast, for as long, as humanly possible. Somehow I'd stirred an urgent, passionate reflex in the depths of my being and found Shawn's words swimming in my head. Except for the Nikes that remained on my feet, the moment might have been contrived from a slice of time ten million years ago. I sped across the vast desert landscape with the same abandonment that my ancestors might have felt in the hunt for game-- as if I'd returned somehow to a pedigreed nature of stalking prey!

For a nonathlete I know how crazy this sounds. Even for some athletes it might even sound a little off. But I've talked with enough runners to know that others have had similar sensations or experiences.

On a similar note, the "runner's high" has been scientifically proven noting a chemical, endorphines, that release into the brain during strenuous activity that not only masks pain but disguises it as pleasurable!

"Perhaps you have too many endorphines running ramped through your brain," I joked with Jennifer. "God knows you like to sleep and run. Life must be a round-the-clock heaven for you."

"So you don't think I'm crazy?" she asked.

177

"Of course not," I said. "Nothing to worry about."

So I'm convinced that there is more to this cerebral experience than meets the eye. Every animal has instinctive behaviors. Are we so far removed from our ancestry that we never subconsciously revert back to these traits? Even in dreams? I rather doubt it. After all, we may be human, but in the end we're still just animals in search of food.

TWENTY FIVE

There's an air of excitement that blows in from the north in late autumn; a chill in the morning, frost on the ground, and the scent of chimney smoke. A sea of burnt orange and rust colored foliage is splashed across the horizon and the front range mountains are capped with newly dropped snow.

I grew up in the Sonoran desert. Until I had moved to Denver I'd never witnessed the onslaught of color in fall, listened to the aspen leaves chime in the wind, felt the crunch of fallen leaves under my feet, or even thrown a snowball. So when it came to this "playground" I was no more than a child, eager to get out to experience these things first hand.

I needed to share them with Jennifer. I asked her to come away with me for the weekend to the mountains. Keystone had just opened with a twenty inch base; it wasn't much but it would serve its purpose. I needed a fix.

When Jennifer told me that Ed had scheduled a double for her on Saturday and a long run on Sunday I was disappointed.

"It's not going to hurt your training," I said. "You could use time off to enjoy..." I stuttered in finding the only word that seemed appropriate. "...life."

"I agree," she said. "The Trials aren't until February."

So Jenny and I made plans to go.

As we anticipated Ed wasn't happy about her decision, but I reminded Jennifer that he wasn't her keeper and that he would have to accept it.

And he did. Although, I received a call from him later that night.

"I don't want you to start messing with her schedule," he told me. "She has the most important race of her life coming up."

"In February," I reminded him.

"Do you want her to be embarrassed in Columbia?"

"Of course not," I said hastily. Ed was an ass. He obviously wouldn't shut up until he'd said his peace.

"And I don't think she should be skiing at all," he continued. "It's too dangerous. She could fall and break something."

"Ed, you sound like a protective parent," I told him. "Jennifer is not new to the sport of skiing. Nothing is going to happen!"

After I hung up the phone I realized how we both sounded like two angry, divorced parents, each in conflict, vying for custody, hiding our selfish motives behind a facade, disguising them as concerns for

Jennifer's welfare. We were blinded with the battle we raged against each other, ignorant of Jennifer's feelings.

When I recognized this I called her immediately and asked her what she wanted to do.

"If you think your time is better spent training then lets forget about the ski trip, "I said.

"Don't be ridiculous," she told me. "I can't wait."

"That's great," I said. "I'll be by to get you at six."

"Oh, one more thing," she said, before hanging up. "Ed just called. He asked if he could join us on Saturday."

My heart skipped a beat.

"You didn't--" I stopped.

"How could I tell him no?" she said. "Besides he's just coming up for the day. You and I will have all weekend."

"You're right, Jenny." I tried to hide the disappointment in my voice but I think she heard it anyway.

"We've never done anything fun with him," she tried to sell me. "You might see another side of him."

"And I thought Ed had an ass on both sides," I said, under my breath.

"What?"

"Oh, nothing." I was determined not to let this little glitch ruin the upcoming weekend.

*

I had taken a small jump and come down awkwardly, landing on one ski and out of control. Jennifer veered sharply to her left to avoid me and caught an edge. Now *she* was the one out of control.

What happened next seemed to go in slow motion. I still see it that way. She had fought to stay upright on one ski, looking like a high-wire act, about to fall. In her panick she put her weight on her uphill ski, causing her tips to cross, violently launching her forward. Jennifer went over a cornice and plummeted ten feet into the woods. A loud thud could be heard from where I was standing. I skiid over to the top of the embankment and looked down. My heart was racing. My stomach: liquid. Jennifer lay there like a broken puppet, her right leg was twisted horribly behind her back. I anticipated a scream, but she just lay there silent, unable to speak.

I popped out of my bindings and jumped from the cornice. Jennifer lay with her eyes closed. She was in terrible pain. There was a large tear in her bibs and I saw a blueness wash through her leg. There was internal bleeding, at least. I took off my jacket and placed it on her to keep her warm. I held her hand until the ski patrol showed up.

"I'm sorry," I repeated time after time. It was the only thing I could say. I couldn't stand seeing her in pain. I couldn't handle knowing that it was I who was responsible. Tears flowed freely.

All the time Ed's cold black eyes glared at me from atop the cornice, violently shaking a fist at me, yelling at me "I told you so! It's your fault!"

That was the day I wanted to die. From the moment I looked over the cornice and saw Jennifer lying there, twisted, I was void of any reason to live. It was I who had asked her to go skiing. It was I who caused her to lose control. And it was I who was responsible.

And Ed let me know it every chance he got.

I told you so! It's your fault!

*

The accident changed everything--for better, for worse.

That Monday Ed came to see Jennifer. Although She answered the door on crutches she was smiling, pleased to have company. "Come in, Ed." She hobbled into the living room and Ed followed. They sat opposite each other. Ed's eyes gravitated toward Jennifer's injured leg.

Her knee was wrapped with an Ace bandage. Her thigh was the color of a bruised peach.

Toni was in the kitchen. She looked up from behind the open refrigerator door. "Hi Ed."

"Hey there, Toni. Looking very fit," he commented.

He then looked back at Jennifer. There was contempt in his eyes. An undisguisable look of disgust washed over his face.

When Jennifer saw this she quickly lost her smile.

Ed immediately launched into an attack, questioning her commitment to the sport.

"It was a stupid decision to go skiing!" he said, clearly having lost his cool. "I can't tell you how disappointed I am in the commitment you've shown me!"

Jennifer was taken aback. Ed had not even bothered to console her on the injury. She was speechless and only answered him in thought.

"All the time I've put in..." he was saying.

I've put in much more, she thought.

"...all the motivation I've offered..."

It was me who did the running.

"...all the plans I had..."

It was my dream!

"All for naught." And Ed showed his true colors. The whole time talking of only *his* heartbreak in the matter.

There was a long silence that followed: Jennifer: too angry to speak. Ed: not wanting to for effect.

Toni walked into the room, unaware. "Anyone want a coke?"

Neither Jennifer or Ed looked at her. Toni backed out of the room as if she'd suddenly stepped in ice-water.

Finally Ed spoke.

"There's the meet next week. The girls will want your support, Coach. Think you can hobble on over?" The sarcasm in his voice was powerfully delivered. It was too much for Jennifer to take.

"Sure, I'll be there to offer my support," she said with a blank expression. "But I won't be there as their coach."

"Fine!" Ed stood up and started to walk towards the door.

"Fine?" Jennifer asked. "Fine? You're just going to walk out?"

"There's a recruit I need to interview," he added. It was Biology 101 and Ed had found a new frog. "Now *she* could be somebody!"

"Good ridden!"

And that was the end of Ed Cooley.

*

She'd never even gotten around to telling him that the injury was less severe than initially thought.

There were no broken bones and an MRI revealed no tears in the cartridge. In that way she dodged a bullet. She did, however, suffer strained ligaments in and around the knee and a torn thigh muscle. But with the proper rehabilitation, which I would remain steadfast in helping her through, she would heal in about eight weeks.

Ed obviously had felt that the Trials were no longer an option. But in reality they were only questionable.

Not that that took away any of the sting. In fact it made it worse. Gray areas in life always seem to do that: there's *nothing* to look forward to, there's *everything* to look forward to. *Time spent with your head in the washer on the spin cycle.*

It would have been easy for Jennifer to call it quits, cut short her dream, and concentrate on running in the next season. But Jennifer had great fortitude. She remained optimistic, telling me she fully expected to toe the line February 10'th in Columbia, South Carolina.

I'd hold her hand whenever she mentioned this to me and tell her sincerely, "I know you will."

But we both knew the sad truth behind the optimism. Even if she healed in time to run the Trials she would likely show up poorly trained. A good case scenario would give her about six weeks of actual training, a formula destined for failure.

Nonrunner's typically don't understand the difference between running a marathon and racing one. They are simply impressed that you've been able to complete the miles. That's fine, and appreciated, but at Jennifer's level they often miss the point. Even at my level the point is often missed by nonrunners. For example, at the Twin Cities Marathon I dropped out at sixteen miles. A nonrunner friend told me not to be disappointed. "I have a hard time driving sixteen miles," he said. His heart was in the right place but I found it irritating that he didn't understand that I wasn't out there to simply complete the thing. I'd put in many runs of twenty miles or more in preparation. The distance was a given. I was out there to lower my PR, to race at my competitive level.

So for Jennifer it wouldn't be enough to simply show up and run-- to put it mildly. She didn't have visions of challenging the contenders for a birth on the Olympic team but it would be less than gratifying for her to show up unable to compete at full strength. It would be a disheartening experience.

So we kept a positive outlook, but the unspoken word was that she might decide to not even show, healthy or not.

*

Now, as for me, I couldn't look in the mirror without seeing a total stranger staring back at me; a thieve of dreams, a robber of heart. *I told you! It's your fault!* Since the Trials only come along once in every four years I knew I had taken much more from her than a couple short months. In reality, it was as if I had stolen *four* years from her. A lot can happen in that time. Who knows if the opportunity would present itself again? I was stricken with guilt.

Jennifer wasn't blind to my feelings. She'd witnessed Ed unleash a gauntlet of fury at me from atop the cornice. She knew it had stuck. So even though she fought to stay positive about her own injury she took the time to console me about my feelings, telling me it was only an accident, that I wasn't responsible. But her leg, swollen and bleeding-blue, was a constant reminder of my fault. I thanked her for her condolences but the damage I suffered was heart-felt. It ran too deep for words to heal.

Guilt: it's a powerful and peculiar thing. It has a way of compounding itself like simple interest. The guilt I felt when the

183

accident first occurred was heavy but nothing compared to the guilt I felt as time passed and the Trials loomed closer.

I found more time to dwell on it. It was foremost on my mind when I woke in the mornings. It gathered speed as the day went on until I lay in bed at night unable to think of anything else. A day doesn't often seem that long a time, but when one day blends into the next and your thoughts never change other than to build upon themselves, the day can seem like an eternity. It was so clear to me now that I was the cause of all her troubles. It was because of me that Jennifer no longer had a coach. Additionally, Ed had fired her from her job. Well, actually she had quit before he would have inevitably asked her leave. She hadn't even put up a fight. I supposed that was my fault too.

I replayed the image of her going over the edge of the cornice a million times. *If I hadn't made the jump and landed out of control. If I had listened to Ed. If she'd never met me...*

That was the real killer! What if she had never met me? Might she be better off? I had always fought to steal her time. *Time when she could have been training.* And from the beginning I acted like a skeptic, questioning the great level of effort she devoted to the sport for the simple reason that my dream, when I pursued the bear, ended in a laughable failure. *She might have realized her dream if....*

And the circle spiraled downward and before long I was worthless. I found myself unable to work. Running was out of the question. How could I with Jennifer unable?

I woke one day thoroughly convinced she'd be better off without me.

*

About a month after the accident Jennifer's optimism began to pay off. She was now able to run a slow pace.

However, something else transpired that lifted her spirits even greater.

Janet Kurth, who had postponed her retirement plans in light of Jennifer's resignation, had forwarded Jenny's presentation to the Mayor's office. She'd included a letter of apology which ended, "I've worked very hard on this presentation. Call me if you have any questions."

The Mayor scanned the documentation on projected levels of contaminates in the ground water. He picked up the phone and called Janet. "This is the best presentation anyone has ever given me," he said. "However, I do have a question as to how you came up with some of these projections."

Janet fumbled for and gave an unsatisfactory answer.

The Mayor was not a stupid man. "Put that young woman on the phone--Jennifer something--maybe she can explain it."

"Jennifer Ledge?"

"Yeah, that's the one."

"She no longer works here," Janet said, reluctantly. "Perhaps if I call her and--"

"Never mind," he said, cutting her off. "She left a forwarding number didn't she?"

A minute later the Mayor was on the phone with Jennifer.

The conversation was lengthy and the Mayor, being impressed, offered her a job as an advisor and aid to his cabinet.

"By the way," he said, "what do you like to do in your spare time?"

"I like to run--"

He interrupted. She'd hit on his hot button. "What a coincidence. I do too. Why don't you bring your shoes in some time and we'll put in a few miles together."

"That sounds great!" said Jennifer. *What the hell?*

"But I've got to warn you," the Mayor continued, in a stroke of his ego. He reached down and felt his left high; it was rock-hard in his mind. "I've been running for years. Hope you can keep up."

Jennifer thought back to how I told her his ass looked like two Sharpai puppies fighting each other when he ran.

"You've never hiked the Appalachian Trail, have you?" she asked, smiling from ear to ear.

*

That same day two things happened which sent me in search of God knows what.

I was on the phone with my boss trying to explain why my numbers were down for the month and why I didn't really seem to give a damn. *How can I explain depression? Guilt?*

I heard a loud knock on the door.

"Can you hold for a second?" I asked him, setting down the receiver.

My landlord stood in the doorway. I swear he was wearing the same unlaundered T-shirt and brown polyester pants he was the first day I met him. His teeth seemed a bit more yellowed however.

"Yoos lease is up," he informed me. He held a pen up. He had a new lease in his other hand all ready to sign.

"Come in, Harvey. I'll be off the phone in a second."

Harvey stepped inside tracking mud along with him.

I picked up the receiver. "I need some time," I told my boss. "What would you say if I asked for a leave of absence?"

A few minutes later I hung up the phone.

"I don't think I'm staying," I told Harvey.

"Look, if it's da price?" He had a pleading expression on his face.

"It's not--Da price," I mimicked him, irritated.

I walked to the French doors and looked out to the balcony, beyond that, the track.

"If it's dat damned track bodderin ya I could knock off a few dollars."

"It's not the track," I said. *Maybe it was.*

"Then--"

"It's--" What's the use? I thought. "I'll be out in a few weeks."

"Jeez Christ, Kid. Yoos got a screw loose," he mumbled, turning to leave.

"Hey, what about my deposit?" I asked him.

He stopped and rubbed his gray-stubbled chin. It was a simple question I'd asked, but Harvey looked puzzled. Apparently this was a tough one. Finally he looked up. "You, uh, interested in an old Jeep?"

TWENTY SIX POINT TWO

Four weeks after I left Denver in the beater-of-a-Jeep I bought from Harvey I find myself on this desolate stretch of unkept road in Southern Arizona. The town of Oracle comes into view. I can see the tops of buildings, tin roofs perhaps, glimmer in the afternoon sun.

I've forgotten how difficult a twenty-plus mile run can be. My breathing is uneven and heavy, the toes on my right foot are numb, my nipples have each rubbed raw leaving two red dots stained on the white cotton of my sweat-soaked shirt. My mouth is lined with dust but I'm so parch I can't gather enough saliva to spit. Still, I turn my legs faster knowing that each step brings me that much closer to Jennifer.

I'd seen Jennifer through her rehabilitation. I worked the weights with her, helped her stretch, and when she was able to eventually lace up her running shoes I ran along side of her offering words of encouragement. I wasn't the only one.

Toni, Barb, and Luz all did their part in seeing Jennifer through this tough time. The girls rallied around Jenny. And soon the tension that I had earlier sensed in the household faded away. It always amazes me how the misfortune of people--or a single person--can bond the hearts of others. You see it all the time. When someone's house burns down and neighbors join hands to lend their support to the grief-stricken victim. On a much larger scale, when floods besiege an area and surrounding counties and states offer any assistance within their means. There was really no difference in this case.

So when I left Jennifer I felt she was in good hands. She was even talking of bringing on a new coach. "Ed taught me a few things," she'd said, giving him some credit, "but there's more than one way to skin a cat. I've talked with a woman with tons more experience than Ed has or will ever have. She's convinced me that Ed would have just burned me out as quickly as I had jumped on to the scene."

My sentiments exactly.

Jennifer had also started her new job. She loved it. "I get to go home at four," she'd said, "and the Mayor understands how important my training is, how lofty my goals are."

I have to laugh at that thought. I wonder how long it took Jennifer to humble the Mayor? Probably about a half mile. I think about the newscasts I've seen of President Clinton jogging alongside of Uta Pippig after her victories at Boston. (He'd invited her and the men's winner, Cosmos Ndeti, down to Washington to--well, I don't know-- pose for pictures I suppose. Politicians love to be seen with winners.)

Next to these remarkable athletes Clinton looked like a big, happy Saint Bernard plodding along, clumsily and unsure. Just don't step on Uta's foot, I'd thought at the time.

So things were looking up for Jennifer, more or less. Still, I silently grieved.

*

It was my turn now. Time to heal. Time to search. And I think Jennifer understood this because when I lied to her and said that I was leaving because "it's a dream vacation that I've always wanted to take," she just told me to "go and come back happy, but you won't find what you're looking for in Arizona."

Like a coward I fled anyway. In search of answers, atonement.

One evening I sat on a hillside overlooking a vast, desert basin and watched the sun turn an explosive red and melt into the horizon. It was a pretty site but it only left me with the stark realization that as it fell so too did Jennifer's dreams to run the Trials.

The following day I watched it drop again. And once again it punished me with the thought that February 10'th was just another day closer. Jennifer was right. I wouldn't find what I was looking for out here in the desert.

I used to judge good days from bad days by whether or not I saw Jennifer. So now I could honestly say that they were all bad. The funny thing is that it seemed like such an easy thing to fix. Yet something kept me from turning my Jeep north and heading back to Denver. And I knew what that was. I was a defeated man. It didn't matter that Ed was no longer in the picture. His legacy left me questioning my value towards Jennifer. So I'd just sit on those hillsides night after night feeling sorry for Jennifer's and my misfortunes. At least I've been lucky enough to have cared, I thought. At least I've experienced a love stronger than many people will ever know. Even if I did consider myself coming out on the wrong end of this mess I at least knew happiness for a while.

One night I called Jennifer. She told me stop dwelling on the past. That I was acting like a fool. I suppose I was but it didn't make me feel any better.

"Stop watching those sunsets," she told me, "and start watching the sunrises."

Her meaning was clear. A setting sun somehow implies an ending. A rising sun implies a beginning.

A week before the Trials Jennifer informed me that while she felt undertrained she would make the trip to Columbia anyway. "My new coach is so much different than Ed was," she told me. "She's a positive influence and reminded me that I've earned the right to be there."

I was ecstatic for Jennifer and felt a great sense of relief knowing that I had not kept her from the Trials.

"Paul, I want you to be there with me," she said.

"I wouldn't miss it for the world," I told her, "but I'll have to meet you there. I don't think this Jeep will be able to make the thousand mile drive back to Denver."

"But you *will* come back to Denver once this thing is over with, won't you?" she asked.

It took me a second to answer.

"It's not that easy," I finally said.

Silence.

"Jenny, be honest with me. Do you think I hold you back?"

"Ed put that idea in your head, didn't he?"

"That's not important," I said.

"It is important," she insisted. "Look at the source. Ed was an ass! Unfortunately he was good at planting seeds."

Planting seeds....

Wasn't *that* the truth! The man definately seemed to arrive at an end to a mean, no matter how far in advance he had to plan.

And there it is, I thought, as clear as if the sky had fallen on me. What I had been looking for all the time!

I'd always had my suspicions that Ed was nothing more than a self-serving coach. He'd convinced me time after time that whatever he did was in the best interest of Jennifer and that I was only interfering in the coach-athlete relationship anytime I begged to differ. Even when I had accused him of setting up Jennifer to fail at the Bolder Boulder he had justified that, if he did indeed do it, it was for her own good. "The mind is like a muscle," he'd said. "It must be broken down in order to get stronger." I hadn't necessarily agreed but he had managed to sell me on the idea of staying out of his way. Then there was the incident of his truck breaking down on the most important day of Jennifer's job at DOE. I honestly felt he had something to do with that. Yet I hadn't been able to prove anything much less voice my opinion. But now....

"Did you ever tell Ed that someone had called and threatened your life at one of those public meetings?"

"Excuse me?"

"The meetings," I said, rushed, excited. "Did you ever mention them to Ed?" *Please, God, tell me you didn't.*

"Of course not," she said. "It would have given him more fuel to pressure me to quit."

189

I had him finally! I thought back to the time that Ed had told me that Jennifer would have to quit her job if she wanted to concentrate on really lowering her marathon time. Specifically, he'd said: "The girl can't be worried about someone blowing her away at one of those public meetings while she's trying to take minutes off her marathon time." Well, if Jennifer didn't tell him about the call, then how did he know? There was a simple answer. So simple that Ed must have silently cringed after he'd said it, hoping that I wouldn't pick up on his error. And for a long time I never did. But know I knew. It was Ed who had made the call! He'd "planted the seed" that added to Jennifer's intolerance of her job. I was sure of it.

And now I finally had my opportunity to undermine his credibility, to toss aside the harsh words he'd thrown my way.

I smiled wide. *To hell with Ed and all his accusations.*

I hadn't noticed my silence over the phone, but Jenny had. Apparently, in that nick of time, she'd figured it out too.

"Why?" she asked. "Do you think--"

"I'm sure of it," I said.

"That bas--"

"Jenny, I need to ask you again," I said. "Do you feel like I hold you back?"

This time when she answered I'd be able to take her word for gold. Ed's accusations would no longer trouble me.

"Don't be ridiculous," she told me.

"In the past I've felt like I might have been holding you back. And when Ed mentioned this to me I turned away, thoroughly convinced that he was right," I confessed. "And when I caused your injury I honestly felt that you'd be better off without me. I thought I'd ruined your life and taken your dream and--"

I could have gone on and on, but Jenny stopped me.

"You don't get it, do you?" she said. "You've never taken anything away from me. Even if I had chosen not to run the Trials this would be true. You've only given to me."

"But I nearly took away your victory," I said. "At the very least I'm responsible for hampering your training. If you'd had these last two months to train properly--"

She interrupted me. There was a tone of anger in it.

"Sure I want my victory," she said. "But if you think I measure victory by the ticks on the clock you insult me."

"I didn't mean to imply--" I was saying.

But she went on, cutting me off again. "Running means a lot to me, but it's just one part of my life. You, of all people should understand that! You showed me the beauty in the process and brought balance into my running, and more importantly, my life. Besides, victory isn't about coming in first. It's about doing your best and being comfortable with that whether it leaves you running in first or last."

"But Ed--"

"Back to Ed again?"

"Ed told me there was no beauty in the process where you're going."

"If you honestly believe that, then I have nothing left to say."

"Again, Jennifer, I didn't mean to imply that I believed him. It's just that--"

"What's more," she continued, "victory is about so much more than running. It's about overcoming obstacles that we face every day. It's when we found each other and fell in love. Now that's a victory we both chased and won. And--" she paused.

"And what?"

"And the rest is icing on the cake."

I spent the next several days waking early to watch the sun rise. She was right. It had a better feel.

Now, a week after that conversation with Jennifer, I've finally made it to Oracle.

I'm exhausted, yet excited. One mile closer to Jennifer.

The town is small and interspersed with small businesses the likes of coffee shops and food marts. There is no taxi service here.

I spot a service station. It's an old, pink adobe structure with two gas pumps and a rusted Texaco sign swinging from a wooden post. Parked along side is a tow truck. *Perfect!*

I walk inside. A tall, wirey man in overalls is busy tinkering under the hood of a pickup truck.

"I need a tow," I say.

I've startled him. He drops a wrench. I hear it clank on the truck's engine and fall to the concrete floor. He hits the back of his head on the underside of the hood. "Shit! Ouch!" He rubs the sore spot and looks at me disdainfully.

He's just a kid, tall but thinner than any runner I know.

"What'd ya say?"

"I need a tow," I repeat.

He launches a chewed wad of tobacco from his mouth. It lands ten feet from him. "You look like shit, Mister."

Polite kid, I think. At least he calls me Mister.

"You don't look so good either," I say. There's an unhealthy grayness in the color of his skin. It looks like a bad make-up job in a low-budget horror flick. Then I realize it's just a layer of grease that's found its way onto his face.

I use the sink in the restroom to wash the salt and sweat from my face and body. I dry myself with a coarse paper towel that feels like sandpaper. I wet my head and throw back my hair and change into the clothing I'd stuck in the day-pack. Within minutes I've hopped in the tow truck and we're driving down Highway 77, towards Tucson. Strangely enough I'm aware that this is the same route the Tucson Marathon is run and I find myself studying the rises in the road, picturing myself on the course. *Always a runner.*

"Now, where you say she is, Mister?"

"South Carolina," I tell him.

"South where?" His eyes are bug wide. His Adam's apple jumps.

I point to the dirt road we just now pass and say; "the Jeep is back there about twenty miles towards Redington. But I don't care about that. I need to get to the airport fast!"

I take out a hundred dollar bill and hold it up to his face.

"I ain't no taxi, Mister." He turns his head away from me and spits tobacco. The window is closed and some of it begins to trek down the glass. Most just sticks to it. "Aaah shit! I hate when I do that." He takes a wipe at it with his sleeve.

"If it makes you feel any better you can pick up the Jeep on the way back." I reach in my wallet again and take out two more hundred. "This should cover it."

"And then some!" he says. He takes the money and stuffs it into his front pocket. "Could you buy me some beer?" he adds.

I look at him a little closer now. He may be taller than me but he hasn't had his first shave yet.

"Sure," I tell him. I was once sixteen.

*

Now, I'm sitting in a stopped taxi in Columbia, South Carolina. I'm panic stricken knowing that the race is nearly an hour old already and I am more than late!

I was supposed to have met Jennifer the night before the race. But as things turned out I had not made my flight after all and was forced to take a later one. "I'll be there first thing in the morning," I'd told a disappointed Jennifer. Then, the connecting flight out of Chicago had been delayed due to snow. I'd spent much of the night in the airport pacing back and forth like an expectant parent in a hospital waiting room. I hadn't dared called Jenny when that happened. I doubt that she had slept well, given the magnitude of the event she was about to undertake, but I didn't want to take the chance of waking her just-the-same.

Finally, when my flight boarded, the plane spent another hour on the runway as it had to be de-iced. That's where I watched the sunrise this morning. The pink de-icing liquid sliding down the outside of my window, looking like melted strawberry ice-cream as it mixed with the soft light from the morning sun. I don't think this is what Jennifer had in mind when she told me to watch the sunrises.

Now I'm sitting here listening to a taxi-cab driver explain to me why we're not moving.

"Must be construction. I'll turn around, go another way," he says.

I put my head out the window for a better look. Wooden, orange barriers block the street in front of us sure enough. *Damn. Just my luck!*

That's when I almost miss it.

A flash of a woman with bright red hair and a long, beautiful half-moon stride runs by.

"It's Toni!" I shout to the driver. "This is the course!"

I jump out of the cab and throw a twenty to the driver.

They run by intermittently, mostly in small packs.

I'm hungry for information. I strike up a conversation with a man next to me who tells me someone named Jenny with a high seed is leading the race.

My God, I think. Could it be "my" Jenny?

"Jennifer Ledge?" I ask briskly.

Although it takes him only a second to respond, I lose my balance and nearly fall into him anticipating the answer.

"Sorry, wasn't Ledge," he replies. "I'd know that on account I got a cousin livin' up in..."

His words trail off as I focus my attention back to the race.

From my vantage point on the sidewalk I can see a sign indicating the ten mile mark. Next to it is a digital clock that reads: 59:30, and counting. I do the math. It had been a briefly pleasant thought to think that it might have been Jennifer *Ledge* leading the race but I know all too well that she would not yet have reached this point. Although, she should be coming any minute, I conclude.

And there she is! I see her from afar. She slowly appears over a rise leading a tightly knit pack of five.

Suddenly, my eyes are wide and full of the moment, certainly oblivious to anything else that surrounds me. Everything, other than Jennifer, simply blends in a nothingness! Do you know what that's like? When it seems that everything but the only thing that matters has turned stale, and a stillness washes over you? When you forget to breathe because even the air in your lungs has ceased to circulate? If you could see yourself in a mirror you'd notice red blotches appear on your skin. You'd see "goosebumps" well up over your body, perhaps a bead of sweat drip from your brow. Someone next to you might take you for ill, but if you could, you'd tell them the opposite, that you've never felt better.

My heart lifts. My eyes threaten to float away carrying with them the vision that I hold of her.

There are few moments in life worthy of being described as perfect. Quintessential moments when all that is good, all that is right, come together. These are the times when your spirit lifts. When nothing, not even your own modesty, can cap it. In music; the time I stood in Washington Park and listened to the orchestra play Copland's Fanfare To The Common Man. In nature; waking to the soft glow of the morning light as it slowly washed over the majestic Tetons in Western Wyoming. And now, in sport; watching Jennifer in this race.

While I know that the moment truly belongs to Jennifer--after all, it is her out there who is racing and effectuating her long-sought aspirations and dreams--I too am heartfelt with this recognition. And in this way I feel that I share in this quintessential moment with her.

Because she appears from behind a small rise, she's slowly revealed to me from head to toe. Painstakingly so, I'm thinking. I almost don't recognize her. Her long hair has fallen out of the braid she typically wears when she's racing and now sways back and forth like honey-brown wheat fields on a breezy summer's day. The sport glasses she wears hide her eyes; there's a coldness to her that's intimidating. And I realize why. Just like the time I'd seen Toni on TV at the Bolder Boulder I am now seeing Jennifer in a different light; as a remarkable athlete on the playing field with her peers. Her face is even, unrevealing. A few more steps over the rise and I see her torso. She's pumping her arms, working the hill, and I see the rippled effect of lean muscles in her shoulders. A few more steps and she's over the rise, back on normal stride. There's no wasted motion here; there rarely is when you see an athlete of her ability. There's a fluidity that accompanies her gait, a motion that has been perfected over years of practice and thousands of miles run and is nothing short of beautiful to watch. I am aware that as I watch this, as whenever I see someone that has perfected a skill, I am in awe of her talent.

Then, in a moment of clear-headedness, a million thoughts flood my senses, coming to me in pieces, like little bursts of energy-- whispers pulled from the past. There was Arturo Barrios passing Martin Pitayo in the closing meters of the Bolder Boulder in the most remarkable show of guts I'd ever witnessed. There was Jennifer and I on our first date, in the dim light of Josephinas sharing drink and laugh, a candle flame licking the air between us. And later, her running with me at Boston, pleading with me not to stop, to search my soul and realize my dream. And Toni's group faithfully gathering at the track every Thursday night in search of speed. And of course there was Ed, shaking his fists at me from atop the cornice, letting me know it was all my fault.

I now smile in appreciation of them all, good and bad. For each experience has worked in its own way to unite this moment--the finest moment of my life.

Jennifer comes closer and I shout some encouraging words to her. She sees me and I watch a faint smile appear on her lips. She points at me and runs on by.

As she does so I watch her stride. There's a lift in it that I'd not seen before. A touch of confidence in her step.

And I know why.

She's running her dream, in the pit, battling the bear.

I spend much of the race thereafter pleading with other spectators to let me ride with them to different vantage points along the course. I cheer for Jennifer every time she runs by.

At the finish I am there for her.

I tell her I love her and hold her closely in my arms.

"Love you too," she says, exhausted.

Jennifer's parents are there too. "Wonderful. Wonderful," they say.

She turns to them and says to her mother, "I didn't let one Kenyan beat me today." We all laugh.

Someone bumps me from behind. I turn to see that it's a reporter who's fighting for position among other media personalities. In the middle of them is Toni Jamison answering a flood of questions being thrown at her. Toni's eyes are wide. She has a gigantic smile plastered on her face. I can only wonder if she's made the team!

Jennifer sees her too. They give each other a thumbs up sign.

Jennifer, her parents and myself, walk away. As we do, a darling little girl, wearing a floral dress and curls in her hair, makes eye contact with Jennifer. The girl's eyes are wide and blue.

"Did you race?" she asks, small, meek voice.

Jennifer stops and puts her hand on the little girl's shoulder.

"Sure did," says Jennifer, proudly.

As innocent as her age, the curious eight year old asks, "why?"

Well, with this, Jenny and I exchange looks and burst out laughing. She's stumped to find an answer. I am no help either.

Veterans of thousands of miles and hundreds of races run and neither one of us can come up with a quick answer.

But really we know why. The answer is so obvious that it's often overlooked and rarely given much thought. Racing is a testament without end. It validates our efforts and lends credence to our heart's desires. In short, we find out what we're really made of.

I think about telling this to the little girl but of course I don't. For obvious reasons it would be futile.

"I don't know," Jenny finally says, surrendering, leaving the girl with the same bewildered look in her eyes.

We walk away.

Jenny has her right arm draped around her father, her left arm draped around her mother.

All around us are elated athletes and their loved-ones sharing in a woven moment so warm that it could melt the hands on a clock and stop time.

Later, Jennifer and I are in her room at the hotel.

"My flight leaves in an hour," I tell her. "But as soon as I get back I'll get the Jeep fixed and drive back to Denver."

"Don't bother," she says.

"But--" I'm startled. I guess I blew it after all.

"I promised dinner with my parents tonight. But I'll meet you in Tucson tomorrow," she says, smiling. "I could use a few days in the sun."

Relieved, I tell her, "you just had a day in the sun."

"Ok then. A few days in a warm climate," she rephrases.

"I know just the place," I tell her. "It's up in the foothills."

"By Sabino Canyon?"

"Yes." I'm surprised she knows the canyon. She sees it in my face.

"I ran Sabino late one night when I was down there at a conference on nuclear waste."

"You ran the canyon at night?" I ask, skeptical.

"Haven't you?"

"Never."

"You should." Jenny looks away, remembering. "There's talk of a magical, roan horse that runs the canyon when the moon is full. Supposed to grant wishes or something if you see him."

More than a century ago, a poet named Henry David Thoreau cited the richest man to be the one with the simplest pleasures. Well, not much has changed since then.

I believe this wealth to be hidden in all of us. For a runner, the chase unlocks it. Whether we're ten miles into a marathon, or alone on a forest trail, a smile is forthcoming.

I'm in the canyon now. The moon is out and looks heavy. An owl hoots at me as I run by--I see it perched atop of a saguaro cactus, silhouetted against the night sky. *Jennifer was right,* I'm thinking. *This place is special.* I listen to the beat of my heart at play with the task at hand, acutely aware that the stretch of undulating road in front of me offers more fun than anyone should be allowed. It's been a long time since I felt this way, but there's no question about it--I'm in love again. The simplicity of the run has me firmly in its grasp.

There's a haunty current that runs through this four mile chamber. I sense its pulse. I think it odd that most people would stand here and sense only a hollowness about it. Perhaps they'd shout and listen for the ensuing echo to bounce back and forth between the canyon walls validating their thought. But I see this chamber in a different light altogether. It's not a dark and hollow canyon at all! If you listen closely, if you open your eyes a little wider, you'll see it in the same way that I do. A place like this is a vast stage where dreams are born and fantasies come true. Locked within its walls are the aspirations of those who have run here before me. In this way it breathes.

And soon I surrender my thoughts to my heart's desires. Jennifer will be at my side tomorrow and everything will have fallen into place. We'll lounge by a pool and bask under the noon sun. We'll talk of our lives together and make future plans. Perhaps then she'll want to loosen her marathon weary legs and we'll head out for a short and slow run. Perhaps not.

But tonight I run alone, accompanied only by the watchful eye of the moon. I look up at it--its resonant glow is mirrored on my face-- and wonder if Jennifer might be staring up at it too.

In the distance, somewhere up ahead and around a corner, I hear the unmistakable sound of hooves striking the pavement in full gallop.

You may order additional copies of *Chasing the Bear* for $12.95 by sending a check to:

Saguaro Publishing Co.
690 Pennsylvania St. #4
Denver, CO 80203

Please enclose the following information:

* Number of copies you wish to purchase
* Your name and address
* Check, made out to Saguaro Publishing Co.

Please enclose $3.00 for postage and handling for the first book, .50 for each additional book. Colorado residents please add 7.3% ($12.95 X 7.3% = $13.90)

Please call (303) 832-6524 for bulk purchases which are offered at a discount. Prices are subject to change without notice. Valid in the U.S. only. All orders are subject to availability of books. Please allow four weeks for delivery.

ISBN 0-9655984-0-3